FOREVER UNTAMED

FOREVER LOVED BOOK SIX A PARANORMAL SHIFTER NOVEL

L. J. HAWKE

ISBN: 978-1-7350479-5-9

❧ Created with Vellum

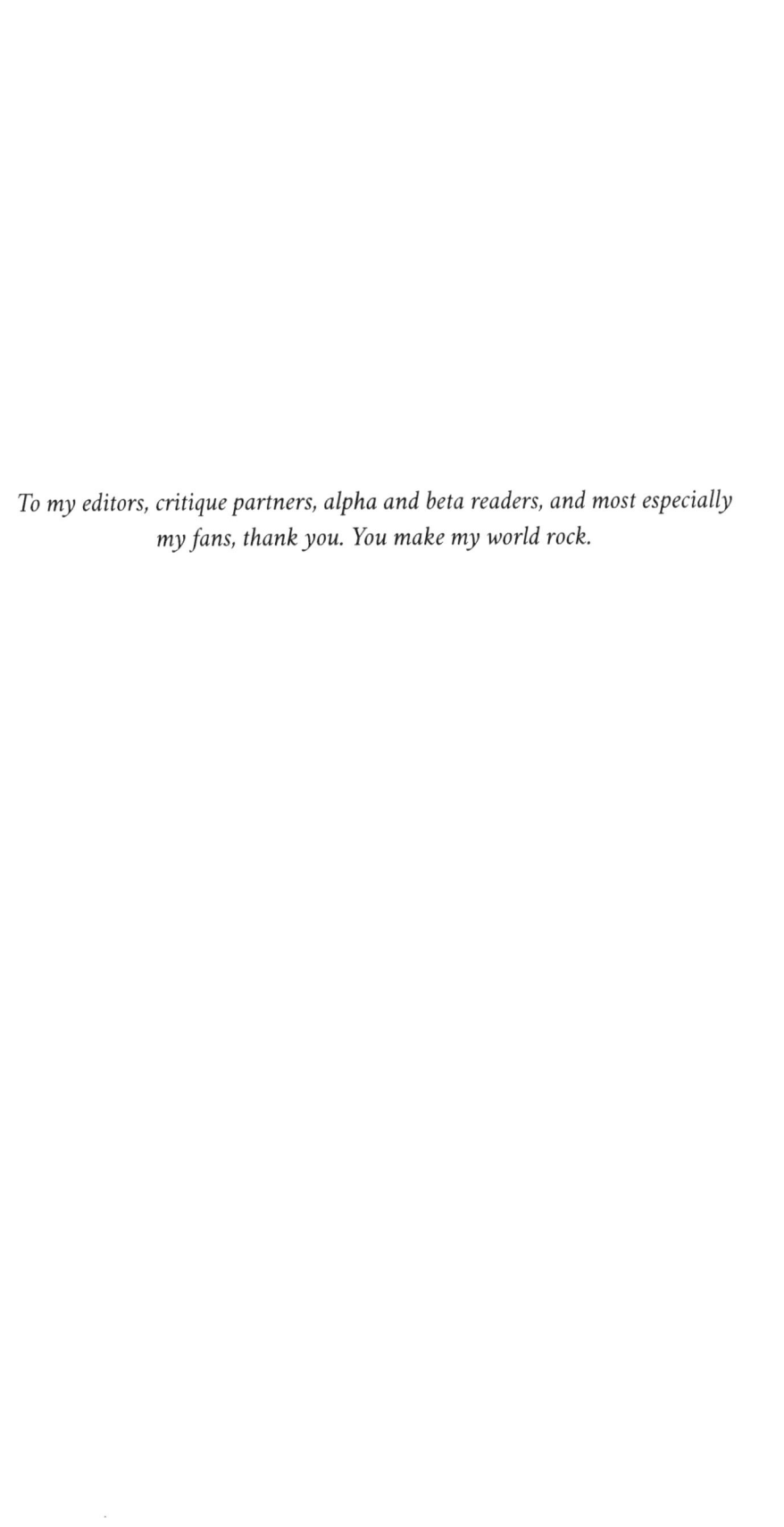

To my editors, critique partners, alpha and beta readers, and most especially my fans, thank you. You make my world rock.

STUDS

*P*enny took the lull as an opportunity to wipe down all the tables and chairs. An ice cream shop got messy if not cared for. Libby Camber, her next-door business neighbor, had a sweets shop, *Sweet Thoughts Bakery*. Penny loved Libby, and they sent business to each other daily. In winter, they planned to destroy the wall between their tiny businesses. Libby had a complex family that Penny, as a single child of a single mother, couldn't fathom. Libby's sister-in-law Kandace had a best friend-like-a-sister Corinne, who had moved to town a few months ago in order to be close to Kandace. Jared Weston, Corinne's brother-in-law, had been the forerunner. He had moved himself and his dog into the county and had scouted a farm with lots of land. Then, Corinne had moved in with her men James and Mitch, and the Camber family had suddenly gotten even bigger with the addition of the Westons.

Jared came into Penny's business, *Flavory*, from Libby's side of the business. Libby's kids Beau, Ricky, and Denver followed him like ducks. A yellow hard hat covered Jared's short military-cut brown hair, and he wore a flannel shirt, jeans, a tool belt, and steel-toed boots. His chocolate eyes were hidden by safety glasses. He moved like he had a purpose, all strong lines and grace. It was odd to see him without his German shepherd, Shadow, but the dog would not be good for Penny's business license.

Jared strode over to the wall separating Penny's business from Libby's. Beau, Ricky, and Denver kept on his heels. They all wore clean jeans and hiking boots and long-sleeved shirts in primary colors. Denver was eight, a towhead who loved to talk and move. Ricky was six, with curly dark hair and huge brown eyes. Beau was five with blond hair and a wide smile.

Penny was stunned when none of the three boys approached her ice cream counter. Libby, her sister Meri, and their spouse Nat had adopted the boys after their birth mother had died in a house fire. Lorraine had been an indifferent parent and had let her boys do anything they wanted.

Penny sped up her cleaning, needing to be ready in case the kids needed food. Instead, Jared went to a corner and had Denver scan the wall with a handheld device until it beeped.

"Ricky, give Beau the end of the measuring tape."

Penny watched, open-mouthed, as Ricky carefully fed the tape out to Beau, who walked it back to Jared.

"Call it out, Ricky,"

"Two feet six inches."

Penny grinned; the little boy sounded so serious.

"Ricky, walk up to where Denver is. Okay, Denver, keep walking. Beau and Ricky, stay the same distance apart. The studs should be in at regular intervals."

Denver kept walking, and the machine beeped again. Beau and Ricky smiled and walked forward.

"Same," Ricky called out.

Jared wrote in a little notebook. "Good."

Penny put away the spray bottle, washed her hands, and went to the boys at the wall. "I assume that little gray box is a stud finder?"

"Why, yes, it is." Jared grinned. "Found me and these fine boys, didn't it?"

Penny snorted. "I thought we weren't knocking down the wall until Thanksgiving."

"We think we can do it faster, cheaper, and earlier. We just need to demo in between the studs, make pillars, and have the same color walls on each end. Both floors are black and white, and keeping the same styles of cafe tables will differentiate your two related businesses. The differences are minor since both of you used the same going-out-of-business service to find them."

Penny nodded. "Before Halloween?" That was both Libby and Penny's busiest time of the year.

"Six days, starting Sunday after closing." Jared turned and pointed. "Ricky, put it on the floor unless you want your fingers pinched. Beau, let go."

The tape measure zipped itself up and spun. Ricky carefully picked it up, and Jared took the measuring tape from the boy's hand, locked it, and put it on the space in his belt. Denver gave back his stud finder; Jared turned it off and put it away in another pocket.

Jared reached into his pocket and brought out a handful of stickers. "Two each, because you did the same job twice." He handed two black Iron Man ones to Denver, two red Iron Man ones to Ricky, and two Spider-Man ones to Beau.

The boys pulled more stickers out of their pockets. They counted stickers, and Denver crowed, "Nine!"

Penny knew nine stickers were enough for The Works, a banana split sundae with both sprinkles and nuts. Libby's sticker reward system had been adopted by many local parents. The stickers could be anything—superheroes, sports stars, literary or cartoon characters. They had to be unique to each child or family. The math was as complicated or simple as the parents desired, and the chores or behavior required to earn them varied. Parents bought cards from local businesses and allowed their kids to redeem products and services for stickers.

Penny grinned as Jared pulled out Penny's chocolate-sundae card from his back pocket and exchanged it for three stickers from each boy. Beau took possession of the card, and all three boys ran to the glass to determine which three scoops they wanted. Penny went behind the counter and scooped out peanut butter cup fudge, mint chocolate cookie crunch, and salted caramel. The sauces were caramel, mint fudge, and strawberry.

"I can't decide about pee-cans or choco-wate sprinkles," Beau said.

"You can have half and half." Penny changed to the half-scoops when Beau nodded.

The boys sat down, and Jared approached her. "Do you want us to start on Sunday?"

"Who is 'us'?"

Jared pointed at the salted caramel. "Cone of that."

Penny scooped out the cone.

"Markour Contracting called Libby today and canceled."

Penny finished scooping out of habit. "They what?" She pitched her voice low so as not to alarm the boys.

"Libby was a lot louder. Anyway, I've built tiny houses with my dad. I've done contracting work since I was twelve and could pick up nails and scrap metal. I've talked to Silver Construction. Emmie's going to be with me, and I'm going to have my brothers from both families help with the demo. Drywall, make the pillars, and paint. Lots of hands. It will take a certain amount of time because hanging drywall takes time, painting and sealing takes smelly time, making pillars takes even more. We will let you both back in the minute the inspector inspects it."

"Good." Penny remembered what her hands were doing and put the scoop onto the cone. She handed him the cone wrapped in a napkin and rang him up. He paid with another card. "I can't believe we wasted all that time and energy." She gasped. "Our deposit!"

Jared held up a hand. "Vic and I got it all back. Every cent. And we're about to save you twenty thousand dollars. The deposit should cover most of it because family works for ice cream, baked goods, and pizzas."

Penny tried to hold back the tears. "That's just…"

Jared kept his hand up. "If you cry, I'll cry, and then the boys will."

Penny turned aside, wiped under her eyes with her thumbs, washed her hands, and turned back. "Thank you. You prevented me from keeping unsustainable hours to pay for this."

Jared backed away slowly, as if Penny held a grenade. Penny laughed. Jared turned and sat at a table next to the burbling boys. Burbling, not running around like maniacs, spilling sprinkles on the floor, or hitting each other. They were slower, more deliberate. Their new family was working wonders with them.

Penny filled up the cherries and rainbow sprinkles, listening to the boys burst into laughter. She smiled and hummed as she filled up on anything running low for the after-school-activities crowd. She replayed the conversation with Jared and said, "Sunday!" to him as he stood to leave with the boys. The boys put their dishes and spoons away properly and used sanitizer to clean themselves. Penny tried not to drop her jaw at their polite behavior.

"See you Sunday!" Jared gave a wave, and then he was gone.

Penny texted her fabulous mama Adelle the good news, then fed the herd of late-season baseball, basketball, football, lacrosse, soccer, swimming, track and field, and other athletes. She had plenty of healthy snacks, and they denuded her sugar-free case. Right behind them, the language, math, glee, and science club members came in a thundering herd. Some had parents or other family members with them, some not.

Penny saw Farrah through the window and sighed. Her assistant, Dana, noticed Farrah's helmet hair and purple-flowered muumuu and hissed out through her teeth. Dana had magenta hair held back in braids and green eyes that seemed to pop out of her tanned face. Dana had just turned sixteen. The young woman was part of the internship program with the local high school.

Farrah stomped in, nose turned up, and the door closed behind her. Penny was one of the few business owners who still served her. Farrah was the mother of a fallen vet, Morgan, one of Penny's closest friends in high school. Morgan died five years into her tour in a place Penny had never heard of before. Farrah was simply a nasty person and had been arrested for being hateful to all sorts of people, including Libby next door and Kandace, Libby's sister-in-law. Maddie, Penny's best friend and Farrah's only living daughter, had moved away and long since given up on her mother. Penny had a tiny hope that one day Farrah would get help.

Penny helped bash through the line, hoping Farrah would behave, but it was not to be.

Beau came in with his brother Denver and stood off to the side. "Miss Penny, Unca Jared says seven on Sunday."

"Thank you, Beau," Penny said and handed a cone to the next customer. "Tell your uncle thank you for me."

"Hey!" Farrah said. "I'm in line before they are!"

Penny watched Beau's face fall, and she'd had enough. She tapped Dana to be sure the teen could cover the rest of the line, and Dana nodded. Penny walked out from behind the counter, walked past Farrah, and went down on one knee to talk to Beau. "Thank you for your message. You and Denver go get a sticker, huh?"

Beau nodded. Penny touched his shoulder. Denver glared at Farrah, then turned away. Sadly, Farrah couldn't let it go.

"What you lookin' at, boy? You cut in line!"

Penny stood and very slowly turned to Farrah. "Farrah, you are no longer welcome here. I remember Morgan and know that you lost a daughter, but I let you berate me and treat me like garbage in front of this entire town for the last time. You just yelled at these two little boys who were doing nothing but carrying a message to me. Go on, get out, and good riddance." Penny knelt back down and hugged Beau and Denver. "Go on back to Jared."

The boys bolted out.

Farrah looked around at everyone staring at her. "You can't kick me out!"

Penny stood up and looked her former next-door neighbor in the face. "Farrah, you never treated your daughter correctly. You berated her constantly. You tried to crush her spirit. Morgan died because of insurgents and because she decided to join the military. But let me clarify to you that Morgan told me directly that she signed up to get out of the house away from you and get college paid for. An insurgent killed her, but you set the situation in motion that got her killed."

Farrah took a swing at Penny. Penny leaned back, and the fist went past her nose. Lacrosse coach Henrietta Jenkins got up and reached towards Farrah, and the entire lacrosse team leaped up and stepped forward.

"Get away from her!" Tan Xi, the team captain, yelled at Farrah.

But, Deputy Nat Sandawan was faster. Nat came in the door, crossed the room, and grabbed Farrah's fist, cocked back for another swing. Farrah was in cuffs and being read her rights before she could take that second swing. Farrah began to squawk, and Nat silently dragged her out of the shop. Everyone in the ice cream shop clapped.

"I'm sorry, folks." Penny found it hard to breathe in.

"Don't you dare apologize." Henrietta looked like a Valkyrie, a blonde with huge blue eyes and the tan of someone who was either on a field or on a horse. "I wondered why you put up with that nasty female and just now discovered it was because her daughter died as a veteran. You've been at every veteran's funeral in the area for years, but I didn't put two and two together until today. Honey, there's cutting her some slack, and there's putting up with abuse. Let her go with no looking back, girlfriend." There was a lot more clapping when Henrietta and Penny hugged.

Penny smiled at everyone, walked back to the counter, washed her hands, finished the line, and cleaned off the tables.

Dana came out to help her when their thundering herd of students left. "Finally stood up for yourself."

Penny mock-glared at Dana. "I was eventually going to ban her."

Dana nodded. "Yeah, after she took a swing at you."

Penny realized something. "You pressed the police button on the cash register."

Dana nodded. "Darn straight. She doesn't get to act nasty to kids. Not on my watch."

"I...thank you." Penny bagged the trash. "I've got to be trashy now."

Dana snorted. "Go right on ahead."

Dana finished the floors, and Penny had her checklist finished twenty minutes before it was time to lock up.

"Go on ahead," Penny said to her assistant.

Dana walked out, her carbon-copy green-eyed, red-haired mother just outside the door waiting to take her home.

The door rang after Dana had put the money in the safe and washed her hands once again.

Adelle came up and smiled at her daughter. "My hero!" Adelle had brassy blonde hair, perfect makeup, and a raucous laugh. The woman was tanned all year because of her gardening, cross-country skiing, and 10K runs.

Penny made sure everything was cleaned, locked down, and/or turned off and walked to the door. "Don't start."

Adelle laughed. "Third happiest day of my life. First, the day you were born, second was when my former next-door-neighbor Farrah the Scary moved out, and today when my daughter got over her terminal niceness and stood up for herself."

Penny set the alarm and locked the door. "Terminal niceness?"

Adelle put her arm around her daughter. "Pizza, pasta, Thai, Chinese?"

"Pulled pork."

Adelle grinned. "Excellent choice."

They headed to Adelle's car. Adelle programmed in The Shack, and the silver car pulled out. Adelle poked buttons on her dash to order ahead; the little shack on the edge of the woods would close in a very short time. Adelle ran in and ran back out with the sack, got back in the car, and sent the vehicle back to her own house, knowing her daughter would be happy to stay over in her old room.

They got inside and had pulled pork sandwiches, potato wedges, and fat double chocolate mint chip cookies with sweet tea.

"Heard that our nasty former neighbor took a swing at you."

"She did. Remember those kickboxing classes I'm taking with Nat, Libby's spouse?"

"Did you sweep her legs out from under her?" Adelle asked, leaning forward.

"What? No. I got the hell out of the way." Penny sucked on her tea.

Adelle's eyes went flat. "That woman better pray she gets real jail time."

"Psychiatric will be better. Real time, so she gets on real meds."

Adelle sighed. "You keep seeing the best in people. Some people are just evil."

"Or sick." Penny took another potato wedge and dunked it in honey mustard sauce.

Adelle grinned. "Heard you kicked her out for good."

"Did. Told her she's responsible for the set of circumstances that led to Morgan getting killed."

Adelle whistled. "I agree. Surprised you stood up for Morgan after all these years. Wish that woman had signed the paper."

When the girls were in high school, Morgan and Maddie spent as much time with Penny and Adelle as possible. Adelle had tried to get Farrah to sign guardianship papers to give Adelle custody several times, but Farrah had refused. The police had been called for Farrah's verbal abuse many times, and each girl had moved out on her eighteenth birthday.

Penny reached out, took her mother's hand. "You are the best mom to Maddie and me."

Maddie called Adelle 'Mom' and had walked Maddie down the aisle when she married her true love, Bronson Hughes, a blue-eyed, dark-haired Irish veterinarian a two-hour drive away. Farrah had no idea where her daughter was or her married name.

"I try. Gilmore Girls? Queer Eye? Stranger Things?" Adelle loved watching TV shows on Netflix.

Penny snorted. "Queer Eye. I may get ideas." Adelle laughed.

They popped popcorn and got more sweet tea from Adelle's stash. When they paused in between shows, Penny told her mom all about the new shop changes, nearly forgotten after dealing with Farrah. Adelle was thrilled.

"That's incredible! Libby's family is so kind! Go shower, and I'll French braid your hair."

Penny nodded. "Be right back, Mom." She went to shower and came back out in her ancient blue sweats and soft socks. "I am so tired." She sat down on a cushion in front of her mother.

Adelle nodded. "We'll watch one more episode. Then, bedtime for us both."

Penny purred as Adelle brushed her hair and wound the wet hair into a French braid. Penny had many happy memories of her mother's deft fingers in her hair. Penny slid into some sort of twilight joy place, her eyes half-slit, watching the Queer Eye guys put someone's life back to rights.

Adelle had been a cashier for years until technology made that nearly obsolete. She had gone back to school and now wrote the programming for self-driving cars. She could have moved out of the small house years before. Instead, she had remodeled, putting in a nice kitchen and raising the roof to make the house airy and light.

Penny lived in the tiny apartment over her shop in order to save money for a nice house. Her mother had gone without food many times, feeding three hungry girls. Penny didn't want to take any of her mother's money despite Adelle's desire to help.

Penny eventually ended up on the couch, her feet in her mother's lap, her mother's favorite chenille throw on her body. Adelle passed Penny a brownie caramel mint cookie ice cream sandwich from Penny's shop and laughed, then groaned as she ate her own sandwich. Penny grinned. Dana loved assembling the sandwiches. Penny was going to have to give her teen worker a raise.

INVITATION

*J*ared was at Libby's shop the minute it closed. He barely had time to get the strong coffee from the coffee shop down the street into his system. Mitch and James were both there. Kandace and Corinne had both decreed that they would help, so there it was. Men who didn't listen to women didn't last long in the shifter world. Everyone knew men could howl all they wanted to, but the women had long reaches and even longer claws. They also had the cubs and defended them in ways that were just stone crazy. No one wanted to see a feral woman.

Libby was in her jeans and a plum top. She had all her tables and chairs in the middle because the middle of the wall separating her business from Penny's would be demolished and the interior wall painted. She pulled over a heavy tarp and taped it down, then stomped on the tape with one foot.

Jared took his sledgehammer over to the other side; he would start from the back, and they would start from the front.

"Hey." Jared smiled at Penny of the copper hair and sea-green eyes. "Can I help you with that?"

Penny carefully whipped a tarp on her glass case like she was putting a tablecloth on a giant table. "Nope."

Jared grinned as she taped it down. He went back over the measurements and used the stud finder once more to ensure they had marked out all the right places. He taped down the floor tarps and grinned as Penny went to lop off her back room with enough tarp to blanket the Camber farm. Penny had gone beyond Libby's preparations. Her chairs were on her tables, already covered with tarps and taped down. Penny wore black jeans and a mauve top, and Jared noticed how those jeans looked on her.

Jared was out of coffee and past ready when Charlie came in, sledgehammer in his massive hands.

"What are you waiting for, boy? An engraved invitation?"

Jared huffed out a laugh and shouted, "Incoming!"

They tapped out three-two-one, and Charlie and Jared both swung at the wall. The drywall split with a satisfying crack. They were in the rhythm, and the wall broke apart. Three-two-one, swing. *There is nothing more satisfying than demolition*, Jared thought to himself.

They could soon see Mitch and James swinging sledgehammers on the other side, farther down the wall. Jen, one of Charlie's wives, picked up huge pieces of drywall and threw them into a wheelbarrow. The door flew open, and Libby pushed a wheelbarrow in the door. Penny rushed to help her position it, and then Libby was gone without a word. Penny grabbed drywall with heavy gloves, filled up the wheelbarrow, then swung it out to the alley to fill up the Dumpster they had delivered the night before.

"Hold!" Mitch said. That was the cue to pull out any wiring or metal. There were no pipes; this was an interior wall between two businesses. The pipes were farther back in the kitchens and the restrooms. The restrooms were being turned into larger unisex ones with enclosed stalls, and they would replace the urinals with much smaller kids' toilets and sinks to make a kids' bathroom.

Jen, Libby, and Penny went into the bathrooms with the sledgehammers, their timing a little off until they caught the rhythm. Jared went to clean up while Charlie, Mitch, and James were on the unenviable urinal-removal duty. The females kept up a steady pace. Jared was surprised at Penny's ability to keep up with Jen and Libby, both shifters. Libby's muscles bunched and lengthened under her mauve shirt. She soon had her shirt tied around her waist, a purple sports top peeking out underneath.

Two wheelbarrow trips later, they were banging out the last of the wall. Jared cleaned off the studs, making them ready to be turned into columns. He sanded down the wood, then used a shop vacuum to sweep the floor after getting the last of the drywall off the floor and out to the Dumpster. He sealed the studs with polyurethane; he needed to give them time to dry before encasing them in pre-carved decorated wood painted in garish colors. The lower half of each column would be painted with whiteboard paint and include ledges for whiteboard pens so bored kids could draw.

Emmie of Silver Construction walked in with an unhurried stride. She had a hatchet face, short-cropped silver hair, flannel shirt, jeans, steel-toed boots, and tool belt bristling with tools. "Sorry I was late. Got caught on a roof and couldn't get off. Long story. Anyway, you've made a little progress."

Jared snorted. "Water's off. Solar lights on." He pointed at the spotlights with an elbow. "Have a team in each bathroom."

Emmie sighed. "Gotta make sure they aren't mucking that up." She strode to the bathroom on the right.

Jared snorted again, got off his stool, and began painting polyurethane on the middle of the last column with long, even strokes. When he was sure he had every bit of every column, he went to Libby's far wall, which would be painted in a slightly darker purple than Penny's wall. He had a coat of primer to put down. He looked up and contemplated the Lego-style lights he'd found. They would look great and unify the space. They would also be over Libby and Penny's budget. The women were going into their busy season, which went from Halloween to New Year's as people bought holiday sweets. Fallow time was between January and March. He could install them then. Or, he could install them at the same time they were finishing the wall and use his own funds. He shrugged. He had enough money; he might as well make everyone happy, including little kids. Who didn't want to make little kids happy?

Jared taped the wall, put on his mask and moon suit, and began spraying. He turned off the loud sprayer when Emmie came back from the bathrooms.

"So far, so good." Emmie grinned.

"Better to do Lego lights now, or later?"

Emmie snorted. "Now. Don't have to install more wiring; they will fit just fine and take up less space than those dangly things they have now that don't really match."

Jared had ordered the lights on a whim. They were in his truck. "Let's do it, then."

Emmie pointed opposing arms at each bathroom. "Tell them. Women hate surprises." She took off her tool belt and started putting on a 'moon' painting suit in white.

"On it."

Jared painted a third of the wall, then Emmie took it over.

Jared shed his moon suit, took out his cell phone, took a deep breath, and was able to catch both women sucking down water at the cooler while the other men filed past with buckets of shattered tiles. "I want to give you ladies a gift, but it has to be installed tonight."

Libby opened one eye and looked at Jared. "What, exactly, is this magnanimous gift?"

Penny grinned. "Show and tell, sledgehammer man."

Jared choked out a laugh and passed over his phone. Libby stared, then Penny. Libby held the phone upward towards the ceiling, then Penny took the phone from him and did the same thing.

"Fine." Libby nodded.

"Fine." Penny grinned.

"But, we pay you back later." Libby's eyes shone.

"A lot later." Penny snorted and handed the phone back.

"You're welcome." Jared took his phone back. Both women, dripping with sweat, grinned at him. They went to their respective restrooms.

Jared checked the fast-drying polyurethane. He began assembling the column covers and started at the bottom. Emmie kept spraying, making a perfect, even coat on the wall. When she finished, she cleaned the sprayer, got out of the moon suit, and checked on the bathrooms again. Jared went outside for the lighting and ladders, and they temporarily turned off the power while they installed the lights. Charlie helped Jared with his ginormous gorilla arms while James and Mitch worked on the other side, so they soon had the lights tested and the power back on.

Emmie kicked them out like a mama protecting chicks. "Go the hell home and sleep!"

They filed out, exhausted, and clanged up the circular metal stairs out back to Libby's ex-apartment, now Penny's place.

"Kitchen sink," Mitch hollered over the clang of his boots on the stairs.

Penny shucked her shoes just inside the door. "Mushroom, olive, red bell pepper, bacon, and Italian sausage."

Jared raised his eyebrows, impressed. "I'm with the lady on this one."

Libby snorted. "Three extra-large pizzas, third one vegetarian." She waved her fingers at her HUD glasses. "Ordered. Penny, it's your shower, first crack at it."

Penny snorted. "Why, thank you for letting me use my own shower first."

Jared looked around, impressed. There were built-ins that hadn't been there before when it was Libby's place. The kitchen sported a spice rack that separated into various types of cuisine. There were lots of cubbies and drawers for kitchen tools, and a blender, food processor, small convection oven, and microwave oven were all on a separate cart. There was a couch with dual recliners and fat pillows. Rufus, Penny's huge orange and black cat, opened one eye from his spot on the back of the couch, then fell back asleep.

Penny petted Rufus, then headed to her bedroom. "Shoes off! Sodas and juices in the fridge!"

Mitch nodded. "Yes, ma'am. This is sweet." He went to the refrigerator and started throwing sodas. James and Charlie caught theirs with ease.

"I'll take a..." Libby caught a can out of the air. "Okay, black cherry lime works." They got their shoes off and used wet towels to get the worst of the grime off.

Penny came out, fresh-faced from her shower. Rufus deigned to admit she existed, padding over to rub against her legs. "Libby's next."

"Girls stick together," Libby said, with a snort from her brother Mitch. She walked back towards the shower, grinning.

"Clothes?" James asked, confused.

Penny grinned. "She leaves some here. We work a lot and sometimes she showers here. She attends a lot of kid things."

Jen laughed ruefully. "You have no idea how many times you will be out of your house when you have kids. Soccer, martial arts, crafts, coding..."

"Your kids are under seven," Mitch pointed out. They had four, two sets of twins, as was proper with bear shifter families. The girls were wonderful, the boys a handful due to their playful bear natures. The girls would be more difficult to handle as they grew older.

"They code with little robots they put in order." Charlie puffed out his chest at the pronouncement. The doorbell rang, and Charlie stood and lumbered towards the door while Penny fed Rufus a little wet food with his dry crunchies. They could hear the cat crunching his dinner from across the room.

Charlie shut the door and was unsurprised to find Mitch ready to take the boxes and hand out pizza. Penny distributed plates and napkins, and James picked a comedy about a cat psychiatrist. James moved to give Penny the recliner. Libby came out of the bathroom with wet hair wearing blue sweats. They put pizza on plates and ate like wolves.

"Next," Libby said.

Mitch sighed. "Too tired to go that far."

Charlie stood, held out his hand, and helped Jen stand up. He led his wife to the back.

Mitch closed his eyes tight. "I do not want to..."

"How do they even fit?" James asked, eyes wide.

Penny laughed so hard she almost dropped her lime water. "I widened the shower stall. Rufus likes to shower with me sometimes."

The giant cat padded up to her, leaped, and lay across her legs. Penny scratched behind his ears, and he rumbled.

"So, columns tomorrow, retile bathrooms, put up stalls." Jared sighed.

Mitch threw a napkin at his brother. "Shut. Up. The cat is going to analyze Scruff, the boss."

Jared laughed and sat with his back against the side of the couch close to Penny. He reached over and petted the cat's huge head.

"Now you've done it." Penny laughed. "He'll consider you a best friend and demand love, attention, play, and snacks for the rest of his life."

"Shadow already does that. She's at home, waiting for me. I'll have to leave after this episode."

"I hear she's been in combat. She saved you?" Penny's blue-green eyes were serious, her gorgeous red hair escaping its clip.

"She did. I couldn't let her down."

Penny nodded. Mitch shushed them. They demolished pizza and laughed at the show.

Jared stood up as soon as the credits began to roll. "Got to get home to Shadow. Thank you for the pizza."

"Thank you for the lights." Penny touched his hand.

"You light up her life. Nice. Now, get on with you!" Mitch growled.

"What's with him?" Jared said as he hauled his sweaty body to the door.

James sighed. "Wife is having girl time."

"Oh." Jared didn't get it. He put on his boots, opened the door, and rattled down the stairs. He wasn't surprised when Jen and Charlie followed him down. "Have a good night," he said to them.

Jen touched his shoulder. "You be good to her, Jared. Girl's been through... things."

Jared knew better than to ask a woman what another woman had gone through. "I'll be careful."

"You do that." Charlie held out his hand, and he and Jared shook.

Jared smiled, went to his truck, got in, and headed for home.

Jared found the interaction with Charlie and his family a little strange. Bear and wolf shifters hadn't mixed much before. He realized with a start that the women were behind it. Corinne married his wolf brothers James and Mitch. Kandace married Libby's brothers Len, Davis, and Vic, making a sprawling bear family. Kandace and Corinne considered themselves to be sisters, so they mixed everyone together. Now Corinne wanted to live near Kandace, and Mitch and James needed more wolf pack members to stay sane. Or so Jared's mama Rachael had said.

So, here they were halfway across the state. The thing was, Charlie, his terrifying little blonde wife Jen, and his less scary wives Lynette and Jetta were acting like James, Mitch, and Jared were all family under their care and protection and had familial responsibilities and obligations to each other.

Hanging Lego lights after a day of search and rescue training for dogs and their humans made Jared sore and exhausted, but he felt right, somehow. Like he'd changed families. Still part of the Westons, still able to go back and take care of family if needed. But his parents Gunny and Rachael and his adopted cougar sister Stretcher had adopted another cougar shifter named Lydia and her non-shifter boyfriend Lucas into their family. They had their hands full there. Rachael had been clear. *Take care of your brothers*. No one ever intentionally pissed a shifter woman off. So, Jared moved to this small town and remodeled his new blended family's businesses.

Jared got home and took Shadow on a walk through the silent neighborhood. Jared followed leash laws, but he could walk Shadow through Times Square without a leash. She had her name for a reason. Her loyalty matched her intelligence. He had already fed her, but he gave Shadow a treat. Jared showered, put on sweats, and climbed into bed. Shadow asked with a near-voiceless whine if she could come up, and he tapped the bed. She hopped up and slept at his feet, guarding him. Here, no one was going to burst through a door, guns ready to fire. Here, they were safe. He hoped he could convince the dog of that.

He hoped he could convince himself.

∼

*J*ared and Shadow had their run. Jared was in a rented townhome with a tiny yard until he could find a place for himself and Shadow. Until he could make sure Mitch, James, and their woman Corinne were staying. Jared knew in his gut they were. The house they found had the right bones, it was within acreage-touching distance of Kandace's house and her bear husbands, and it had a clear path to the Camber farm. Bears and wolves both knew to go to a safe den. Jared knew he sucked at lying to himself. He was here, and he had to settle down. He'd have babies to guard soon, he and Shadow. Both Corinne and her best friend Kandace were pregnant.

Jared did a figure-eight around and through the dog park. There was a wide lake full of ducks quacking at each other. Shadow held back from chasing fat rabbits growing out their winter coats. Shadow loved Jared more than rabbits. She kept close to her human, making sure he stretched out his legs and ran in bursts, then slowed to a jog. Jared did some of his PT by the lake, then jogged home to give the dog her food and water. He lifted weights in the garage, went after the kickboxing bag, then showered.

Jared fed the dog, then ate yogurt with fruit and granola, one egg poached hard, tomatoes, thick-sliced bacon, mushrooms. Shadow watched him gravely with big brown eyes. "You're on the perimeter, inside. I have to work on a business for a girl I like."

Shadow guarded the door. Jared petted her, played with her, gave her a treat, then put her back on guard. He took fruit and nut bars and both coffee and cherry water with him.

The truck took him where he needed to be. It was still early, with nearly empty streets except for the farm people on their morning chores or heading to the diner for breakfast. Jared knew both his punch list and Libby's entry code. He let himself in, got into the moon suit, and sprayed the wall a shiny amethyst. Emmie showed up to inspect his work, then she and Jen installed the bathroom toilets and sinks, then Jared helped them with the wall tiles. They were careful not to damage the floor tiles. Charlie, Penny, and Libby showed up, and they got all the tile work down. Jared and Penny put up the back-splashes in the kids' bathroom; Charlie was far too tall for the job. So Charlie and Libby did that job in the other one while Jen and Emmie sealed everything.

They had lunch at the barbecue place, then they came back, and they put up the mini-stalls in the kids' bathroom and the larger stalls in the adult one. Jared smiled at the lights as he made sure the polyurethane was dry on the columns on his water break. They put tarps down and sprayed color on the walls in the bathrooms, a rich gold to go with the shine of purple, blue, and gold backsplash and wall tiles.

They made sure the entire punch list was done, then went on a cleaning spree. The women were ferocious with their spray bottles and scrubbers.

Emmie ran the punch list again. "While the walls are drying, you could paint or poly the chairs all the same color to give yourself some cohesion in here. Then I'll come back with the plumbing inspector."

Jared refused to moan, cry, or give in to despair. Instead, he leaned back and cracked his back. He set up a sprayer station with double plastic under his feet. Libby went for more paint while Penny and Charlie taped the backs and Jared cleaned the sprayer. Libby came back with gold and silver paint, and Jared ran the sprayer while Charlie fed him the chairs. Libby and Penny took off the tape and sprayed the backs of the chairs.

"They look surprisingly royal," Jared grinned as he took off his moon suit.

Penny agreed. "They do."

They got rid of the painting detritus and washed up, then went to the diner. Penny and Libby sat across from the men. Dora came up to take their orders.

Penny ordered first. "I need a BLT, wedge fries, chocolate Coke, and a slice of apple pie with cinnamon ice cream for dessert."

Charlie poked at the menu. "Same thing, but with the Reuben."

Libby handed over her menu. "BLT, same order."

"Me too. What Libby said." Jared stretched, and something else in his back popped.

Charlie grinned. "This is going faster than expected. Be done when the paint dries."

"I need a vacation," Penny moaned. "I can't feel my hands."

Jared reached over and snagged her right hand. He dug in with his thumbs into her palm, then gently stretched and massaged the rest of her fingers.

Penny moaned. "You have forever to stop that."

Jared grunted, then started on her other hand.

Libby laughed. "Do we need to give you two some privacy?"

Charlie made everyone smile with that great gut-deep laugh of his. Jared tried not to let his eyes mist over. He missed his dad, Gunny. Gunny's laugh was even louder.

Gunny shook his massive head. "No, I don't think they'll scare the children or the horses."

Jared snorted and finished stretching out Penny's strong left hand. The woman lifted and scooped ice cream all day. She had fingers of iron. "Stretch out like this, too." He let go of her hand. He put the fingers of his other hand on his palm and stretched his hand palm forward, fingers down. "You can also put your hand against a wall and turn away from yourself."

Penny nodded. "I do that one too."

Their lunch arrived, and they were dead silent as they attacked their food.

When the pie and ice cream arrived with more chocolate Cokes, Charlie sat back in the booth. "Come to the house. We're having a picnic tomorrow while the paint dries."

Libby goggled at her dad. "Um…"

"Lots of people, very overwhelming," Charlie warned Penny. "I know it's been just you and your mom. How is Adelle?"

Penny grinned. "As amazing as usual. I would still be there, but the apartment opened up, and no commute sounded good when I'm saving up for a house."

"Tiny apartment, minuscule rent." Libby grinned back. "Of course, we cheated and had three people in our home. Having Nat the police officer also helped. Keeps the neighborhood safe." She grinned sweetly at Jared. "Move into our neighborhood. With your dog Shadow on patrol, we'll be the safest people ever."

"Maybe I'll come." Penny grinned. Charlie grinned back, and Libby looked concerned. Jared stretched again. "I need a break."

"So do we." Charlie leaned back, and his spine popped. "Every single one of us."

SECRET

*P*enny didn't know what one brought to a family picnic. She knew they would have a ton of food. She doubted flowers were a good idea, or candles. She'd never been to the Camber house before but doubted, with three women living there, they'd need decorations. Besides, with four small children under the age of seven, plus three more from Libby, Ned, and Meri's household, candles or vases or anything breakable seemed like a bad idea. So, she took some gallons of homemade cinnamon, butter brickle, and peppermint stick ice creams, put them in the cooler, and hauled them with her.

The day was crisp, the air carrying smoke from illegally burning leaves. They were in piles of crimson, gold, russet, and brown in nearly every yard. Penny pulled in, and Mitch had her cold box out of the trunk and in the house before she could fully close the door. There was a giant leaf pile on the side of the house, and two corgis and Shadow jumped in and out of the pile with a herd of giggling kids —Bethany and River, their brothers Adam and Bobby, and Beau, Ricky, and Denver. They sounded like banshees, laughing so hard the dogs had to help them up. Penny stumbled across the lawn toward them, drawn to the giggles and shouts, the dog herding the kids back out of the pile so they could jump back in again.

"We have to get a dog." Libby stared at the pile of leaves and children. "They started a sticker campaign to figure out a number. They're willing to give up TV and Lego and all the other things for a dog. I can't lie to myself and say they aren't good with animals. They're even good with Nat's Siamese cat Spook. They listened to every word we've ever said, every word their new uncles Mitch, James, and Jared said about animals. They've even started reading dog training books. We can't get a little dog. We need something good-sized."

Penny pointed. "The animal shelter is over there." She tapped her sunglasses to bring up her HUD. "They've got a black lab, a...wait. A russet dog."

"Where?" Libby took Penny's link and tapped her own sunglasses. "That's..."

Penny saw the look on Libby's face. She was in love. "I'll go. You'll be missed."

"No, as a mom, I have to sign." Libby sighed. "Ned is going to kill me."

"I'll cover for you." Penny walked over to the picnic table, grabbed a collapsible director's chair, snagged a soda from a cooler, and sat while Libby slunk away. The kids and dogs ran, jumped, fell, got up laughing, and did it again. Every once in a while, Penny pointed to the rakes a distance from the mound, and kids would rake the leaves up. Then, the leaping thing began again. Penny took a million pictures for the doting parents, grandparents, uncles, and aunts and sent them all to Charlie to pass on. Charlie sent her a link to a folder, and Penny slid the pictures in. She also shot some videos.

Meri came over to give Penny a bathroom break. Penny snagged a bowl of salsa and some chips on her way back out and watched the kids dive in some more.

"We need to bottle this." Meri brought over and opened up another camp chair.

"*Eau de kid joy.*" Penny grinned, dunked a chip.

"Exactly. Or *Unlimited Energy.*" Meri took off towards the kitchen again. Penny suspected treats were in the offing.

Penny counted herself exceptionally lucky to have been filming with her HUD when Beau saw his mother Libby's car drive up. He pointed and began jumping up and down. Denver looked over, then saw a red head sticking out of the car window. He was off like a shot. Libby got out, and the Irish setter lunged to the front seat and hopped out after her. He was a boy with a coat that had been neglected but was coming back into its russet goodness. Denver knelt, and the dog kissed him. He hugged the dog. Libby threw him a ball, Denver threw it to the side, and boy and dog were off.

Beau was moving his little legs as fast as he could when his brother Ricky passed him. A second dog lunged out, this one a yellow and black brindle greyhound. The dog ran up to Ricky and quivered. Ricky knelt, and the greyhound lowered herself in a play pose. Ricky twitched, the dog started, and Ricky followed the dog when she took off like a shot.

Beau finally got to his mother, and Penny's heart dropped at the tears in his eyes. Libby opened the back door and grunted as she lifted a gray French bulldog with a white stripe on her belly and huge jowls and deposited her on the ground. The dog promptly took two steps to Beau, sat on his feet, and slobbered. Beau leaned down, stricken with love, and petted the dog's head. The dog looked up with absolute adoration. Libby grinned, and Penny gave her a thumbs-up.

It took a while to get a very slow boy and even slower dog back to the Pile of Dog and Kid Joy. Libby sat with a thud in the second camp chair. Penny got sodas, put them in the chairs' drink holes, and sent two little girls and their brothers in with Jetta to take a bathroom break. Charlie came out with a tray full of strawberry-lime frozen pops, and the kids rushed outside for a treat. Beau and his dog made it in time for Beau to sit down and eat his ice pop while the dog slobbered on his foot.

Charlie grabbed a chair and sat down. "Beau, what's your new dog's name?"

Beau looked at Libby.

"Nyx," Libby said.

"It means night." Penny grinned at the dog. "She kind of looks like dusk, when the sky goes gray."

"I love her." Beau patted his dog's head. "She is a very good dog."

Charlie nodded. "I see that Rusty and Lemonade are very fast."

Penny grinned. "Good names."

"Do they answer to them?" Libby asked her father.

"They do." Charlie went back in with the freezer pop detritus, came out with another camp chair, and plopped down.

Libby sighed. "Beau doesn't need speed. He's never had a problem going to sleep or getting up on time. What he needs is…"

"Love and adoration," Penny said.

Charlie nodded. "I can see that."

Beau smiled at his mom. "Thank you for bringing me my dog."

Libby's eyes went misty. "I love you, kid. And, good news. You don't have to give up your stickers."

"Yay!" Beau grinned. The dog licked his face.

"But, your dog needs food, water, walks, brushing…"

"Especially the Irish setter." Charlie pointed with his chin.

"And lots of love." Libby smiled.

"No problem." Beau patted his dog.

"You can't forget. If you're sick or need help, you have to ask for it. But you only get sick days twice a year."

"Got it." Beau knelt and gave a tummy rub. The dog groaned in happiness.

Libby grinned, her eyes moist. "I trust you with the dog, buddy. Your brothers may have to… wait, I'll just program their schedules."

Charlie laughed. "Do you remember when Jen programmed your schedule?"

Libby laughed. "I was so overscheduled that I nearly had a heart attack!"

"You were coltish and very nervous for a while." Charlie grinned while Libby grimaced. "She was trying to get you focused. Your grades did go way up."

Penny laughed when Adam and Bobby ran towards the house, most of the dogs in tow. "We probably need to eat."

"That involves getting up." Libby groaned.

Charlie stood and pulled Libby up. "I hope you have enough food, dog dishes, and a mountain of grooming products for Rusty."

"I do, but I have to get it all out of the vehicle."

Penny laughed. "You do have Meri and Nat to help."

"Nat's on graves and is, therefore, able to spend more time with the boys. Nat gets them to school, sleeps, and then wakes up to play with them after school."

"Why is a small-town cop on grave shift?" Penny asked.

"Cleaning up paperwork. They did another raid on those idiots living in the woods." Charlie left the 'cartel drug manufacturer' part out of the conversation.

Penny stood and helped fold up all the chairs. "I understand. Must have created a paperwork blizzard."

"Three more weeks of mind-numbing paperwork. And less rescuing cats from trees."

Libby reached down and picked up the very slow dog. Charlie picked up Beau and put the kid on his shoulders. They walked up to the big table. Charlie put Beau down, and Libby put the dog down.

"Hand washing first," Libby informed Charlie.

Charlie picked Beau up and took him at a lumbering run to the outside sink. Libby guarded the dog while Penny went to go wash up. Jen came out and wordlessly put a huge bowl of potato salad in Penny's arms. Penny hauled it to the table. Nyx began a slow trek towards her missing boy. Charlie and Beau came back with water for the dog. Beau carefully put the bowl under the table. Nyx edged over to the bowl and lapped up the water. Beau sat down in his little chair, and Nyx put her head on his feet again.

Penny nearly died from the adorableness. "Good news. You'll always be able to find Beau."

Libby snorted. "Yuk it up. You're the dogsitter."

Penny sat, her jaw on the ground, as a steady stream of handsome men came out with the food—Libby's brothers Len, Davis, and Vic, and Mitch and James and their brother Jared. There was fruit salad in a watermelon 'bowl' with the melons cut into little balls, making a little lake of green, orange, and red. There was a pasta bake with shredded red pepper, chicken, bacon, and melted cheddar and mozzarella cheese on top. There were baskets of bread twists, a green salad with several cruets of dressing, baked potatoes, baked apples stuffed with nuts and honey swimming in a caramel sauce, and grilled pork. Jen came out with the kid food, sandwiches, and fruit on plates. Rachael and Jetta came out and put the kids in kid camp chairs at the much lower kids' table. The dogs followed, and to their credit, lay down under the table. The corgis and Shadow chose the adult table, wisely looking for dropped pork or chicken. The kids giggled and discussed dogs.

Penny sat next to Libby on one side and Jared on the other. The food and hot apple cider spiced with cinnamon and nutmeg flowed. The food was amazingly delicious. There were jokes, stories, and so much laughter. Penny sat there and soaked it up.

Jared looked Penny up and down. "Overwhelmed?"

Penny smiled at his concern. "No, exhausted. And gratified. Don't get me wrong. My mama is everything. Adelle is the best of the best. She took in two girls who weren't hers. My next-door-neighbor Farrah had two daughters, Morgan and Maddie. They both got out at eighteen. They both stayed with us until graduation. Morgan became a Marine."

"I heard about her. Her service was amazing, from what I've been told."

Penny nodded. "She was the best of the best, no joke. So, Maddie went off to college, and I got through two years of community college. Maddie moved away and is married with two little girls. Anyway, my mama went hungry some days to feed three teen girls."

"Your mama is the hero." Jared poured more cider for them both.

"That's why I am living in that teeny tiny apartment over my work. I'm saving up for my own place. My mama has money now, but I'm not going to take a dime from her."

Jared nodded. "I get that."

"What about your mama?"

Jared laughed. "Rachael is a force of nature. See Jen?"

"She scares me," Penny spoke in a teeny-tiny voice.

Jared laughed. He snagged a baked apple and gave it to Penny. Then he snagged one for himself. "I get that. She would make a fantastic drill instructor." Charlie laughed and winked at Jared. "Anyway, Rachael is tough, kind of a ribbon of steel hidden in that soft mama body. My dad is Gunny, not nearly as big as Charlie here, who is a mutant freak of nature."

Charlie gave Jared a thumbs-up from across the table.

"Sounds like you have a strong family." Penny bit into a bite of apple and moaned.

"Mama gave Jen the dunked apple recipe." Jen gave Jared a dirty glare, and he ducked his head as if she'd thrown something at him. "Anyway, my mama took in Stretcher. She's ex-military, very strong. And Mitch and James' parents died, and they ended up with us. Then they left, and now they're back. And now I'm here."

Penny tried not to moan while eating the rest of the apple. "What is it like chasing after all of these kids all the time?"

Jared laughed. "Fun. I look forward to chasing even more of them."

Penny gave him a side-eye. "Are you trying to tell me that you're a baby daddy?"

Jared threw back his head and guffawed. "No. No girlfriend, so no." He looked down at his lap. "In fact, I think I've forgotten how it works."

Penny snorted. "I kind of vaguely remember. Try starting a business that is very seasonal. New levels of both hard work and terror."

Jared smiled. "Try moving to a new town and becoming a trainer. Scary new job. Get to work with my dog all day, though."

"Where is she?" Penny asked.

Jared pointed. Shadow was herding the very fast Lemonade back towards the table. Lemonade made it to the kids' table and flopped down. Pleased, Shadow trotted back to the perimeter. "She's decided that it's her job to herd the new dogs."

Penny grinned. "Well, she is a shepherd."

Somehow, Penny and Jared ended up washing the kids up after eating and watched them as they headed inside as the temperature dropped. They got out the giant Legos and began putting them together to make an actual small house in the living room. The dogs guarded the children, Shadow on the perimeter.

Beau walked up to Penny, Nyx on his heels, and looked up at her. "You have to leave soon."

"I was planning on it anyway," said Penny, a little hurt. "I've got to get up early to get the work we did in my place inspected, then open my shop."

Beau shook his head. "I'm not trying to be mean at you. It's just that, the kids get to stay in, and we have a sleepover with Ned and Aunt Corinne and Aunt Kandace. But, you gotta go."

"Okay. Why?"

"They kinda change. Ooo."

"Ooo?"

"Bears and wolves." Beau looked at Penny, begging her to believe him with his eyes.

"Shifters." Penny kept her voice low.

"Yeah. But it's a sea-cret."

"It's okay. I won't tell."

"Good. Bye bye."

Penny hugged the little boy close to her. He smelled of leaves, sweat, and dog. She crossed the room and spoke to Jared. "I've got to go. Early day tomorrow."

"Sure. Just let me call Mitch or Jetta or someone in. I'll walk you to your car."

Penny smiled at Jared and his chivalry, then put on her jacket. Corinne came in with Kandace, and the two of them bookended the kids. Kandace had her hand on her stomach, and so did Corinne. Penny realized what Jared had been talking about earlier.

When they got onto the porch, Penny said, gently, "You are shifters."

Jared stopped moving forward. "Who told you?"

Penny said, slowly, "Beau wasn't just watching movies he's too young to watch, was he?"

Jared stared at the enormous full moon, silvery and low in the sky. "You can't tell anyone."

"I'm not crazy. I go for hikes in the woods. I see bears and wolves. Saw a cougar once."

"That may have been Lynette."

Penny sighed. "It was. I saw her change, put on her clothes, and walk off. I was in a tree downwind. Still like to climb them."

Jared stared at her, his face frozen, his eyes huge. "When was this?"

"Almost two years ago."

"Does Libby know you know?"

"No, and the fact I know and didn't tell her will probably hurt her. It's just that... I was in the tree because it's the anniversary of the day Morgan died. I didn't think it was my secret to tell. In fact, I thought I was going crazy, although I was stone-cold sober."

"Thank you for keeping our secret."

Lynette stepped out from her hiding place on the porch. Penny jumped a little. "I heard you cry as a cougar. I changed and didn't see you as a woman. I wanted to tell you that the pain of losing a friend is horrific, but it does get better with time."

"It does, but it still sucks."

"It does. It gets better, but it doesn't go away. I am so sorry you lost your heart-sister." Penny stepped forward, and Lynette folded the younger woman in her arms.

Jared smiled a little and walked around the side of the house.

Once the tears stopped flowing, Lynette said, "I have to join my family. They'll be wondering where I am." She stroked Penny's long hair. "Do yourself a favor and go home. You have my official permission to tell your mother. I know Adelle well and know you're an apple under her tree."

Penny choked. "And how do I explain this, exactly? Mama, I know this family that changed into cougars and..."

"Bears, wolves, and a very large wolf-dog." A huge black dog with yellow eyes came around the corner. "This is Mitch. He has a wolf form too."

Mitch looked at Penny with those yellow eyes. He looked like he was laughing at her.

"Okay." Penny nodded once, hard. "Okay. I'll hold off telling Mama quite yet."

"Have her call the house. Corinne or Kandace will explain."

"Wouldn't want to get locked up in a rubber room." Penny smiled through her tears.

"They really don't do that anymore." Lynette let Penny go.

"You were willing to expose your secret to comfort me."

"Girl, you are definitely worth it." Lynette waved, and Penny walked to her car.

~

*P*enny didn't remember telling the car to drive to her original home. She alternated sobbing and laughing, wondering if she was, in fact, insane. She wiped her tears and got out of the vehicle. Adelle already had the door open. She dragged her daughter inside into the warmth and held her close. Penny cried a little for Morgan, who never got to see her sister's kids. Then she cried for the young woman in a tree who thought she was going crazy.

They sat down on the couch. Adelle handed over a box of tissues. "I just had the weirdest call from Lynette. She said you will tell me something that sounds crazy, but it isn't crazy and not to have you committed. I'm afraid to ask. Very afraid." She sat up very straight. "Lay it on me."

"It's actually Lynette's secret." Penny spilled out the story of the tree and Lynette's ability to change into a cougar. "Lynette says you can call the house and talk to Kandace or Corinne. They can't change into anything, by the way. They apparently stay with the kids while other people change."

"This is going to sound crazier than what you just told me, but that actually explains a lot of things." Adelle looked thoughtful, not shocked or horrified. "The bears and wolves around here are extremely polite. I pay attention."

"I... Mom, I was afraid you'd call someone to take me away."

Adelle shook her head furiously. "If anyone comes to take you away, they have to go through me."

Penny smiled and held her magnificent mama close.

TREED

*J*ared entered Libby's half of the sweet bakery/ice cream shop, hoping to get some nut butter-filled gluten-free goodness. The scents of the season assailed him. Pumpkin, spice, cinnamon. He had no idea why people bought pumpkin spice lattes to drink, pumpkin pie tartlets, or indulged in pumpkin spice ice cream. He didn't hate pumpkins; he just didn't want to smell them everywhere. There were people with laptops pounding out words or code, moms and dads with babies in packs on their bellies or in strollers, and a couple of people eating treats and staring off into space or looking at their HUDs.

Mary Beth was behind the counter when Jared came up with his mix of cocoa-nut butter treats. "Where is Libby?" he asked. "I don't see Penny either."

"At the police station."

Jared nearly dropped his treats. "What?"

"You know about Farrah, right?"

"She used to be Penny's neighbor. The woman that walks around saying hateful things to people all over town, right?"

"That's the one. She's apparently in a psychiatric hospital and is in deep denial about how much trouble she's actually in and what's really

34

wrong with her. Chief Taylor is asking everyone who's had to deal with her over the years to come in for an interview to explain exactly what happened. He's also throwing in all the body cam footage from the cops who have had to deal with her over the years. Anyway, she harassed Libby last year, then Penny this year. She also screamed at Ned, Meri, and a lot of other people. Most of the business owners have refused service to her. They're getting a lot of footage to help the doctors help Farrah."

Jared nodded. "If it helps at all, that's probably a good idea. But, those poor people have to relive everything they've had to deal with that woman. Mary Beth, can you tell me exactly where the police station is located?" The teenager pointed a little bit down across the street. "Thanks. Let me have some of these snacks to go."

Jared ate a cacao peanut butter ball, walked across the street, and found the municipal building with very little trouble. It was a squat building, all stone. Jared was just beginning to trudge up the stairs when Libby came out, her arm around Penny. They made their way partway down the stairs.

Jared jogged up to meet them. "Rough session?"

Libby smiled grimly. "I sure hope this helps. I really hope it was worth it. I had no idea Farrah had done so much damage. The woman belongs behind bars or in a rubber room until she figures out how to behave properly among other humans."

Penny nodded. Her beautiful blue-green eyes were teary and red. "My mother and I both want her to stay where she is until she learns how to be an adult among other adults."

"I know it's a little early, but do you ladies want some lunch?" Jared asked.

Libby nodded. "We've both been up early. Penny has started working out with us in the mornings. Ned is making us stronger. So, yeah, sounds good."

Penny gave a watery laugh. "I'm still freaked out that you only have to get from 70% to 80% of your resting heart rate to be effective with high-intensity interval training. My weights are low to start until my form is perfect."

Jared grinned. "If for some reason Ned can't make it, I'll be happy to help. I've got to get into better shape myself."

Libby gave him the side-eye. "I thought you did interval training with the other dog trainers."

"We do. If we expect our dogs to stay in shape, we have to be in good enough shape for taking them all the places they need to go."

They made it to the diner, and Jared opened the door for the ladies. The lunch rush hadn't hit yet, so they were able to get a booth looking out on the town. People wore jeans, slacks, or corduroy pants, and flannel tops or sweaters. The breeze was brisk, swirling the leaves.

They all ordered strong coffees, sandwiches, and fries. Tammy, their server, came back with a black open-your-eyes Kenyan blend. She had a broad face and dark eyes and a braying, infectious laugh.

"You ladies have to go to the police station? I gave my testimony at the crack of dawn. Hope it gets that woman's head on straight."

Libby pointed at herself, then Penny. "Preaching to the choir." Tammy nodded, whirled, and went to go top off the coffee at another table.

Penny grimaced. "Let's talk about something else. Like how much I've had to order, and how I'm making ice cream at 5:30 in the morning so I have enough for Halloween."

"Do you have any idea how much almond flour costs? It isn't just people with a sweet tooth who buy more for Halloween. My gluten and sugar-free people need something to deal with that night." Libby added more cream to her coffee.

Jared nodded. "I eat gluten-free snacks, too."

Penny nodded. "I literally can't make enough of them. I had to get Libby's sister Meri to make me a batch while she makes her food for her shut-ins."

The food came, and they were all quiet as they ate their grilled chicken burgers. The fries were curly and salty and absolutely perfect.

Halfway through lunch, Penny was finally able to talk about it. "It really wasn't bad—the interviews, I mean. They were just recording us talking about our experiences with Farrah. That was the entire question, tell me about your experiences with her. It's not like we were raked over the coals. The therapist guy was really nice. His name is Reggie. I remember him from high school. Used to play baseball. He has the kindest eyes. Anyway, he explained that Farrah keeps ending up on full lockdown with all her privileges removed for being rude and hostile to the point that her comments can be classified as hate speech. She's on meds, but until she can see herself as she truly is, she won't change."

Libby nodded. "How many therapists does it take to change a light bulb?"

Penny and Jared both groaned. "One, but the light bulb has to want to change. Your grandma told us, remember?" Penny pointed at Libby.

"The good thing about being raised poly is the grandparents. Charlie's parents died in a car crash when he was in the service, but all three of my moms have their moms. Jen's mom is just as scary as she is. By the time she leaves, something in the house is much cleaner than it used to be."

Jared laughed. "Gunny's mom is about a third of his size, with dark hair and very dark eyes. She has his laugh. I swear you can hear that woman laughing in another state."

Libby ate her last fry. "Jetta's parents are backwoods, quiet, country folk. Like us." Everyone at the table laughed. They were country, but none of them could be considered quiet. "Charlie decided that they needed a wedding present for having birthed his new wife, so he bought them a new truck that gets them back and forth on a single charge. They end up spending half the time on their visits with the poly community's beekeepers. It turns out they're doing all sorts of work to make bee colonies recover all over the state. I swear I've never eaten so much lavender, clover, and other kinds of honey. I buy honey from the poly community beekeepers and use it in a lot of my desserts. I also make lavender honey cream as a topping."

Penny opened her eyes wide. "Bears like honey."

Libby grinned. "And she catches on."

"I don't howl at the moon, change in bathrooms or in front of other people, and I didn't play guitar as a teen. I have also never pined after a sparkly vampire's girlfriend." Jared ate his last fry and smirked.

Penny moaned. "All the stereotypes! They're crushing me!"

Libby grinned. "I do love sweet things, and I do cook with honey. I started cooking because I have two very busy moms and a busy dad, and we teenagers ate like moose. I either ended up with sad little lunches that didn't fill me up or learned how to make them. One of my moms hired a local chef boy before he went on to become quite famous in St. Louis. Meri and I learned various aspects of cooking like ducks take to water. I like making sweets, even gluten-free, once I got on that kick when the teenage boys started howling about carbs."

"Do bears howl?" Jared gave a little *roo*.

Libby reached across the table and smacked his arm. "Doofus. No, we don't. Parents get very big, and growl, and will do anything to defend their young." Her eyes narrowed. "Jetta was a very special case. She wanted two sets of twins and planned to leave immediately upon having the second ones. Her husband was violent. Apparently, the second birth was terrible, and she was sick for quite a while."

Jared clenched his fork. "I take it, the father…"

"They found the skeleton a while ago and a creek bed. No one seems to know what happened to him." Libby grinned ferally. "Couldn't have happened to a nicer guy. Jetta had been long gone by then. She got her clan stipend for being a widow."

Penny lowered her voice. "Shifter social security?"

Libby nodded. "Very secure investments, trusts. I was very put out with his clan until I found out Jetta's husband had been living in the woods like a survivalist and no one had known where he was."

"So, clans police their own members?"

Libby and Jared both nodded like bobbleheads.

"Let's just say that certain things are not allowed." Libby narrowed her eyes at both Jared and Penny.

Jared literally hung his head. "I'm in a lot of shifter trouble right now for talking about what we are. Jetta is going to get a lot of free babysitting for a long time, and if anything goes wrong with your shop, either of you, and I can help, give me a call."

Libby grinned. "Everyone loves the Lego-style brick lights. People come in just to look up at them, then they smell things and order them. I'm at nearly twelve percent over last year. What about you, Penny?"

Penny's voice was very small. "Same for me. Jared, I'm very sorry I got you in trouble. I just thought that I had gone crazy."

Jared patted her hand. "I should have thought first before I spoke. Seems to be a problem with me."

"Well, Jared, stay here and have pie. The two of us work with sweets all day, and we've got to get back to our shops." Libby stood and stretched. "Since you're in so much trouble, you'll pay the bill, won't you?" Libby's voice was as sweet as her dark cherry tartlets.

"Of course. Have a lovely day, ladies. I think I'll just have some peanut butter pie with the chocolate cookie crust. It may not be gluten-free or good for my middle, but it's incredibly delicious." Jared patted his flat stomach.

Libby kissed his cheek. "Thank you, new brother."

Penny kissed his other cheek. "Thank you, Spiller of Secrets. I foresee your having some very active children over Halloween. I'll see you in a few days." She smiled a slow, sweet smile that made his entire body ripple, and then she was out the door.

Jared pondered his new name. He had always considered himself to be particularly trustworthy. He had never told anyone non-family what he was. This episode had been rather traumatic and somewhat unforgivable. He could have been censured, forced to return home, even gotten the bears arguing with the wolves, which nobody wanted. Penny had looked so sad and confused and had believed herself insane. He couldn't let the woman that he had begun to care about feel that way.

He liked her smile, her ready laugh, and the way that she interacted with kids. She could get a wailing toddler to coo in seconds. Of course, it helped that she had the magic of ice cream behind her. Still, the way she spoke to children was remarkable.

Jared loved children and hoped for a large family. He didn't care if his fatherhood was biological or via adoption. He just wanted to feel that gut-wrenching thing he knew Charlie felt with four young children in the house. What Mitch and James were going to feel when Corinne gave birth to twins, and Kandace had hers. Gunny had been a fantastic father, even when Mitch and James broke their hearts by moving out, wrecked by their parents' deaths. Now Rachael and Gunny were helping a young woman named Lydia come to terms with being a cougar shifter. Lydia's father had died when she was young, and her non-shifter mother had died relatively recently. Lydia wasn't alone anymore. None of them were.

Jared finished his pie, paid, washed his hands, walked out, and got into his vehicle. His racing thoughts about Penny and the packs cut off when he told the truck that he wanted to go home to pick up Shadow for training. He was on his way home when he heard the code for child abduction, and Jared encouraged the vehicle to go as fast as possible to pick up Shadow.

Chief Taylor called while Jared was a block from home. "A little boy is missing. We'd like you and Shadow to help. We're meeting at North Pine Road."

"On my way in two minutes."

The sheriff hung up. Jared got out, reached in the door, grabbed the go pack, and put Shadow's coat on her. Shadow perked up. She loved to work.

They met partway up on the far side of the mountain at the base of a little-used trail. Shadow was ready. Deputy Nat Sandowan looked grim.

"The boy's name is Skyler Salter. Skyler, his parents Rudy and Lucia, and his little sister Grace were hiking up this trail from the other side."

Ned sent a picture to their HUDs. Jared stared at the picture of a brown-haired boy with an elfin face, tilted green eyes, and a very dark tan wearing blue jeans, a long-sleeved red shirt, and brown hiking boots.

"We're lucky because this picture was taken this morning. This is exactly what he's wearing."

Mitch, in his huge black wolf-dog form, moved closer to James. Shadow wagged her tail. She liked Mitch in either form.

"Skyler ran ahead to jump in the stream, as little boys do. He got through a break in the trees. His sister, father, and mother all agreed that he was taken by an individual with hair dyed black because all three of them mentioned seeing brown roots. Tan skin, brown hiking pants, very scuffed hiking shoes, a black shirt. It only took a second for him to pick up the boy and run. Skyler is five years old. We will find him, and we will return him to his family. Blackie, east, Shadow, west."

Ned held out two socks. Both dog and shifter-dog sniffed the socks, getting a snootful of the boy's scent. James and Jared bumped fists, and then the dogs were off in opposite directions when Jared gave the order to find. Jared had a backpack with him in case he wanted to change into a wolf himself. But men and dogs made better pairs, and a human could carry the boy out better than a wolf could.

Shadow knew exactly what she had to do. She kept her nose to the ground, following the trail. The abductor would probably use getting in and out of the river to hide the scent, but that wouldn't fool the dogs for long. They had a plan and a purpose. The Cambers and Westons knew every bit of that land because it abutted their property. Mitch, James, and Jared had all been out here as wolves. There weren't any cabins or other places for someone to hide, no hidden caves. With bears nearby, that sort of thing would have been found and mapped.

Shadow knew where to sniff. She went back and forth between the edges of the trail and surged ahead. It was a cool, crisp day, better than if the call had come out in the middle of summer. Jared knew the abductor would have a car somewhere and would be an experienced hiker. The abductor had used a split second, which told Jared this had probably happened before. An experienced abductor was a dangerous creature. Jared longed to get his teeth into the abductor. Once they got DNA, Jared suspected that a host of crimes that had been committed on mountains would be closed.

Jared heard a deep aroo. "New plan, find Blackie," Jared ordered Shadow. Shadow was off like a shot, following a deer path. Jared struggled to keep up with her without breaking an ankle. The forest floor was covered with leaves in various stages of decomposition, and a good pile of wet leaves could lead Jared into injury rather than saving the boy.

The deer path crossed the stream. The abductor was trapped in the middle of the water, Blackie/Mitch in the water with teeth bared, and James barrelling up to his brother.

Shadow ran past them towards a tree. Skyler had climbed up high, too high, and had wedged himself in between two branches. Shadow put her front paws on the tree, frustrated because she couldn't climb. Jared ignored the man's cries as his brothers' pincer movement in the stream closed in on him.

"Skyler, my name is Jared. I'm working with the police department to find you." He tapped his HUD, sent the feed to Nat. "You did really good by getting up in that tree. You're such a smart boy."

"Is the doggie going to eat me?" Skyler's voice was rough with tears.

"No, Shadow is trying to climb the tree like a bear. She forgot she's a dog." Jared gave a hand signal, and the dog immediately sat. "Good girl, Shadow, good find," Jared said in German and gave her the pink whale squeaky toy. The toy squeaked with abandon as Shadow shook the toy. "The police are coming, along with your family. It'll take them a while to get down here because it's a bit slippery on the leaves. You can stay up there, that's fine. We can wait. Or, if you want to, you could climb on my shoulders and sit on top of me like a tree."

Skyler gave a half grin through his tears. "My daddy likes to carry me on his head, but he says I'm getting a bit too big."

"Cover your eyes," Jared ordered the boy as the abductor leaped out of the stream towards the deer track Jared had come in on.

Jared gave a command in German, and Shadow dropped her toy and took the man down. The abductor screamed as if he were being eaten alive, but Shadow had been trained to hold someone still and not to kill unless on command. Jared spared a glance to find Blackie laying his considerable weight over the man's legs so he couldn't go anywhere. James approached the man with plastic ties, so Jared told Shadow in German to stay still.

Jared looked back at Skyler. The boy looked absolutely terrified, his eyes huge. "It's okay; we're arresting the bad man. Shadow and Blackie have not hurt the man. They are just holding him in place."

"Okay. Can I get on your shoulders now?"

"Sure."

Jared maneuvered himself directly under the boy and reached up. He took Skyler's feet, and Skyler stood on his shoulders. He reached up to the boy's ankles and was ready when the boy fell forward with a scream. He lowered himself and held on until the boy's arms were around his waist. And then James was there to help turn Skyler over. Skyler grabbed onto Jared like a monkey.

"I am so sorry that was scary." Jared held the boy tight as he heard crashing above.

Nat came down, surefooted. Nat wasn't a shifter but had a gracefulness and a calm implacability that the shifters trusted. "Skyler, we are so happy to see you. Jared, please call off your dog. Blackie, stay where you are."

The abductor was making little mewling sounds. Jared called Shadow back to him. He checked her teeth for blood, but there was none. She got her squeaky toy back from Jared and shook it.

Nat nodded once, hard. "Jared, do you have a problem walking Skyler up to the trail?"

"Not a one."

Shadow gave Jared the toy back, and Jared put it in the pack. Ned, James, and Blackie stayed with the suspect while Jared and Shadow carefully took the deer trail up to the main trail, Skyler on his back, the boy's grip surprisingly strong. Jared started singing "The ants are marching one by one," and Skyler's little boy voice joined in.

Sheriff Taylor, a largish man who had slimmed down a lot so his uniform sagged over his belly in folds, looked down at them from farther up the hill. The sheriff sang as well, as did the EMT, a young woman with dark hair and kind eyes. They sang all the way through a quick checkup. By the time they were done, Skyler's family had surrounded them, and Jared had been divested of his limpet little boy.

Shadow sat quietly and allowed a very scared older sister to hug her and cry. Jared knelt down next to Grace. "I am so sorry this happened to your family on your nice hiking day. You can drive home if you want, but I know of a really nice place that has ice cream and brownies."

Grace nodded. "Sounds nice. Did your dog find my brother?"

"Her name is Shadow, and yes, she found him in a tree. Another dog named Blackie found him first. James, his human, trapped and kept the bad guy in the river. Then Deputy Ned came and arrested the guy. So, you don't have to worry about anything."

Grace wiped her eyes. "On TV, when that stuff happens, cops ask a lot of questions. Can we put in an order and have the stuff delivered?"

"I'm stuck up here in the mountains with you, but I know someone who can help. Why don't we talk about what's in the shop? My sister-like friend Libby runs the bakery side, and my good friend Penny runs the other. I seem to recall there being butter brickle, chocolate cookie mint, rainbow sherbet..."

Grace's voice grew stronger. "My brother eats anything with chocolate and sprinkles on it. My mom likes anything with mint in it and dark chocolate, and dad likes anything with nuts in it."

"What about you?"

"My mom says I'm a little baby chocoholic. But I like anything with peanut butter in it too."

"So do I," Jared confessed. "So, I think we have enough information to get an order in. I'll tell Libby and Penny what your family wants. Someone will be up to the trailhead with the entire order. How does that sound?"

"That sounds nice. Our dog Sunny is small and white. She's at the groomer's today. We decided to take a hike after lunch, and we're going to pick up the dog on the way out. Stupid plan, huh."

"No, not a stupid plan. It's a very good family day plan. I'll call the groomers and make sure your dog gets some extra special treats while waiting. How does that sound?"

"Omigod, so awesome." Grace smiled and swiped away the last of her tears, and Jared smiled back. Shadow licked her face, and she laughed.

∼

To his surprise, Jetta was at the trailhead with everyone's order, including coffee and extra brownies for the parents, rescuers, police and EMTs, and hot chocolate for the kids. The kids ate their ice cream, which delighted their parents so they could stop panicking enough to have a little bit of ice cream themselves. Penny had wisely only sent enough ice cream for one cone each for the parents, knowing they'd be too upset to eat much. The kids, however, devoured the sweets.

Everyone gave their reports and signed the paperwork, leaving Sheriff Taylor and Deputy Nat Sandawan to transport the prisoner and fill out their mounds of paperwork. FBI techs came up, delighted to get evidence against a serial kidnapper. They took custody before Nat had even gotten into the front of the vehicle.

Nat shrugged. "Less work for me." He sighed. "This outcome was worth losing sleep." Both sides signed transfer of custody papers, and the FBI vehicle left, leaving the tech van and techs behind.

Jetta walked back to her truck. Jared and James and their canine friends got into their vehicles and followed her down the hill. She had insisted they come, and no one in their right mind argued with the shifter female.

Once they had all parked their trucks at the farm, Jetta rounded on Jared. "You earn some points. That was good thinking, and it made those kids feel better. Mitch, you go change. James, you and Mitch are heroes for catching those people, and Jared, you got that boy safely out of the tree. We're all happy about that. But, Jared, you're going to have a heck of an adrenaline crash. Right now, I want you to go chase Bobby and Adam. They're in the backyard in a tree right now. Don't pull a Kandace and try to get them out of the tree if they get stuck. Just call one of us."

Jared nodded once, hard. "Yes, ma'am."

Jared was glad that he had postponed training until later in the week. His new rescue story would get everyone showing up on time and doing what they needed to do during the rest of the week. He crossed over into the backyard, and, sure enough, there were two black bear cubs in a fat oak tree, striking the tree with their paws and watching the leaves fall down. Jetta came back out with a camp chair and a soda for Jared, and Jared sat down to watch his new family play. Shadow sat and played with her pink toy elephant and ignored the bears. It was a good day.

HALLOWEEN

*A*s Halloween crept up on them, the dramatic rescue was the talk of the town. Parents who had previously allowed their children to walk alone or with older siblings on Halloween had a change of heart. So did Penny.

"Why don't we have a party with the cover charge on Halloween night? Now that there is no wall, we have space. We can have a costume contest, have kids bob for apples, pin the Velcro tail on the plastic donkey, stuff like that."

Libby laughed. "We make enough money not to do that. Besides, someone is going to have to watch all these games you're talking about, and we're not going to have time to breathe. We can, however, have the kids and their parents put pictures of the costumes up on the pillars, and have a vote for the best ones."

Penny laughed. "Good use of pillar space. I think what we can do is just have the pictures put up and have little stickers up for the kids to informally vote on what they would like best. The top three get free food. You're right; we won't have time to do much more than get the food out and clean."

Libby nodded. "I like your costume. In fact, I'm rather jealous."

Both women had decided to wear costumes that made it still easy to move. Libby was dressed as a black cat, with cat ears and a very short cat tail. Mary Beth was dressed as a Roman matron, her hair in ringlets, a circlet on her head. Her dress was cut in such a way that it was still easy for her to move. Penny's assistant Dana was dressed as a punk rocker with fake tattoos and a spiky pink-haired wig. Penny was absolutely gorgeous as a fairy. She had plastic pointed fairy tips on her ears, a gorgeous blue sparkly gown with layers, sparkly fabric on the skirt, and her red hair with strawberry blonde highlighted a cobalt blue.

Penny pointed to her hair. "Blue wax."

They made sure there were extras of everything, including garbage liners in the cans, toilet paper in the bathrooms, and stuffed refrigerators and freezers so they could quickly put out new food items. They put out thirty percent more than their usual stock and opened an hour later so that they could stay open later on the other end. Libby went to the drugstore for some instant disposable cameras and stickers, then they opened the door.

The day hit them like a freight train. There were numerous Halloween parties going on because parents wanted to keep their kids indoors. Some had the intelligence to order things in advance, and some did not. Penny was delighted that she had made extra ice cream cakes in case of this eventuality, and Libby had made hundreds of spooky cupcakes, including gluten-free versions. One rush came in, there would be a lull, and Penny and Libby ran around like maniacs cleaning up and restocking before the next.

Their usual round of authors and coders avoided them like the plague except to fill up their carafes with drinks and their backpacks with snacks. They were going to inhabit the coffee shops and library and sneak off in the bathroom in the library to eat treats.

Even the parents wore costumes, so there were quite a few witches, vampires, monsters of various shapes and sizes, ghosts, werewolves, giant animals, superheroes, and robots. The disposable instant cameras were hit, and pictures began covering these columns, adults on the top, kids below. Voting was done in the form of smiley faces and hearts. A little girl who had come in as a superhero nurse was in the lead.

Jetta came in to pick up things for the kids, and she helped with cleanup in order to give all four of them bathroom breaks. She got free bat cookies and a pint of fudge brickle for her trouble. "When you guys close, if either one of you were still standing, come to the farm. We're going to have movies."

Penny nodded. "We're closed tomorrow, so if I'm still standing up, I can make the attempt."

"Come in your costume. You are absolutely lovely." Jetta wore a bear costume, just the ears, face painting, and a furry sweater, which made Penny and Libby laugh.

"I will." Penny waved. The lines were suddenly much longer, and they were slammed again.

By the time they shut the front doors, they had sold nearly everything in their stock. "Thank goodness we are not open tomorrow. It's going to take me two days just to replace everything." Libby shook her head.

"My ice cream makers are going to fall apart." Penny finished her checklist.

They had taken out the trash and cleaned and scrubbed the minute their lines slowed down. Mary Beth and Dana escaped, off to enjoy their own Halloween parties.

"Let's go get some food at my parent's house. My dad has a barbecue addiction. I'm sure we'll have great food to eat in addition to all the sweets they're going to be serving." Libby grabbed Penny and dragged her out the back door. Libby locked and set the alarm and continued to drag Penny to her vehicle.

Penny tried to pull away but almost fell over with exhaustion. "I have to get back here at a reasonable hour tomorrow in order to start making more ice cream."

"Be reasonable. Sleep in, then we'll come back here, have a nice lunch in the coffee shop, and we'll both get to restocking. That sound good?"

"Fine, but I don't have…"

"I happen to know your gym bag is in your vehicle. Wear your sweats tomorrow." Penny grabbed the bag out of her trunk, and they took Libby's vehicle.

There were still trick and treaters out as they went to the farm. They made it there alive, ducking kids throwing toilet paper on their hated teachers' lawns. Nat caught the miscreants.

Libby grimaced. "If I had done any of that when I was a kid, my parents would have lined up to kill me."

Penny nodded. "My mother is awesome, but mayhem would have put me on her chores-for-a-month list. I knew I wouldn't die if I showed up pregnant or after a jail sentence. Or after a pregnant jail sentence."

Libby snorted. "Both at once would probably be bad."

Penny held up a finger. "I wouldn't die, but my mother taught me that there were consequences to everything. She taught me to cook and bake, how to make my own clothes, how to budget, how to make a dollar stretch and squeal. She helped me with my homework until the point that I got it, then I had to do the rest of it by myself. She would have been disappointed by a pregnant jail sentence, and she would have made me go through as many consequences that she could stand."

Libby nodded. "We're shifters, and we're bears. We've got secrets to keep, huge families and businesses to run, and no time to put up with a kid acting a fool. Most of us are twins, so there was always a tattletale. I couldn't get away with anything. Dad is really big on consequences too. Nothing that would actually kill us, but we found it really quickly why you don't run around in the snow with no coat in human form. My mothers say that I was tinged blue before I figured it out."

They made it to the farm without further incident and quickly got themselves into the house. Charlie greeted them at the door, but it was Jared who got Penny's attention.

Jared's jaw hung down and his eyes grew wide, then he picked up his jaw with his fingers and put it back in place. "You look amazing." Penny laughed. "You look like me."

Penny was stunned. "You play Lothairian Redux too?"

Jared nodded, in full elf mode, with a blue doublet trimmed with silver filigree, dark blue pants, low soft boots, a handmade silver shirt with drawstrings at the top, white hair pulled back, and elven ears. Jared reached out and touched the tip of her ears and smiled. "Beautiful work."

"Ribs!" Libby crowed. "Biscuits with honey, corn, twice baked potatoes."

"I'm in." Penny clutched her stomach. "I haven't eaten in eight hours flat. Do chocolate sprinkles count as a meal?"

Jared laughed. "Come, milady, and have your fill." He bowed and extended her his elbow.

Penny put her arm through his elbow. "Lead on, sir elf."

They all ate as if they had never seen food before. The spread was amazing and delicious, and Penny found herself lingering over hot chocolate with cinnamon whipped cream and some sort of melting chocolate toffee extravaganza in a bowl she shared with Jared. There were still occasional knocks on the door from trick or treaters. Charlie was dressed as Frankenstein and enjoyed answering the door, scaring the kids, and passing out candy.

Their own passel of kids had already been out, and the stampede of boys were playing some very complicated fairy game that involved saving a pillow tree and sneaking up on the bad guys, played by Mitch and James. The dogs were all assisting except Shadow, who watched carefully to be sure everyone was okay. Bethany and River were having giggling fits in the corner, stacking up glittery plastic cubes and knocking them over. Charlie was giving his wives foot rubs when he wasn't answering the door, necessary after a long day herding children. Meri and Libby passed out little bowls of popcorn in chocolate, salted caramel, toffee, and almond flavors.

They watched a kids' show about a group of friends attending a magical school, including teenage witches, werewolves, pixies, dryads, and one water nymph. The water nymph kept getting everyone wet, and the witch kept having to use increasingly complicated spells to dry them out. It was surprisingly funny and well-written.

Somehow the kids managed to get through their sugar high and were carted off for stories in bed. There were three trundle beds for Meri, Libby, and Nat's boys. Sadly, Nat was on call and had been arresting various miscreants all night. Vic picked up any damaged revelers in his ambulance, and Davis was at the hospital patching them up.

Adam, Bobby, Denver, Ricky, and Beau and assorted dogs enjoyed Mitch's complicated ghost story. Since Penny and Jared were already dressed as elves, they put on the girls' gossamer wings and acted out the story of a fairy princess who had to save her entire kingdom and her bumbling suitor who kept messing up her plans to the giggly little girls. Meri, Libby, Charlie, Jen, Lynette, Jetta, Corinne, and James ended up on the floor in the hallway outside, listening to the story and laughing as Penny and Jared brought the silly story to life. The girls had their last drink of water, and the adults all went back into the family room. The dogs stayed with the kids except Shadow, who followed Jared.

Corinne sat on the couch, and Mitch rubbed her back. "I have never seen anything funnier than that. You should have your own TV show."

Penny accepted more hot chocolate, this one with mint whipped cream, from Jared. "We accept your kudos and applause. We would also like large amounts of money."

Kandace laughed. "Here, here." Len got his wife a cherry tart and cherry water.

Libby groaned. "At this point, we actually have large amounts of money. Mitch, thanks for the assist earlier tonight." Mitch had swung by on his motorcycle to take their deposit and drop it off at the bank.

"No problem. Besides, I got some sweets for my trouble."

James glared at him. "Did you remember to bring any home?"

Mitch grinned. "Yes, and I dropped them off with Len as well. Corinne and Kandace will be happy for a week."

Len looked around, wide-eyed. "I was supposed to save those?" Kandace threw a pillow at his head.

They did a mash-up of horror films, from *Swamp Thing* to *Scream* with a little *American Horror Story* thrown in. In between, Penny and Jared narrated more hilarious fairy antics. All of the adults doubled over, screaming with laughter.

"Have to film... for Nat," Meri said, gasping for air.

Kandace grinned. "Have been, for Davis and Vic. I'll send you a link."

"It must be a pain in the ass to have so many family members on call." Penny sat down next to Jared.

Jared nodded. "I am as well, actually. I'm hoping nobody gets lost tonight. Parents are keeping a much closer eye on the kids since...." Jared closed his mouth about the abduction attempt, knowing there were quite a few skittish parents in the room.

Charlie grunted. "That guy is getting so much jail time; he won't get out till the next millennium. Rescued some kids. Closed quite a few cases. And that's enough said about him."

Libby nodded. "Mitch, James, Jared, and Shadow, thank you all for being there."

Jared shrugged. "You donated the snacks, and Penny the ice cream."

"I can't even imagine," Lynette said, with a shiver.

Jetta narrowed her eyes. "I can. Let's just say that we all have an eye on the kids."

Charlie held her close. "We do, and with so many people in our family, there's always someone willing to help."

Penny raised a hand. "I can help Jared with the kids. I've always wanted to have them. It would be excellent practice."

Jen grinned. "I'm going to shoot myself in the foot here and say, Penny, you should never offer babysitting services to such a large family. You will forget how to sleep, eat, take a shower, go to the bathroom. Forget what it's like to attend soccer, baseball, basketball, or any other sports activity alone. Track meets and dojo visits are in your future. You will ask other people, even adults, if they need to use the bathroom. You will start cutting up the food of the adults next to you."

Jetta laughed. "That's exactly it! I've talked in a sing-song voice to cashiers!"

"You'll speak in a little squeaky voice all the time," Charlie said in a voice that sounded as if he had been huffing helium. Everyone laughed at that one.

Meri grinned. "You'll make enough food for ninety people, even if there are only two people in the house. I'm very lucky because when I do that, I can use it for lunches with my clients. Jetta, Jen, Lynette, and Charlie are not so gifted."

Jetta nodded. "We freeze a lot of food. We actually only have to cook twice a week at this point. Meri taught us how to put everything in boxes. Our boys do the same thing hers do too; they take out their own boxes and cook them in the microwave."

Libby sipped her hot chocolate. "Beau loves being in control of his own food. The others would eat almost anything you fed to them. They probably wouldn't eat dirty socks, but other than that..."

Meri snorted. "They used to be so picky. I delivered their food to their mother before she died. But, now they absolutely love food. They get a choice, so if they don't like something, they can eat something else."

Jared pointed at Penny. "Take notes."

Penny tapped her skull. "I am."

There were cots for the adults, numerous blankets and sleeping bags, couches and recliners, and a guest bedroom. They scattered around like apocalypse survivors, exhausted after playing with the kids and watching so many movies. Penny somehow ended up on the floor next to Jared on an air mattress. He removed his wig, changed into sweats in the bathroom, then positioned the mattress near the heating vent and piled on the covers so Penny didn't get cold.

Penny changed into her sweats in the bathroom, then looked at the bed. "I'm going to get hair wax all over these pillowcases."

Jared laughed. "It'll wash out. And if not, I think I can spring for a pillowcase."

"It was fun. I thought being around such a large family would be complicated, but things have been really cool." Penny grinned when Libby dropped off an old towel so Penny could bind her hair.

"I love my large family and wouldn't trade them for anything. But, I think I want things a little smaller."

Penny looked at Jared with surprise. "So many people around you are poly. You're not?"

Jared grinned. "Wolves mate for life." He kissed Penny's nose, helped her tuck in the towel wrapped around her hair. Then they both fell into an exhausted sleep.

~

*O*n the morning, there were carafes of coffee and orange juice, and tartlets with cheese, mushrooms, tomato, bacon, and sausage. Penny was eager to help.

"How do you make these?"

"The bacon goes in the microwave while you dice the veggies and grate the cheese, and the sausage can be microwaved or put in with the bacon in a frying pan." Meri cracked one small egg each into a silicone muffin tin, then added the cheese, mushroom, and tomato mixture. She mixed them up with a fork, then put the crumbled bacon and sausage in. Another twist of the fork each, and they were ready to go in the microwave. "Less than seven minutes total and these will stay in the refrigerator if you wrap them up. They're a great breakfast and perfect if you're on the keto diet."

Libby grinned and stole some bacon while Meri and Penny cut up more veggies. "Keto people account for a huge percentage of our businesses. Remember how I talked you into the sugar-free sorbets and ice creams, and we got a duplicate case for more gluten-free snacks for your side?"

Penny nodded. "The peanut butter dark chocolate ice cream and matching gluten-free snack bars sell to everybody."

Libby laughed. "You pay me and Meri to make the gluten-free stuff, and we both sell all our stock almost every day!"

Nat took the muffins out of the microwave and dumped them into a basket. "The percentage of keto people keeps rising. Most of the paramedics, firefighters, rescue personnel, and doctors are on the keto food plan in this town. Low carbs, high fat, and veggies. The farmer's market people are delighted. They sell veggies to their hearts' content."

"Relax, honey," Meri said to Nat. "You must be fall-down exhausted."

Nat sighed. "Six arrests, two slashed tires, three stranded motorists, but, for a change, no lost children. Everyone kept track of them." Ned snagged a muffin and a cup of coffee and sat down.

Meri pointed at her plate. "The kids love the gluten-free snacks and breakfasts like this one. I need to figure out how to make a seed and nut bar dipped in dark chocolate."

Penny raised her eyebrows. "If you figure it out, I want in on the business with you. You and Libby never steered me wrong, and I'm actually making a living even though it's a seasonal business."

"Eat up," Libby said to Penny. "Charlie said we could do our prep here. He's got two giant ice cream machines, and we can have Davis pick up anything you need in the way of containers or ingredients on his way home from the hospital."

"I can get used to this." Penny poured herself some coffee, added some coffee sweetener, and sat down with two muffins.

"Shower first," Meri suggested. "You're still blue."

They all laughed.

TRAINING

The dog training facility was a huge farm on a lonely road in what seemed to be the middle of nowhere. There were two one-stoplight towns on either edge of the mountains, the farm nestled in between. Rolling open fields surrounded the white farmhouse, trees spilling crimson and gold onto the ground in the distance. The great red barn sat on a low hill surrounded by white fences enclosing jumps and tunnels, play and training areas, and a second floor with apartments for the trainers. There was also another barn off to the side, blue with black trim, slightly smaller than the great red one. A train car sat off to the side, painted a bright yellow and surrounded by late-season flowers.

Dogs were trained for personal protection, drug-sniffing, and far more commonly, as support and comfort dogs. Some dogs could detect seizures, tell when a child's breathing or heart rate had gone wonky, open special cabinets and doors for people with a wide variety of mobility issues, and help treat a wide variety of disorders from autism to PTSD. Every single dog was a rescue.

Yanna Beltran ran the facility, an ex-marine with a wide smile and a gimlet eye. She trained dogs for law enforcement forces all over the world, then raised funds online to complete her facility to make sure dogs were matched with the correct training and skills and then with the best people. Thesite was huge, with many veterans and ex-law enforcement employees.

It was just past breakfast, both human and dog versions, so the place looked surprisingly empty in the golden light. Normally, the hills were covered with dogs, trainers, and new law enforcement officers or civilian trainers working with their new canine friends. The sun had cleared the trees when Jared parked, a tad jittery from consuming coffee liberally dosed with monk fruit extract instead of sugar so he wouldn't end up the size of a house. He opened the truck door, and he and Shadow leaped out.

Yanna Beltran came out of the barn and greeted them, her close-cropped hair dyed a burnished copper. Yanna was ex-military and ATF bomb squad and was missing two fingers and a chunk of her right leg, so she had a leg brace. Her right eye was glass. Her coonhound, Roger, sat at her feet, ready to demonstrate commands and techniques. Jared stood facing her, ready to follow Yanna's lead. Jared had known Yanna in his military life and was grateful for the hour and a quarter commute each way to do something useful with himself and his dog.

Yanna gave Jared a quick rundown as people streamed out of the barn on the right. The dogs were trained to sniff for drugs and explosives from puppies, although some older dogs did well. Most of the older dogs became reading or support canines. The people they trained that morning were law enforcement from all over the midwest United States and one from overseas, ready to learn how to work their new dogs.

Yanna did the initial lesson and demonstration, then Jared took half the class aside and took them to their train car. In the blue barn training segment, they also had a fake airport luggage room, two apartment mockups, and several 'suspects' they had seeded on the property. Jared liked the train car for a first lesson. The small size made training a bit easier.

Jared ran Della Vu through first. Della was from Singapore and had been visiting relatives in Virginia when her promotion to canine officer came through. The officer had long black hair kept in a tight braid, a flat face, and a ready smile. She arrived for each class half an hour early. Della had chosen a coonhound. Daisy was a champ, ready to go at any moment.

Jared smiled at them both. "You've got a great dog there. I trained her myself."

"I can't wait to do more training! We'll be training together in Singapore as well." Della couldn't stop smiling.

The setup was in two parts, luggage purchased from several yard sales and a few bored commuters standing in line at the other door, actors hired from the local community college. Daisy found the scents of both explosives and drugs on clothing, stacks of luggage, and one very forgettable young man with a goatee in rumpled khakis who seemed to be waiting to board a train or flight. She did her tell, sitting after a sniff.

Jared praised both dog and human. "Excellent work! Go on, playtime."

Della gave Daisy her blue snake toy reward and took her off work mode to go play and get some water.

Jared took Roberto Swinso and Katie Quell through next. Katie was first, a short, sturdy, methodical officer from Kansas City with a beagle named Vi, and whippet-thin Roberto from 'all over' had a black-and-white pointer named Huey. Jared took them one at a time and had Katie learn to criss-cross the space. Katie's normally porcelain face was flushed; Jared sent her to get water for herself and her dog.

Roberto and Huey were perfectly in sync. The ATF agent was slight, with dark eyes and a wispy beard.

Jared sighed. "Roberto, you can't go undercover and leave the dog."

Roberto shook his head. "They don't use me for that anymore. I'm going to be testifying in trials for years when I'm not walking Huey here through sites."

Huey grinned, and Roberto took him for a play session and a drink. Huey had a yellow squeaky three-eyed monster for his reward toy.

They all met up for more training, this time finding two suspects, one of them a ten-year-old girl with a bag of weed. Roberto and Katie had seen this before, but Della was stunned.

Della put her hands on her hips in outrage. "Her parents should be arrested!"

Yanna nodded. "They would be. That's my daughter, and there are only two seeds in there and some kitchen herbs. Thanks, pumpkin."

"Mama, my name is Reece, not pumpkin. Halloween's over." Reece grinned, a towhead with big white teeth and a sprinkling of freckles everywhere.

Yanna laughed. "Go on, Reece."

"Wait." Jared put two small bags of peanut butter-infused snacks in Yanna's hand. "Gluten-free, seeds and nuts."

Yanna took one of the bags, put it in her pocket, and handed the other one to her daughter. "I know. I order them by the case from your sister-like entity Meri."

Jared handed the snacks out to the rest of the trainees. He also handed out dental bones for the canines. "For after the last round."

The humans pocketed the snacks. Then, they went for training in a noisy, enclosed fake airport with a lot of loud people, including piped-in announcements about fake flights. The trainees laughed when they recognized announcements for flights to Mars, the Moon, Venus, and the asteroid belt. Each dog walked through separately with the trainer, and each dog found luggage or people with explosives residue. Then, it was time for play and treats and water for both people and canines. All the scenario extras, trainers, and actors from the local community college drama club headed out.

Jared met Yanna for a post-training rundown. They had to be sure everyone knew their assets and vulnerabilities. Della had to get over the surprise that parents would use their children in criminal enterprises. Some trainers had jerky movements, and some needed to be more precise with their commands. They wrapped up, and it was Jared and Shadow's time to go home.

Jared decided to go a little farther and make it back to the Weston farm. Nestled in the foothills, the farm was surrounded by tiny houses that the Westons and people all over the valley used for extra income. Holler people had turned aside from their own criminal enterprises like growing or running drugs some had turned to when the factories closed and the money dried up. Instead, they had banked on their beautiful views and had tiny houses all over the valley for hikers, snowshoers, trailblazers, leaf peepers, photographers, birdwatchers, artists, writers, and any other group of people that would like to rent a tiny house or cabin in the middle of the woods.

Jared found leaf peepers on the edge of the Weston property, two women and a man wrapped up in what seemed to be a bit too much clothing for the crisp fall weather. They had jeans, hiking boots, heavy sweaters, and woolen hats and gloves.

"Folks, I'm Jared. I live around here. There's a trail right up over there that has some beautiful leaves." Jared pointed.

"We thought we heard goats," said a woman with chubby cheeks and hazel eyes. "Over there." She pointed.

Jared whistled, and Tuna, the gray and brown girl, and Pitchfork, the black and white boy, came at a run. He handed out carrots to the delighted tourists. "Hold them with the tips of your fingers at the end of the carrot, or you're liable to lose your gloves or even fingers. Pitchfork is smelly because he's a goat boy; he does get regular baths. I'm surprised he's not out munching kudzu. In the late fall in early winter, our boys go to Georgia, Alabama, and other places that are overrun with it, choking out plants and wildlife."

"We're from Florida, the panhandle. Seen lots of that horrible vine," said the man, who had gray hair and a shuffling gait. "I'm Wayne Adams, and this here is Lucille and Petra." Lucille was the hazel-eyed one. Petra had a blade face and brown eyes and hair, from what little Jared can see poking out from under her dark blue cap. "We were at the Amish town a ways down and bought us a bunch of fudge. Ate some, then got on a sugar high. Thought it would be good to stop and walk it off. Y'all have beautiful trees."

"That we do. I'm Jared Weston, and this here's my parents' farm. Tell you what, I've got some lemonade in cans in my truck. Why don't

I get those, and I'll walk you to the trailhead? I'll even give you a trail map."

Wayne smiled so hard his eyes nearly closed. "That would be right kind of you."

Jared passed out the cans of lemonade, looked both ways, and walked them across the country road. Petra and Lucille had the map open in front of them and stumbled because they weren't looking where they were going.

"You're here." Jared pointed to first the map, then the bottom of the trailhead. "You have enough daylight to walk this loop around and back down and still have time to get to wherever you parked your vehicle."

"Right over there," Vernon pointed. Sure enough, a fat brown truck was parked across the street and down the road a bit.

"Y'all go on ahead." Jared pointed and plastered a big smile on his face. He waited until they were out of sight before unlocking the gate with his code, drove in, and locked the gate again. He gave the goats more carrots and shooed them to go run and play.

Rachael came out, her black hair pulled back, bright red lip gloss on her lips, a saucy cant to her walk.

"You look like a 50s pin-up girl," Jared said to his mother. He kissed her cheek, then she bent to greet Shadow. "There's some outside folk walking the mountain. I think I'm going to change and follow them in wolf-dog form."

Rachael nodded. "Put your pack on when you change so you can change back. Some of those tourists are plumb stupid."

Jared laughed. "They're all going to smell like lemonade, so I can find them easily enough."

Rachael nodded. "Run along now. We'll have barbecue chicken and biscuits with honey for you when you get back."

"Thanks, Mom." He kissed her cheek again and went to grab his wolf pack out of his truck. The straps could be configured in such a way to where they stayed on his body after the change, and the pack held a complete change of clothes. Of course, Shadow followed his every move.

He and Shadow found them with ease. They were just wandering about, taking pictures, talking about this and that bird. He kept yellow eyes on his prey. Jared's wolf dog was white and black with yellow and russet patches. Therefore, he could easily hide in the leaves. His wolf was the white and black of the pack. He hadn't known he had the ability to change into two forms until Mitch had shown him he could. Both boys had been eleven years old at the time. Shadow, well, she wouldn't be seen unless she wanted that to happen. Jared often wondered if Shadow was actually part cat.

Jared was delighted when the touists stayed on the proper track, went back down the mountain, walked to their truck, and got in. He made sure they had actually left before he crossed the street, slid under the fence, and trotted toward the back door. He hadn't smelled deception on the people, which was good.

He changed, put his clothes back on the mudroom, petted Shadow and gave her a treat, and went to take a shower. The three corgis, Shawn, Wayne, and Rascal, were in the house, so he petted them too. When he came out dressed in clean jeans and a soft blue henley shirt, they had food on the table. Stretcher and Lydia were doing their weird talking without talking conversation. One of them would make a small movement, the other one would make another small movement, and their eyes would meet. *Cats,* Jared thought.

"Brother," Stretcher said, with a tiny wave. For her, that was the equivalent of a long hug.

Lydia actually hugged him. "Nice to see you, Jared."

"Thank you."

Lydia passed Jared a can of Coke. "Let's hear it."

Jared popped the top and sat down. Shadow went with the corgis to drink water, then the dogs stretched out under the table, hoping for crumbs. "Mitch, James, and Corinne are all doing fine. The Halloween party was amazing, and I have videos. And I look ridiculous in an elf outfit, which should make Stretcher here very happy." Jared sent the link to their HUDs and listened to Stretcher and Lydia's coughing laughs while he sipped his drink.

Charlie came in, smiling broadly, bags of delicious-smelling stuff in his enormous hands. He looked like a smaller, sleeker Gunny with close-cropped hair and beefy arms. Both men were ex-military. "Finished, and just in time for two tourists coming this weekend. Just waiting on the last of the polyurethane to dry."

Jared groaned. "I can still smell a whiff of polyurethane in the joint sweets-ice cream shop."

"Even the fast-drying stuff takes a day." Charlie washed his hands, then put the contents of the bags on serving plates.

Lydia and Stretcher set the table, and Jared put cans of soda on the table.

"Let's sing," Charlie said.

Jen came in, washed her hands, and then everyone held hands and sang about how blessed they were for food and harvest. They sat and started passing around barbecued chicken and pulled pork, biscuits, slaw, and home fries Charlie had delivered from the local barbecue joint.

Lucas came in. "Jared! Saw the truck."

Jared got up and hugged Lucas, a highly talented designer of backdrops for video games. He also worked with a local teacher to come up with valid languages for his games, so the games sold like crazy. This was his busy time of year. The same was true for Lydia and Corinne; they both created websites. Lydia was part Navajo and part Crow and did a lot of her work with First Nations businesses. Lydia had been shot by a stalker she had been trying to identify and had slow healing despite her cougar form. She had rented a tiny cabin and fallen in love with Lucas. It was a weird pairing, but they worked together just fine.

"Were you up for a training?" Rachael asked her son. She knew the pull of home was trying to drag Jared back.

"I was, and it went very well. I am grateful that my job is in between here and there, and I can come and visit from time to time."

Rachael nodded at his tacit acknowledgment of her order. Someone needed to watch over the wolves and strengthen the pack. Splitting the pack was no fun, but Kandace and Corinne needed each other. Besides, the wolves and bears were becoming closer. Some shifters needed to stay hidden. The wolves had been outed when a college student attacked his roommate. The victim had turned into a wolf and successfully defended himself—on a live video feed. The bear shifters were not out in public yet, but the time would come when that would happen. The bonds between shifters needed to be strong for that eventuality.

Gunny passed the biscuits, then the butter. "Sounds like you have your hands full over there."

Jared tried not to groan. It was obvious that Gunny and Charlie were having lengthy conversations about what was happening. "I made a very serious mistake, and now I'm the clan babysitter."

Stretcher stared at her brother. "Jared, what did you do?"

"I told an outsider something she already knew. Beau, that's a little five-year-old boy, asked her to leave, essentially so the adults could change and go wolf and bear. She put that together because she had actually seen Lynette change. Penny told her mother, too, with Lynette's permission. Both of them are keeping the secret. Penny works with Libby every day, and now knows that Libby is a bear shifter."

Rachael nodded. "So, no running away, no howling to the press, and Penny feels like a part of the family."

Jared grinned when his mother realized what he had done had benefits. "Penny was over for Halloween last night, and everything went really well. Meri, Libby, and Penny are probably still cooking together; they were when I left at the crack of dawn. They were all so busy with Halloween that they had to restock. So, that means cooking and baking, and Penny's ice cream."

Lydia reached for another biscuit. "I don't see the problem. They're working together, having fun together. I saw the video with you playing with all the kids. Penny was the fairy princess, right?"

"She was. She makes homemade ice cream and sells it in her store with Libby. We got together and knocked the wall down between shops, so she and Libby saved a fortune on a remodel. Penny is saving up for a house because she doesn't want to ask her mom, a struggling single mom, for any money. She lives in Libby's old apartment over the shop."

Stretcher glared at her brother. "There are bears. Lots of them. Even military and ex-military ones. Ones that love dogs and kids and apple pie like you do."

Lydia reached out, held Lucas' hand. "Lucas here loves dogs and apple pie, and we get along just fine."

Lucas shook his head. "I prefer cherry pie."

Everyone laughed.

Gunny struck the table with just enough force to make all the dogs and people stare at him. "The woman has been brought into knowing. Therefore, if my son wants to date a blue fairy woman, then that is his choice."

Rachael nodded. "I concur. While the idea is to fall in love with someone of your shifter animal, the trait is dominant. I did not expect my son Mitch and James to fall in love with Corinne. That woman mellowed our very angry Mitch and brought our boys back to us." She reached out, put her hand over Jared's. "It looks like you have a reason to stay near your brothers."

Jared couldn't help it. Despite being completely infuriated that people were talking about his love life as if they had any decisions to make about it, he had to smile at his mother. Rachael knew how to take the upper hand in any and every situation. It would be a very good idea for him to follow her lead.

Jared stayed for the caramel apple pie; Gunny could bake since he learned to do it in the military. After dessert, he played with the corgis and Shadow, helped clean up, and inhaled deeply. The house smelled like the surrounding pine, the cedar lining his mother used for all the drawers and wardrobes in the house, baking, corgis, warm wolf, and chilly cat. He could also smell one more thing; it was definitely going to snow. He had to get back before going through the valleys became an exercise in sliding over black ice. He hugged everyone except Stretcher. She had made herself scarce, knowing damn well he was furious with her. He hoped that she fell in love with the most non-shifter of humans. He threw off the spiteful thought, called Shadow, and headed back out to his truck.

By the time Jared pulled into the house he shared with his pack, the snow was approaching whiteout conditions. He was very lucky to get out of the valleys before being cut off. He got a text from Yanna that she was closing down training; everyone was far enough along to get certified anyway. He sighed; he would be training a lot less days over a snowy winter. Onsite staff would continue training the dogs and getting them to good homes. He had only one thing to look forward to, and that involved wearing a tool belt for the next few months.

"Looks like we're on baby preparation duty," Lucas informed Shadow as they slipped inside the house.

The two girl corgis met Jared with sniffs but no barks. They had smelled Shadow and correctly guessed that Shadow's human would be close behind. He gave everyone treats, shed his outer clothes, kicked off his boots, and stoked the fire. He also made absolutely certain they had plenty of stores laid aside for the next three days to handle the blizzard.

Jared took a page from his father's playbook and prepped pancakes, making batter in a plastic container. He sliced apples and dosed them with clover honey and cinnamon but kept them in a separate container. Corinne liked the apple pancakes; the males in the house preferred the blueberries in the freezer.

Jared padded down the hall of his room, such as it was. He had managed to strip the paint, put on primer, and paint the room. Two walls for a sunny butter yellow, and two a deep blue. Jared felt like he was sleeping on a sailing ship on the ocean on a sunny day. The base of the ship-bed had been made, so future toddlers could take naps in their playroom. It was a full-size bed because twins liked to sleep together. Jared wasn't a big guy, but he really needed a large bed. He rejoiced at the move from the cot he had used before the built-in to an adult-sized bed.

The house had been started by a poly triplet who ended up choosing a much bigger house for a very good reason—they decided to bring in another husband. The outside had been built, the walls up, the plumbing, wiring, and cable put in before the sale. The house had been missing any drywall when Mitch, James, and Corinne bought it. Jared had been working like a madman with his brothers hanging drywall and finishing the rooms where the adults would sleep and getting the bathrooms in perfect working order. The kitchen and downstairs bathroom had been completed, and now Mitch was working on the nursery upstairs while Jared had moved from a cot to an actual bed by working on the playroom. Sometimes sleeping over after working all day was prudent. Corinne kept a bag of Shadow's food and a box of her treats in the pantry.

Corinne wanted every single thing done by the time the kids came, and Jared could see her position. Who wanted to raise screaming babies in a construction zone? The work with Libby and Penny's business place had set them back a little, but a blizzard was a great way to keep you indoors and working. Jared had a job to do, and he was not going to let his pack down.

TREATS

*P*enny dragged herself through her morning shower. She was falling over. She felt lucky to have gotten home with all her new stock put in downstairs in the shop freezers before the blizzard hit. Three days of being closed would have worried Penny, but she had made so much more business since the wall came down. The side-by-side businesses encouraged buying on both sides. No, she had enough to do with accounting, payroll, quarterly taxes, and ordering to replace her denuded fruit and fresh cream stocks. She also had to exercise. She had hand weights, a yoga mat, and a special Pilates machine she could pull down, use, and put back up. Being folded over ice cream or a computer all day made her back pop like a machine gun when she worked out.

Plus, she was also lucky she had enough to eat over the blizzard. She had soups and stews already made. Plus, she had cheddar, Brie, and shaved Parmesan. She made some lovely focaccia bread dusted with herbs and Parmesan, and the peanut butter and dark chocolate bars Libby taught Penny to make.

Penny caught up on Netflix during the ice-dark evenings, regretting not having a dog. But dogs were expensive, and she was on track to buy a house. She read books, petted the fat cat, took hot baths, used a facial mask, and painted her nails. Her toenails, no. Who would see them in winter? Then she thought about Jared, and she gave herself a pedicure too. She played her favorite video game with the elven princess she'd based her Halloween costume on.

She had stayed up way too late with the video games the night before she got the crack-of-dawn text informing her the snowplow had dug out the store. She sighed, dressed from head to toe in layers so only her eyes were showing, and went downstairs to shovel out the store. She scraped down to the sidewalk afterward. She put away the snow implements and went back upstairs to put her blue-and-silver long-sleeved shirt over her clean, pressed jeans. She layered up again, this time in her short boots with her blue-and-silver running shoes over her shoulder.

The power had never gone out, so all was well. In the shop, Penny changed from boots to running shoes, hung up her heavy coat, muffler, and gloves, washed her hands, did her checklist, then did Libby's checklist when Libby ran late. Libby's first customers were authors eager to get out of the house. She ran both sides until Libby came stomping in.

"Stuck behind a snowplow!"

"We cross-trained for a reason! This is the reason. Don't worry!"

Penny sipped her cappuccino, a small price to pay for serving Libby's people, and served hot chocolate with peppermint ice cream to a group of freezing parents who needed to get out of the house before they killed their spouses, kids, or cats who liked to climb curtains. Some of the stories of what kids and pets got up to when bored were hilarious. Toddler Em Dalton had gotten into her mother's lipstick and decorated the walls. Gage Tarquist had built a fort using every pillow, blanket, and sheet in the house that took up the entire family room. The parents had pictures as proof.

Libby kept busy serving coffees and heated up nearly all of her treats. Penny knew things would be slow on her side; the parents were a welcome distraction. She stocked everything up and received her orders of cream, fruits, nuts, and sprinkles. She sold an entire frozen cookie mint pie to a frazzled dad needing a treat for two children with scratchy throats. Penny began deep-cleaning one of her cases, part of her deep-cleaning rotation for winter.

They had compressed hours once the snows fell. Penny changed the signs. She watched both counters when Libby took lunch with Kandace and Corinne, who were already Christmas shopping. They were gone for nearly an hour and a half. Penny was ready to eat her socks when they came back. She changed into her snow boots and made it across the street without falling. She ate a grilled cheese sandwich with tomato and bacon at the counter. The place was packed with stir-crazy neighbors. Penny walked back, surprised to find she was being followed. Several people from the restaurant, including Nat and Chief Taylor, followed her in.

Penny sold Nat a scoop of peppermint ice cream for the top of Libby's super fudge chunk walnut caramel brownie. Nat smiled at Penny, then sat down on Libby's side. Chief Taylor stayed to chat with Penny, ordered himself some coffee and gluten-free protein balls from Libby and sugar-free lime sherbet from Penny.

The chief had lost enough weight that his pants were beginning to sag, and his face was smaller. They walked to a table, and Penny sat with the sheriff.

The sheriff pointed his spoon at Penny. "You've been busy?"

Penny nodded. "In the last few weeks, sure. But, I think my side of this shop is down for winter."

"You got a side job? I ask because my dispatcher got her CPA and does law enforcement accounting, budgets and stuff. I am taking law enforcement courses, thinking of training a dog for the library so kids who are scared of reading or talking can talk to the dog. Nat gets farmed out to do paperwork for the next county sometimes 'cause they love him. Farmers in this valley are now doing that vertical farming stuff to grow crops in winter." The chief sipped his coffee.

Penny tilted her head. "I'm surprised you asked me that. I just checked out some courses online. I can learn more keto desserts; that will make me some money. I like the accounting thing. I can do overflow accounting, you know, like tax time. I'm not busy until mid-April, just after taxes are due. I don't know. I have to think about it."

"Lotsa people 'round here put stuff online, like crafts. I'm wondering about my neighbors, is all. The idea is interesting."

"You can drop the Mayberry sheriff act. I'm onto you."

The sheriff's laugh rumbled in his chest, like a cat's purr. "It tends to make my job easier if people think I'm just a little stupid."

Penny laughed. "I can see that, but I happen to know Nat respects you. Nat actively hates stupidity." They both laughed. "Back to our earlier thing, I have talent. I can design things. Logos. Plus the accounting. I can also design kitchens."

"A woman of many talents."

"I actually am." Penny sipped from her own cup of coffee and grinned.

"I have another question. Farrah's doctor has one, actually. Can she send a recording to you about what it was like having her as a mother? You can pass it to me, and I'll get it to Farrah?"

Penny felt like she had been punched in the stomach. The next thing she knew, Libby gave her a glass of water, and Nat glared at the sheriff.

"I'm sorry." Sheriff Taylor held his hands up. "I was out of line."

Penny sipped her water. "I... it may actually help Maddie. Farrah is a black hole. It probably won't help her. But, I can say clearly that I can, and will, pass on the message."

Sheriff Taylor stood. "I am so sorry I upset you."

Penny shook her head. "It was... unexpected." Penny leaned forward. "Farrah should have been locked up for emotional abuse. That woman from Child Protective Services, Candy Tayne. I know she got fired a few years ago because some kid in her care almost died. She came by a half dozen times over the years and wouldn't help Maddie or Morgan. Mom didn't have the funds to help them declare themselves emancipated minors. She skipped meals to feed us."

The sheriff nodded. "I was just a deputy back then, and I've got to agree. It's one of my nightmares that I'll miss something I should have seen."

Nat nodded. "Mine too."

Penny stood up. "You just helped me realize I can do something to help my friend."

Nat nodded. "We'll help."

~

*P*enny helped Libby with her side; people were still eating ice cream during the day, but generally not at night. They whipped through the last two customers, Lisa Tuan and her brood of stair-step daughters who had tiny noses and wore their shiny black hair to their waists just like their mom. And there was the rotund and highly energetic Connie Phillips, buying hot drinks for choir practice. Penny convinced Libby to sell coffee carafes with their logos on each side and give a discount for bringing them back. Penny regretted it, despite the profit, when she poured fifteen cafe mochas, peppermint hot chocolates, and something called Deep Cherry, a hot apple cider-cherry concoction Penny made by the enormous catering pot on her side, then moved it over to Libby's when night fell. Penny closed out, and Lisa and her brood, Amber, Jade, and Amethyst, helped Connie walk the carafes three blocks over to the Unitarian church. Everyone was bundled up; the snow had melted, but the wind cut like a knife.

Penny headed back to finish cleaning and get the nightly deposit. Libby swung into cleaning up as soon as the door chimed closed while Penny went to lock the door and put up the Closed sign.

"Omigod." Penny heard Libby's spine pop from across the room. "I need to lie around doing nothing."

"You have a sister, a spouse, and three kids. How is that possible?" Penny got the spray and clean rags and began cleaning the tables.

Libby laughed. "I get reading to the kids. Ricky vibrates the whole time, Denver sings to me—he has a lovely voice. Beau wants to snuggle in deep."

"Who knew he could sing?" Penny was stunned. All three boys used to have terrible behavior, running around and throwing food on the floor before their mother died in an accident. Their behavior had vastly changed since Libby adopted them with her sister Meri and Nat Sandawan, the deputy.

"I sure didn't." Libby hit the button for the end-of-night report, then took the money back to put it in the safe. Penny did her own report, locked up the money, and had the entire front done including chairs on the tables and the floor swept and mopped by the time Libby had the back of the house ready to go. "We've got to go!" Libby crowed.

Penny put everything away and washed up, checked her back door, and put on her boots. They went out into the night.

Penny turned her face up to the sky. "More snow," she predicted.

Libby waved her hands in front of her face. "No! Not until I get home! I won't get there for a week at this rate." Automatic vehicles that drove in snow went very slowly.

Penny handed Libby her deposit bag. "Go!" Penny took her own advice. She circled around the side of the building to her stairs... and ran smack into what felt like a wall. "Ow!" she said and covered her nose.

"Are you all right?" Jared grabbed Penny's elbow to steady her. "I was coming to take you to dinner. Then, I've got to get home before the snow gets bad."

Penny felt her nose, then her wrists. "Nothing broken. Or damaged much." She looked up at Jared, her eyes bright with tears from the sudden stop.

"Omigod, I made you cry. Dinner. Or we can pick something up, and I can rub your feet."

"If there's any barbecue left, I'll take that. If not, half honey barbecue, half ranch wings, and wedge fries." Penny pointed down the street. "Hurry."

Jared let go of her arm. "I'm on it," he said, turned, and hurried down the street to the barbecue joint.

Penny rubbed her nose, laughed, and slowly and awkwardly hauled herself up the stairs to her apartment that she had decorated in what Libby called Early Nerd. The walls were soft blue, and she had Celtic hangings and swords and dirks hanging on the wall from her

Society for Creative Anachronism stuff. Quitting the group to run her shop had been intensely difficult. Nothing drove out mental demons faster than attacking them with a sword. She still went to the Renaissance Faire; her elf outfit had gone over well there as well.

Penny had time for a very fast, hot, blessed shower. She put on her thick, soft socks in a pale blue, black leggings, and a garnet chenille sweater. She made some cinnamon apple cider and put out trays with plates, silverware, and several cloth napkins.

Libby sat but had to stand again to let Jared in. "Missed the snow." Jared brushed one of the first flurries off his shoulders as Penny took the food. She opened the bags and squealed when she found a half rack of ribs, honey barbecue wings, and pulled pork sandwiches. "You can eat the wings tomorrow if we don't finish them." Jared grinned.

Penny laughed. "I ate a very hasty lunch, and Libby's stopped slipping me snacks at every opportunity. She's too busy."

"No gooey goodness?" Jared took off his boots, washed his hands, and sat down to eat barbecue.

Penny pointed to her stomach. "Better that she doesn't." Then, she was lost to barbecue.

Jared smiled as she attacked her food. Jared had a sandwich, half the wedge fries topped with cheese, bacon, ranch, and some wings. He cleaned up while Penny washed her hands.

She came out of the bathroom. "Wait, I was going to clean up. You're a guest."

Jared smiled. "You've been working all day."

"So have you!"

"How do you know? I could have sat around eating Libby snacks all day."

Penny laughed, crossed the room, and sat on the couch. Jared covered her with a blanket. "Libby snacks. I love it."

Jared put her remote control in her hand. "You have the power." He stood. "How did you know I worked today?" He sniffed his arm. "Doth I offend?"

Penny laughed. "You smell like metal and grout. Was there a bathroom involved?"

"Yes, the upstairs one. Have you ever tried to prevent a pregnant woman from getting to the bathroom?"

Penny shook her head and shivered. "That sounds like a bad idea."

"I agree. I hate to leave. I want to watch stupid television with you."

Penny reached out and touched his hand. "Stay. It's not supposed to be too deep by morning."

"If Corinne needs anything..."

"Sit." Penny patted the couch next to her. "I get that James and Mitch are your brothers."

Jared sat. "They are. Annoying brothers, but brothers."

"And they asked you to move here?"

"No. My mother did."

"Wait, that doesn't make sense. Why?"

"We're wolves. My brothers and I. They're pack."

Penny nodded slowly. "Okay."

"And, Corinne and Kandace are like two peas in a pod. They can't be separated. And they want to be pregnant together."

"Okay. And, so, what are you?"

"I... you don't know the Camber or Weston history, do you? How much has Libby told you?"

Penny put her remote down, picked up her cup of hot cider, and cupped it in both hands. "I know that the Cambers, Libby's family, are bear shifters. They all like sweet things, and that makes sense."

"I'm a Weston. Lynette Camber can turn into a cougar, and so can my sister, and a woman my family's kind of adopted. What else?"

"I know both James and Mitch Weston's parents died within a week of each other. And then Mitch went kind of... nuclear." She made a bomb noise and splayed her fingers.

Jared shuddered. "That was a mess. Gunny was involved in... let's just say that James and, especially, Mitch blamed Gunny for losing both parents. Their dad went into the military to afford his wife's cancer treatment and died in a helicopter crash before she did." Penny nodded, wide-eyed. "Gunny was there. Every baseball game, track meet, video game tournament. And neither boy would even look at him. I could see his heart break. He and Rachael adopted them—

distant cousins, so same last name—and they became my brothers. With Mitch, it was like being in the same place as a wolverine crossed with a porcupine. He was insanely angry for years."

"That sounds bizarre and horrifying."

Jared nodded. "Corinne called it a cluster--uh, bomb." Jared rubbed the back of his neck. "I get that. Like spaghetti made up of detonation wire on fire. Anyway, Gunny blamed himself, too. Corinne helped us all see there were no good options, and a lot of self-delusion was involved on all sides. The men in our family just didn't think their mom would die. Anyway, Corinne brought Mitch and James back into the family. Rachael, that's my mom, wants one of us keeping an eye on them. Mitch is still rowdy, still angry deep inside. He tries to bleed it off with kickboxing. But he's close to his wolf side. He's a predator, always will be. Not in the sense that he is a danger to people. In the sense that he loves that side of himself."

"The dark side." Penny smiled. "There is a difference between brooding darkness that isn't used to attack others and people who think they are religious and judgmental who do more damage than Mitch in a ring ever could."

"Who... Oh, I've heard about Farrah. If she's done even a small percentage of the stuff I've heard is true, she's a terrible example of humanity."

"In a mental hospital now. In fact, I have a very nasty phone call to make that I've been putting off."

Jared held her hand. "I can sit here and hold your hand when you make it."

"I have no idea how to ask my friend to relive her childhood." Penny held out her cup, and Jared stood to fill it up, poured his own, then sat down next to her again. "Morgan and Maddie lived next door, and I thought of them as my sisters. Morgan went into the military to get away from her mom and to pay for college and got herself blown up. Broke my soul. Maddie got broken, too. Farrah is her mother." Jared handed Penny her refilled mug. "Thank you."

"You grew up next to that horrible woman? And she had two daughters?"

"Yeah. We were in a tiny crackerbox, a half-step up from the broken-down trailer my mama grew up in. I don't know how you could call my bedroom a bedroom. It was kind of the size of a closet, just big enough to put a bed and a tiny dresser. My mom found an old daybed in the trash and painted it lovely colors. The ones I'm wearing, actually. I've always liked a garnet color." She huffed out a laugh. "If I have a daughter I would name her Garnet, but then everyone in town would think she's one of Lisa Tuan's daughters."

Jared snorted. "They must spend three hours a day doing each other's hair."

"Actually, Daddy is a hairdresser and Mommy a real estate agent."

"Ah, so free hair products. Got it."

Penny grinned. "Yes. Anyway, Mama is incredible. I wore good-looking clothes. Nothing was threadbare. I wasn't a roll-in-the-dirt girl. Mama told me hard work and good grades were the only way out of that tiny house with a neighbor like Farrah, and I believe her. Farrah saw something wrong with anyone and everything, most especially her two daughters. They spent nearly every spare minute not in school or working some after-school job in our house."

"After school? As little girls?"

"Yeah, we walked even smaller girls home from school and hid the money in our socks. Mine didn't go for candy. They went to my mama, who used those quarters to pay bills."

Jared took off one sock and began rubbing her foot. Penny's eyes rolled back up in her head. "I had no idea." He sighed. "Raising goats and selling vegetables won't make you rich, but we were always healthy and fed because Dad was in the military, had some extra money coming in. Construction in these parts won't make you rich either." He pointed out the window at the swirling snow. "Like you and selling ice cream, inthese parts in construction you only work from April to late October. Now they build tiny houses, have a vertical farm, and raise goats. Dad's thinking about building tiny houses in the barn during the winter. He can move them when the weather gets good."

"Made it through a week into November this year before profits fell off." Penny grinned proudly. "I do sell hot drinks. I'm deep-scrubbing everything I can get my hands on, tweaking recipes, learning every gluten-and-sugar-free dessert possible." She made a face. "Some ended up in the garbage. Getting the monk fruit-erythritol balance right is hard. I'm also supposed to use berries, not fruits, except for lemon and lime. Citrus is okay in specific amounts. And nut butter. I'm getting the hang of making my own. Plus how to make cauliflower rice, which is a pretty weird side effect of learning gluten-free stuff."

Jared nodded. "Great for gluten-free bread and for a pizza base."

"Good to know." She moaned as Jared dug into the arch of her foot. "Anyway, I've got a great chocolate peanut butter pie gluten-free dessert, and a gorgeous lemon-raspberry ice. Anyway, I hope to have three to four seasonal sugar-free recipes. Gets the athletes in. I had no idea we had so many athletes. Bruno Rachau lifts weights, and Carmella Benitez can lift him." She laughed. "Runners, hikers, and skiers. Lots of Meri's people on keto or other diets that ban sugar and/or gluten. I have a steady income, mostly at lunch, but I'm probably going to go down to thirty percent of my normal income if I don't get more of these keto things going."

"Okay. The dessert talk is fascinating, and I'm craving your food. But, we're veering off the reason for your tough phone call."

Penny sighed. "Yes. Well, we had the world's most stupid, oblivious, idiotic person working for Child Protective Services. She didn't see emotional abuse as a problem."

"Didn't she learn about that while getting her psychology degree?"

"Social worker degree, and you would have thought so. Farrah had no business having children. They were her slaves to keep her piece of shit house clean, her tchotchkes and Bibles dusted. They were scrubbing the house as really little girls. They were never respected or loved. I can't tell you all Maddie and Morgan went through, but it was horrible."

Jared dug deep into the arch of her foot, and Penny groaned.

"And now, tonight, I'm determined to call Maddie and ask her to make a video for her mom to see, kind of a You Were A Horrible Mom highlight reel, in the hopes that her mom gets it. At all. Abusers and narcissists minimize what they did. 'It wasn't so bad, it didn't happen quite that way, that particular thing didn't happen at all. I was abused, framed, misunderstood.' That woman has been kicked out of businesses, restaurants, churches. Churches! I'm surprised she didn't go join that church that protests funerals. West-something. Anyway, she's been disruptive almost anywhere she goes. She says nasty things and tries to put some sort of religious spin on them to make it okay for her to say horrible things." She realized she was breathing hard. Penny put down her cup, put her head in her hands, and breathed deeply while Jared rubbed her back.

"You grew up next door to a monster. It sounds like you or your mom or someone reported that woman for child abuse, and the kids should have been taken out of their home."

Penny sat up, rubbed her eyes. "I cry when I'm mad."

Jared nodded. "I do that, too. My dad wasn't one of those boys-don't-cry idiots. I don't cry during most Netflix movies, but I have once or twice."

Penny nodded, took a shuddering breath. "I felt completely helpless. I stood up to that woman, even told her off once or twice. She hit me in the face once, and my mother called the police after punching her out." Penny grinned through her tears. "I have no idea who bailed the woman out. My mom told everyone in the neighborhood what she did, showed off the bruise on my face. Told me to show it proudly at school, that it was a badge of honor to stand up for my friend. Told all the teachers what happened. That ended anyone having any patience for her anywhere. Stopped it cold."

"How old were you? And what did Farrah do?"

"I was eight. Farrah called Morgan a slut to her face. Morgan, even at twelve, was so straightlaced she probably could have made your dad look loosey-goosey. Morgan refused to let her mother call her something she wasn't, and I wasn't about to put up with it either."

"What did Morgan do that set her off, if anything?"

"She wore a short-sleeved red shirt and cherry Chap-Stick. The shirt was for a school play. After that, if Morgan tried out for something, she got it, and she was allowed to spend as many hours at school that she wanted. Lillie Navarro, the janitor, paid Morgan to do some of her tasks and gave her the first pick of donated stuff because some of the churches donated clothes and school supplies to the schools. Morgan was able to get some good jobs because she was able to dress in clothes without holes and always had school supplies. Maddie did the same thing. The problem was, Mama didn't have the money to pay to get Morgan and Maddie legally emancipated. She did get us fed, which was a major miracle with growing teens."

Jared nodded. "That's when Libby and Meri learned to create delicious goodness. Len told me he and his brothers Vic and Davis were eating Jen and Lynette out of house and home. They hired a young chef to make boxes of food they could reheat, and Meri and Libby soaked up whatever he had to teach them."

"Good to know." Penny wiped her tears. "I need to make a call."

Jared nodded once, hard. "Do it. Do you want me to lock myself in the bedroom?"

Penny laughed. "This apartment is the size of a postage stamp. You can hear me, or my end of the call, anyway. I trust you. But, I do appreciate the sentiment." Penny took a deep breath and made her call. She quietly and gently explained the sheriff's request. "You don't have to do it, Maddie. You owe that woman nothing. Not a thing."

Jared, who had started rubbing Penny's other foot, heard Maddie clearly. "I need to tell her what she did. She won't change, not for a second. But, venting may help. I want to be a great mother. Having one last confrontation with my mother from afar is okay. I'll do it in such a way that there are no tags. No way of knowing where I am, tracing me."

"Okay. Maddie, you know I use a burner wrist link to call you every time."

"If she shows up, I'll just call the police," Maddie said, then sighed so loud that Jared heard it while digging into Penny's other arch.

"Okay. Send it, and I'll deliver it to the sheriff. I don't know where your mother is."

Maddie grunted. "That witch is not my mother. She's an egg donor."

"You are a product of relationships with your close friends. And Mrs. Zenna."

"Thank all the Powers that Be for Mrs. Zenna. Gotta go, Shiny Penny."

"Love you, Madcap Maddie." Penny hung up.

"Was Mrs. Zenna the drama teacher?" Jared asked. He dug into her heel.

"No, math club. Maddie is a contractor, helping small companies give exceptional customer service."

"Maddie sounds incredible." He smiled. "No thanks to her mother. Thanks to you and your mother."

"She calls Mama every week." Penny grinned through her tears.

"Come here," Jared said. He took Penny in his arms and held her close. It took about thirty seconds of her shaking under his fingers to realize she was stone-cold furious, and a hug was contraindicated. He let her go, stepped away.

Penny stood up and stalked to her cubby, where she kept her workout equipment. She put on workout gloves, blasted some music on her cell phone, put on her workout gloves, padded back to the couch, and called up YouTube on television. She put on a workout video that was the craziest thing Jared had ever seen. There was a short warmup, then there were punches, spinning kicks, knees, and elbows, all with Penny holding weights in her hands. He picked up the coffee table and moved it to the side, glad it was glass and chrome and not some wooden or even marble version. Jared filled up a sports water bottle for her with water, then got the hell out of the way. Penny's face was red, her eyes bulging, veins standing out in her neck. Who would have thought a tiny woman who scooped ice cream for a living had so much rage in her?

To be honest, it impressed the hell out of him. Mitch had been a beast, a monster, his anger obvious, but Penny was happy, cute, contained. Cheerful, kind, great with kids and adults alike. But he hadn't thought about, really thought about, what other kids went through.

Rachael and Gunny believed in dumping love on their kids' heads, that no kids should guess if they were loved. They adopted Jared when he was four and changed into a wolf for the first time. His mom had been a drunken college student who had gotten pregnant at a party. She didn't even know the guy's name. He remembered his mother as someone always in classes. She left him at all sorts of daycare facilities most of the time. He vaguely remembered dark hair and the smell of spaghetti, her go-to meal for him. He held no anger towards his birth mom. She had no idea she'd slept with a shifter. She put up a discreet ad, and Rachael was there the next day with paperwork and a lawyer named Hobart Ringley. For the first time, he really thought about what might have happened to him if Rachael hadn't shown up that day.

Penny's hair was getting dark with sweat, her muscles standing out. She was grinding her teeth. This next-door neighbor must be a real piece of work. Penny's video ended in stretching. She unclenched her jaw, and the veins quit popping out on her forehead. Penny drank her water, nodded at Jared, and headed to the shower.

Jared sat on the couch and thought about how his life could have gone much, much worse. Then he took her burner wrist comp and checked the video camera in it. It would be good enough. He then went to her little dresser and selected foundation, concealer, mascara, two eye shadows, lip gloss, and her surprisingly excellent set of makeup brushes. He went back into the living room and spread it all out on the coffee table. He made decaf and doctored it, then went back to the couch.

Penny came out into the living room, fresh-faced, hair up in a ponytail, in a garnet sweatshirt and black leggings. "What's all this?"

Jared nodded towards the stuff on the table. "Payback. You get as pretty and sophisticated as you can be, you look right into the camera, and you give that woman what she deserves. No yelling, no nastiness, just statements of fact. Incident after incident. Be very clear about what you saw and heard, how old you and Maddie and Morgan were when each incident happened. Make it like a tide she drowns in."

"Okay." Penny nodded slowly. "Okay. Let me put on..."

"May I pull from your closet?"

"Um, yes," Penny said, stunned.

He dressed her in a garnet sweater and put a product she rarely used in her hair that made it shine before he put it back in its high ponytail. He added a garnet necklace and gorgeous drop earrings.

Jared sat her on the couch, stole the hand mirror from the dresser she used as a vanity, and handed it over. "Watch what I do. If you have a question, ask. Did you put on moisturizer?"

"Of course!"

Jared put on a very light moisturizer first, then concealer, then foundation with a sponge.

"You're a military guy. How do you know this? Are you secretly one of the Fab Five?"

Jared laughed. "No, your friend Morgan wasn't the only one who loved drama. I got into it because I had a crush on Opal Dursey. Girl was as skinny as a rail, don't know why I fixated on her." He switched to finishing powder, applying it with an expert hand. "She had the best singing voice. Still does, as far as I know."

"Are you still in touch?" Penny asked.

"Sort of. We joined the military together. She's still there, a colonel by now. Don't know where exactly. She's an in-the-field sort of Marine. Anyway, I can't sing without someone getting a pellet gun and shooting me in the nuts." Penny laughed. "I'm really straightforward. I can only take roles where I play an honest person. I also suck at comedy and, as I've already told you, musicals. That leaves out a lot of parts. I learned makeup because I got to relax and talk with the cast, and it turns out I'm really good at it." Jared did her eye shadow, a shimmering silver with dove gray on the lowest part of the lid. He layered the colors carefully.

"You also got to talk to your girl." Penny smiled at him, her eyes closed.

"Yes, I did. She dated her understudy."

"Oh."

"Oh, yeah. Bisexual, but no interest in me. She liked guys and girls that could carry a tune. When she could, she legally married a civilian contractor named Kila Donague."

"Okay. So the girl that got away."

Jared laughed. "Half a world away." He ended with the lip gloss, a lovely shimmering deep red. "Okay, now I set up the camera, and you start with your earliest memory of the woman next door. We can edit this stuff, but I think you should just keep talking. Want some decaf?"

"Cherry water. I made a batch. It's in a plastic carafe in the door."

"On it." Jared set up the camera on a pile of books and pressed *Record*. He took the makeup back, poured her the cherry water, brought it in, and left it on the coffee table. He pointed to the door, and she waved. Penny needed to let it out, and he didn't need to rifle through her memories. He knew she was strong, and his dog was waiting at his brothers' giant unfinished house. He had a storm to beat home.

STORM

*J*ared was careful with the separators for the tiles. He had a bathroom to finish. Pregnant women needed to pee whenever, wherever. The plumbing was in, done by an actual plumber. The tiles Jared could do. He had learned at his father's knees. The Mexican tiles were in blue, interspersed with sand-colored tiles with a blue gecko, and a silvery blue with an intricate filigree pattern in the center of each block. He put down the thinset, then the tiles. He was slow, careful, and checked everything with a level. He blasted smooth jazz interspersed with some Santana, so he kept the pace slow, steady. He knew he would get it all done in one day.

He finished, humming as he did his work. He put on some Southern rock and went after the backsplash, silver, blue, and golden glass tiles in mesh. Jared felt it was kind of 'cheating,' but the idea of setting each tiny piece of glass individually made his hands cramp.

He finally backed out, cleaned up, and washed his hands. He made himself a chicken, goat cheese, and smoked red bell pepper panini with Cool Ranch Doritos and a black cherry cola. Shadow, who had been in the hallway while he worked, followed him in and got a beefy-tasting dental snack for her trouble. Jared ate, washed up, then took Shadow out. Snow dusted the ground, but it gave Shadow no problem. She ran around, joyous at running free. Jared threw a ball with a hooked neon-green thrower so he didn't harm his abused back and shoulders. He stretched in between throws. The downside of laying tile was creaky, sore knees despite the knee protectors Jared used.

Jared laughed as the dog slid on snow, her mouth open in a doggy laugh. She caught the ball and ran back. He kept throwing until his nose got cold. Then, he headed over to find Mitch in his garage. The first thing Mitch did upon arrival at the new house was set up his garage with heat and air conditioning and shelves for all his motorcycle parts. The second thing he did was set up his kickboxing gear in a corner so his anger stayed under control. Jared heard the pounding music floating over the frigid air. Mitch tore down and put back together bikes for buyers from all over the country. Mitch's other truck was a tow truck for bikes.

Jared shut the door against the frigid cold. "Hey. Bathroom upstairs needs a little more, but getting there."

Mitch grinned. "I am taking distinct advantage of you." He knelt and continued stringing the brake line. "Three hots and a cot do not match you being an unpaid civilian contractor." He stared off into space. "You're getting paid." Mitch nodded his head once. "Keep track of your hours, and you'll get credit on the house credit card."

Jared nodded. There was no point arguing with family. Then he shut the door behind the dog. Shadow padded over to the water bowl, then lay on the dog bed Mitch kept in the garage. Jared sat down on a rolling stool close enough to the tools to hand them over, far enough away that he could avoid getting burned if Mitch wanted to put on his welding equipment and lay down a bead.

Jared kept his voice low, careful with his phrasing. "You know I have the draw from pack money." He meant the money from investments. Gunny had invested every penny he wasn't spending on food, clothes, his construction business, or the farm into a trust, which were then invested in primarily index funds with some liquid capital. At this point, they had to work, but there was a nice cushion. There was money for investments in houses, but Mitch, James, and Corinne's old A-frame house had sold for a pretty penny, so no worries.

"You do, but we're making bank, bro. I can teach you how to do what I do with the bikes. You can do computer stuff, which means you can work from home. Or you can do trail and ski stuff like with James. Or all three, or the dog stuff. Hell, bro, build a barn kennel on our property. Build a house back in the woods."

Jared nodded slowly. "I can do all of that. We know I'm good with my hands, so your stuff for now. But I'll be a baby, make stupid mistakes. Don't wanna have some biker crash because I'm new to this." Jared had helped his brother tear down bikes for a few weeks once, but he hadn't really been much help. He stared out at the light dusting of snow. "If you're dead serious about having a brother here, I can look nearby, maybe find a barn I can move here. Something made of wood at least a hundred years old. They were using heartwood back then, the real thing."

"I have no idea why you ended up here, but I suspect Rachael sent ya." Mitch cut his eyes at Jared.

Jared nodded once, and Mitch grinned. "No harm splitting a pack to make a new home." Jared wondered how he'd ended up defending his mother. He hadn't wanted to come, but now he didn't want to leave. Besides, Rachael and Gunny were exceptional at adopting a horde of passing shifters who, for the most part, ended up staying. Now, Lynette and Stretcher had Lydia, if cats could be said to have packs. Prides, maybe. Cougars were normally solitary as hell.

Mitch nodded. "Never thought we'd end up in the position Dad is in. Building a pack with my hands." He reached out a hand, and Jared scooted over and put the pliers in his brother's outstretched hand. "James is supposed to be the leader here, but he's got hikers coming out his ears. Gotta make 'em happy because we're doing our last long Christmas holiday before the little ones hit us up in late January. Can't believe those ladies figured out how to get knocked up at the same time."

Jared tried not to start and scare the dog. "They did?"

Mitch shrugged and stood up. "Apparently, there were thermome-ters involved." He shuddered. "All I know is, she started chasing us around. According to Len and Davis, Kandace did the same."

Jared put his fingers in his ears. "Na na na," he said.

Mitch snorted. "What are you, six? Get your fingers out of your ears! Let me show you how to check a brake line since you have apparently forgotten."

~

*A*fter some time puttering in the garage, re-learning the parts of a motorcycle, Jared had homework. He listened to an introduction to motorcycles while he took out the spacers after the mortar dried in the bathroom, then put in gorgeous silvery grout. Then, he put down tarps and sprayed the ceiling and walls in the nursery. They had a lot to do there. Everything was already on order, and the wolf, bear, and some cat shifters had already purchased everything via an online baby shower. Jared was determined to get everything ready in plenty of time. The babies were twins and shifters, and both tended to come early. Shadow lay in the hallway with her fat dental bone and slept.

Jared cleaned the sprayer and went downstairs, Shadow at his heels. Corinne had gone from a flat stomach to huge nearly overnight, her babies sitting low. She wore a yellow sweatshirt over black maternity jeans, her long hair in braids and pulled back into a silver clip. The hollows under her eyes were gone; Jared had gotten her a white noise machine, so she slept better. Corinne and Mitch had made tortellini with a sausage and tomato cream cheese sauce, a salad, and individual brown artisan loaves with butter on the table. James came home when they were about to sing, filthy from guiding a hike. He kicked off his shoes and sang with them, then went to shower.

They sat and passed the dishes around, filled up their plates. Everyone was ravenous.

"How did it go today at the salt mines?" Jared asked Corinne.

Corinne had been slamming out a website while Kandace worked; they liked to work at back-to-back computers in Kandace's huge home office. Kandace was working on the math and coding that involved building hyperloops that zipped people between cities. No one knew which ones would really get built, all or none, but Kandace was making an enormous amount of money working on her sub-team of the worldwide team.

"No world domination as of yet. I'm actually doing some overflow with Lydia. The website she's working on is such a mess she's having me clean up the English copy before she translates it back." Lydia, their relatively new cougar shifter family member, worked on websites for Native American organizations and companies.

"Sounds good." Mitch passed the tortellini to Jared. "Jared helped me with the bike today."

Corinne raised her eyebrows. "Are you going into business with my husband?"

Jared nodded. "I could for now. Part time. I'd be a baby mechanic for a long time. But it's good winter work. I don't know if he told you…" Jared watched James come into the room, sing, and sit. It was weird. Jared was older and was a put-together soldier, but James was all quiet strength and control. All alpha. Jared would win in a fight, but he would lose the hearts of everyone in the room. Besides, alpha was not what he was after; he preferred control in his own life.

"About the dogs? Sure, we can have a kennel here. But the rescue dogs and this house stay separate from our corgis." The dogs were on their beds, munching treats. "Some of the adopted dogs will have behavioral problems initially until they learn better. Like my man." She grinned at Mitch, who pretended to growl at her. "Down, boy." Jared groaned, and James glared at their wife. She smiled sweetly and passed the bread.

James poured himself a cup of coffee. "I got the text when I hit the trailhead." James passed the salad and reached for the tortellini. "How close to the house do you want to be? Close, far away, so far away that we can't see you? If you're that far away, getting water, power, and an actual road out there may be problematic."

"I will want to move out at some point." Jared took some salad, then passed it to Corinne. "I'll want to see the house, but the dogs barking will drive you batty if I don't build pretty far out."

Corinne took some salad and passed it on. "Good point. I ran a search for a barn for sale while I did the work. Found a contender in Arkansas. Then, I called Ricardo. He'll be out to grade the land. We can decide tonight, and he'll come out to grade and pour. You need to get it done in the next three days when the snow melts off and it gets warm enough to work, or you won't get done until spring. That doesn't give you much time to decide what the square footage of the accompanying house would be like."

"Yours. Your old one. I like everything about it—the square footage, the A-frame design, the view out the windows."

"One problem." James pointed with a chunk of his bread. "The one we ran into. We were on a mountain, so adding onto it would have been nasty. If you want kids, it's a problem. If you want that style, fine, but I would pour for bigger. In fact, I'd make bedrooms upstairs and downstairs. Having only the one downstairs was a problem. You may have trainers staying with you, right?"

"In Yanna's place, they put in insulation and turned the hayloft into apartments for the trainers with the dogs below. Plenty of room for dog pens, which we make look like living rooms. Comfy couches and dog beds, not crates. Have to pick up lots of used furniture. But, I get your point. No reason why I can't make it bigger, put some good-sized rooms downstairs. Can use the rooms for anyone, really. Trainers, visiting shifters, whatever. It's just that I'll have dogs, and you'll have babies."

"There are hotels, cabins, even bed-and-breakfast around here. This is the backwoods, not nowhere." Corinne dug into her tortellini.

"He has a point. The cabins here are usually full, nearly year-round." Mitch took more bread, buttered it. "Anyway, I've got the plans for our place. We can shoot them to Gunny. He's got an architect he works with. Make the downstairs bathroom fatter, add more counter space or a longer breakfast bar in the kitchen. Definitely more bedrooms."

"Okay." Jared nodded. "Yeah, let's do that."

Mitch wiped his hands, did some poking on his cell phone, and put the phone away. Corinne didn't glare at him; this was an obvious exception to the no-phones-at-the-table rule.

"How was your hike?" Jared asked James.

James shook his head. "I swear, the dad and mom had a clue, but those kids must have crawled out from under a rock. The girl kept rolling her eyes and whined at nearly every step. The boy kept trying to sneak in video games. It's too cold and slick to do stuff like that. They were hiking the area because the mom and dad are thinking of moving here, and they wanted to know the hills. They're both runners. I finally hauled them back to their car, which did have snow tires, and explained to them about the lack of cell reception in a lot of the spots around here. I don't think they'll be moving here."

"That was all day?"

"Nope, went to help Linc with his new tiny house. Got filthy clearing construction debris."

Linc lived at the turnoff to their country road, a software engineer who wanted to get on the profitable tiny house bandwagon. His husband, Greg, still lived in Atlanta. Linc was the forerunner, getting both the fat white farmhouse and their first tiny house rental ready. Greg was a hotelier eager to be an innkeeper.

"How's he doing?" Corinne asked.

"Greg's finishing off the year; he's going to stop working at 11:59 New Year's Eve so they don't pay him into the next year."

"Nice guy. I met him when he flew up to help with the painting." Corinne grinned at Jared. "I heard the sprayer upstairs when I came in. Nursery primed?"

"We'll have everything ready, I promise." Jared groaned mentally; he had a hell of a punch list to complete. It was time to give up his townhome rental. He couldn't let snow get in the way of completing his pack's house on time.

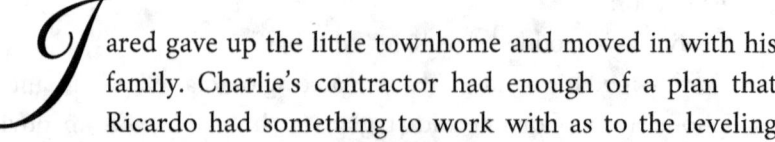

Jared gave up the little townhome and moved in with his family. Charlie's contractor had enough of a plan that Ricardo had something to work with as to the leveling and the concrete pour. Everyone agreed on the places to put the house and the barn, a huge meadow back from the main road.

Dan Oliveras scraped the ground flat with his bulldozer while Ricardo and his daughter Lucia marked out the house, barn, and driveway with stakes and string for the concrete pour. Jared and Mitch helped, dressed in jeans, flannel shirts, and sweatshirts over the top. The bright sun melted the snow, and they got a great day's work in. Jared listened to Mitch's motorcycle podcasts with the flavor of country and Southern rock overlaid, blaring from trucks all tuned to the same radio stations.

They put up lights to finish, then they hiked back to the house. Mitch called for pizza. They took turns showering, and, post-shower, Jared and James checked on the upstairs bathroom. The grout had set. James was pleased.

"Looking great. After the grout sealer, we'll be ready to install the fittings, lights, and mirror."

They went over to look in the nursery. The paint cans were ready for the coats of yellow and pale blue.

James let out a long breath. "Have no idea how to raise two daughters."

Jared huffed. "You'll be fine. Besides, Rachael and Gunny will be over here every time they can get away, plus we'll have the bears over here every five minutes. Bears are good with twins too."

James breathed out, low and long. "Dude, we're piling it on. Getting this house done, and now you'll have your own house, and the barn gets delivered on Tuesday. Got to get it all insulated, then the apartments can go in during the winter."

"That is fast." Jared rubbed the back of his neck. "Cutting off more than I can chew, maybe."

James shook his head. "We learned from Gunny and Rachael, and you were in the military. You know how to focus, find a dream, make plans, implement them. Get the dream as real as that barn is going to be."

"I'm a guy with half a job." Jared raised his hand. "Not any different from anyone else living in deep snow half the year with an outside job, I know. But, I want to be working more full-time. I get it if it's piecemeal, that's fine. It's just that there are some ex-cons. Some of them are in this prison dog-training program on the inside. Lots not locked up for violent crimes. Also, lots of ex-soldiers needing a smoother re-entry."

"Ex-cons?" James asked. He held up a hand. "I get it, really, I do. But the twins…"

"I'll work closely with the trainers, find the best people to train." Jared held up a hand. "I know it's a risk. A huge one. And with the kids… I'll buy the land and put up a fence if you want."

James shook his head. The doorbell rang. "Dinner. Let's eat, then talk about it. Corinne and Mitch have brains, too. We all get to decide."

Jared nodded. "I apologize. I should have opened my mouth before this."

"No, it's a good idea, but we need to be practical as well as emotional. We also don't want the townspeople mobbing us."

They headed downstairs.

"Mobbing us?" Mitch said. "Did you bite someone in wolf form?" The pizza guy's motorcycle sounded from outside. Mitch had three pizza boxes in his hands.

"No, Jared wants to hire ex-cons to work with the dogs."

"Makes sense. They'll be unemployable on the outside even when they've been working for nearly nothing inside." Mitch shrugged. "No sex or death crimes, but other than that, sure."

They got into the kitchen, and James went to get plates while Mitch went to the table with the pizzas, and Jared brought out cherry water for Corinne and pale ale for the rest of them. Corinne came out of the small bathroom, her face a little pale.

"Are you all right?" Mitch asked their wife.

"Fine, just getting kicked in the kidneys. Pregnancy is just lovely. Pizza!"

Corinne had barely made it to the table by the time James came over with the plates. They held hands, sang, then Mitch doled out veggie, super supreme, meat lovers, and a very special pizza with mushrooms, bell peppers, olives, Italian sausage, and bacon. That was Corrine's pizza, and no one else bothered to touch it. Coming between a pregnant woman and her pizza was a very bad idea.

They each got through a piece before Mitch threw out, "Honey, Jared is going to hire ex-cons for his dog training program."

Corinne choked on her cherry water. "What?"

Jared was quick to explain. "There are people who have already gone through learning to be dog trainers in prison."

"Oh. So you're just hiring them when they get out." Corinne nodded her head. "I can see that. They work in prison for nearly free, and then very few people will hire them for any job. Having them already trained in what it is you want them to do is an enormous step forward."

"I apologize for not speaking with you about it earlier. I haven't hired anyone. I've just been looking at programs that do that. There aren't that many of them. I'll get recommendations from the program directors. There won't be that many of them getting out of prison at any particular time, and we can check them out as thoroughly as we want."

"We? It's your business, bro." Mitch reached for another piece of pizza.

Corinne barked out a laugh. "He meant me. He's a good uncle and will make sure the babies are safe."

"We're wolves, we've got bears across the way, and we've got cougars in the family. I think we're good." Mitch grinned and ate his pizza.

"I trust you, Jared," Corinne said. "Just send me the details on the finalists. I'm not worried about that. I'm worried about Thanksgiving. Bathrooms are done, you guys worked on the den non-stop so you could have your video games, the kitchen is great. We're definitely big enough to host ten million people."

James laughed. "We don't have quite that many. The poly people will be having celebrations with their own families, so I don't expect the neighbors."

"Poly people? Oh, the polygamists." Jared reddened. "Sorry. Wolves generally mate a lot then choose one mate for life, so you three kind of shocked the family a little bit."

Corinne grinned. "I really don't care who knows I'm married to Mitch and James. The companies I work for don't care. They want websites, and they really don't care what I do in the bedrooms."

Jared put his hands over his ears. "Too much information. There are some things I just don't want to visualize when it comes to my brothers."

Mitch belly-laughed while James got the conversation back on target. "So, we're big enough. So what's the problem? We've been stockpiling extra food in case there's a blizzard. Oh, that's the problem. We were kind of out of the way, but now we're next to the poly community and all. You're afraid you're going to end up for lots of people in one house for three days straight like last Thanksgiving when Lydia came over." Corinne nodded. "Well, very simple. Along with the food they're bringing, we ask everyone to bring their sleeping bags in case Mother Nature doesn't agree with us. If you're really worried, they can bring extra food in boxes or cans that we donate to the local food pantry if a blizzard doesn't hit."

"That's an excellent idea. Sometimes my brother has a brain." James grinned, and Mitch threw a napkin at him.

Corinne looked across the table at Jared. "I've got two on the way. What am I going to do?"

"We can always pack you in the new van if Mitch and James upset you too much." Jared had bought a transport van for the dogs. The barn was on its way but hadn't arrived yet. They would also need to transport all sorts of equipment and tons of dog food as well. Between the truck and the van, Jared had it covered.

Mitch growled, and James gave Jared a flat stare. "If you take our wife and unborn children anywhere, you're going to be in pieces in the morning."

Jared held up his hands. "I was making a joke."

James nodded once. "That's what I thought. Pass the parmesan."

Corinne gave a sigh of relief when the squabble blew over. "I'll send a text about bringing extra food and sleeping bags. The high chairs and booster seats should be here tomorrow. We're going to need them for our own kids anyway."

James grinned at his wife. "You think of everything."

"I try."

He kissed her hand.

Mitch leaned over to Jared. "Seriously, dude, no joking."

Jared held up his hands again. "I was talking about taking her to the spa, dude. Uncles do that."

Mitch snorted, then reached for more pizza.

THANKSGIVING EVE

Since everyone was coming out for Thanksgiving anyway and snow was expected but not blizzard conditions, the Camber contingent arrived a day early. Of course, delivery of the barn highly interested them. Lucia was the project manager because she had worked on barns before. She was a tiny dictator in jeans, her blue-black hair pulled back in a low ponytail, hard hat on her head. The barn was in fantastic shape. She put any stray Cambers and Westons to work right away. Linc, the software engineer who had the farmhouse on the corner, came over to help. He was huge, with a bald head, full red beard, and very intense blue eyes.

Their interior work involved framing walls, stairs, and putting in the floor for the second level. It was very loud, saws and nail guns running nearly constantly. The smell of sawdust filled the air. Dan Oliveras leveled the ground outside. He also drove the local snowplow, so he was a busy person. Ricardo, Lucia's father, ran the saw. With so many hands, things went quickly. Despite the barn's enormous size, the stairs and flooring went in quickly, and individual rooms began to take shape.

Penny and Libby showed up in their ready-to-work clothes, jeans and flannel, heavy gloves, and steel-toed boots. Libby had her own tool belt and hard hat, both in magenta. Penny was so excited that she ordered a set for herself in garnet. Lucia came over to them with her clipboard and signed them both in.

"Well, get a load of you two. Where did you get that stuff? I've got to get some for me." Lucia grinned and pointed to her black tool belt and then her bright yellow hard hat.

"It's a company that sells tool stuff for females. They're mostly shades of pink, but they've got other colors." Libby proudly displayed her tools, then sent Lucia a link. "Where do you want us?"

"See my dad over there cutting wood?" Ricardo and Lucia had the same deep set chocolate brown eyes and strong noses. "He cuts, he points, you carry. Everyone does a rotation there first."

Penny nodded sharply. "Got it."

They replaced Lynette and Charlie, who were working together to move the wood from Ricardo to where it was needed.

"Thank you, ladies," Charlie said. He put his hands on his massive back and stretched backward. Both Penny and Libby heard his back pop. "We needed a break half an hour ago. When we come back, I've got Ricardo's place so he can take a break. Don't know what the lovely Lynette is doing."

Lynette grinned, dark eyes shining. Sweat beaded her forehead. "I'll figure it out when I get back. Come on, big guy."

"I'll take left, you take right," Libby grabbed the end of the double stack of two-by-fours. "Ricardo, I'm Libby, this is Penny. I know you know us from the shop, but you may not have figured out which one is which yet."

Ricardo laughed tiredly. "I know who you are. Left and up the stairs. I suggest piling them up at the bottom and handing them up later."

"On it," Penny said.

They ducked Mitch on the first floor, throwing refills for nail guns overhead to his brother, who was standing on a piece of plywood nailed in between two studs on the second floor. Jen also caught some nail packets out of the air, and she went one way while James went the other.

They carried the stack to the bottom of the stairs, one board at a time. Libby got on the middle of the staircase, and they passed the wood up the stairs to James. They went back and forth, then passed up two-by-fours and plywood for the base flooring upstairs. The barn had come with heavy beams that were very sturdy. They were working outward from what had been the hayloft.

Penny and Libby's arms were spaghetti by the time they had been there an hour. By two hours, they were delighted to take a break.

"I scoop ice cream all day, and I do kickboxing. Why can't I raise my arms?" Penny asked.

Libby groaned. "Because you're not lifting wood all day."

They drank their hot chocolate and replenished themselves with gluten-free Libby snacks Libby had brought and put in the back of the truck they were using for their breaks.

Penny snorted. "Remind me not to go into construction as a profession."

"We make sweet things. That's our groove, that's our thing." Libby stretched out one arm, then the other. Then, she leaned forward, put her hands together, then stretched her arms behind herself and over her head.

Penny waited until she was done with her hot chocolate and Libby snacks before doing the same thing. Her shoulders creaked. "Back to the salt mines."

Libby pointed at the portable bathroom. "Bathroom break, then I'll show you how to use a nail gun."

"I love you," Penny said.

"That's nice, but she's my wife."

Penny jumped, then whirled. "Nat, you may be the law, but I'm not above throwing hot chocolate at your head."

"Hey! I thought you'd be at the Thanksgiving luncheon with the kids." Libby hugged her spouse.

The deputy nodded. "I was. Just got out. Like you said at the play, the thanks part of the holiday is what we should be celebrating in our current lives, not the foreshadowing of indigenous peoples losing their land. So, Meri made some hot sandwiches, and I brought them over. Besides, this place is going to be for homeless dogs. Who can't get behind that?"

Libby grinned. "I hope she made enough for ten people. That's how many we have in there at any particular time." She helped Ned unload the deputy's vehicle.

"That barn is huge. I can't believe how quickly things are getting done." Penny used her spaghetti arms to pick up the smallest box of sandwiches and followed them to the truck used for catering.

"The power of ten and one goal." Ned put down the box, kissed Libby, and waved goodbye to Penny. "I moved back to day shift. Now I've got to go deal with data work until my eyes bleed unless any people are stupid enough to put their car on manual in order to get in a fender bender."

Libby waved. "Have a great day! See you at dinner! I'm picking up the kids."

Nat waved, got back in the police truck, and headed out.

~

They decided not to have dinner at Corrine's house, which was as clean as a whistle. People sick of sawdust in the chilly barn had painted the last of the upper rooms and had cleaned up after themselves like construction fairies. Jared, battling insomnia, had already put the wood floors down, stained and polyurethaned them, and covered them in heavy tarps. The tarps came off, and the house had many lovely but unfinished rooms.

Gunny made the call. So, as people swept up the sawdust in the barn, the rest of the family unloaded trucks that lined up outside with the pre-ordered furniture. Corinne stood on the bottom step like a pregnant general, yelling out the names of rooms as people carried furniture inside. Gunny and Jen were ready to haul things up the stairs that needed it. Mitch and James went upstairs with Corinne to put the cribs together, prompting cheers and some tears from nearly everyone.

"This is better than a baby shower!" Penny enthused, battling to get a carousel lamp out of its box and unwrap the bubble wrap cocooning it. "The bride isn't the only one to open the presents, and we get to help put everything together! I like this playroom. It's comfortable."

Jared grinned as he screwed the last screw in the bookshelf. The box of baby books was next to his left foot. "It is kind of awesome. I promised I would get things ready on time. Then there was the idea of the barn, adopting shelter dogs to train as support animals. And Corinne ordered the barn. She had to, there aren't that many of them left, and the deal was too good to pass up, and it ended up like being on the back of a bucking bronco. Or, in this case, two of them going in two different directions. I had no idea how I was going to keep my promise." His voice held tears.

Penny gently put the lamp down, turned, and hugged Jared. He held her close. Penny felt the thump of his heartbeat, felt her own heartbeat increase its thudding. She stroked his cheek, then said, "We're all family around here. You really didn't think anyone would show up for a barn-raising in the holler?"

Jared laughed. "It's not like we advertised or anything. The barn came early, and so did the family. I thought the barn would sit there until after the holidays."

"Ned brought Meri's pulled pork and buffalo chicken sandwiches, and they still had to call for pizza when the high school kids showed up." Penny flattened the box the lamp came in. "We special family folk have all been invited to dinner across those trails on the back of your property that lead to the Camber farm. Let's get this done so we can eat."

"I shouldn't even be upright. I started around four in the morning." Jared knelt to open the box of books.

"Sounds like my normal workday. I've joined Meri and Libby working out with Nat." She got the lamp plugged in, then helped him put the baby books on the shelf.

"My brothers keep talking love talk with Corinne all the time. Does it happen with Nat, Libby, and Meri?"

"Nat is a deputy, so no. Libby and Meri crack jokes with each other, but they don't have their hands all over Ned. I've been around the Cambers enough to know that they kiss and hug a lot, but they do that with basically everybody."

Jared broke down the cardboard box that previously held the baby books and added it to the stack of recycling in the hallway. He took out Penny's detritus as well and rejoined her.

Penny opened the box with a changing table. "Poly must be really difficult. Everybody in the relationship has to be sure that everybody else is happy. And, if mama ain't happy, nobody's happy."

"It's not something I want for myself." Jared checked around to be sure only he and Penny were in the room and pushed the door most of the way closed with his foot. "Wolves mate for life. And, this is what we want. Or at least what I want. Kids, food, putting together furniture like this when babies come or toys on Christmas Eve while the kids are asleep." He reached into the box for the changing table, took out the directions, snorted, and began putting the parts into piles.

Penny stared at the piles of parts. "I want kids. I froze my eggs."

"You what?" Jared stilled his hands. He lowered his voice. "Sorry, just surprised."

"Why? Small town, not many prospects. When you've known someone since grade school, there's not a lot of secrets, except like yours, the shifter thing. Everyone remembers when you had braces or flubbed a line in the school play. And, a lot of people just leave. I remember going to a picnic once. In three days, fourteen of those people had gone. School, the military, jobs anywhere they could find them. Not just graduating high school students either. Some people move here, get a load of the winters, and move right back out. A lot of people hate not having cell phone service on some of these mountains. If you want to see a play, it's watching kids or an amateur production. If you want to see a movie, that's what the internet is for. We're rural people, Jared."

"Um, it's none of my business why you froze your..." Jared concentrated on trying to interpret the confusing shelf directions.

"Eggs. Like a chicken." Penny eyed the tiny metal object that was supposed to be both the screwdriver and wrench and took the real objects off her tool belt. "I didn't know where or when I would fall in love enough to want to get married. Mostly everybody paired off really quickly. A lot of people got married in their early twenties around here. Those that stayed, I mean. I didn't want to hit my late thirties and not have viable eggs. Plus, I could get cancer or be in an accident and not have them at all. Leslie Doherty died when she was in her twenties of ovarian cancer. A week later, Karissa Deshawn had a log roll down a hill and hit her. She fought her way into walking again, but she won't be having kids physically. We were all a complete mess for a long time after that. We're a small rural school. There weren't that many people in our graduating class."

Jared held up the bottom of the changing table, and Penny took the other end. He put the side on, then Penny screwed in the screw. "I guess I never really thought about it. Sometimes we will take in cubs. We change at around five years old for the first time. Some people adopt kids and don't realize what they really are. We've also had parents moving to wolf compounds in order to learn how to be parents to wolf cubs."

Penny handed the next screw to Jared. "Now that's real parenting." She stood, got the other side, took a screw, pulled out a second screwdriver from her belt, and began screwing it into the bottom of her panel.

"It is. Heard of it happening in Montana, and another one in Utah. Those parents are amazing."

"Would the wolves and bears here do that? Sorry, stupid question. I don't know your family all that well yet, but the Cambers would without any question. You told me that your family took on Mitch and James, so obviously they would do that too."

"And Stretch, and Lydia, and some of my other brothers. You don't run a pack without having really big hearts. Or, um, den."

"Technically, a sloth. Or sleuth, of bears." Charlie came in, looked around the room. "Stupid name for a group of bears." He pointed to the bed where Jared slept. "You going pirate ship, treehouse, or fairy glen with that?"

Jared stood, grabbed the second shelf, and put it where it needed to go. Then, he screwed in the first screw for the top shelf of the changing table. "I hadn't got much past planning the toddler rope bridge and slide. I think a tree house may be the way to go for now. I want to keep it simple until the girls develop their personalities. Then they'll just need to change a little bit of paint further on down the road."

Charlie opened the box with the kids' table and chairs and screamingly bright primary colors. "Sounds like an excellent plan. Have you ordered the parts for the rope bridge and toddler slide yet? We can get that ordered right now as part of the baby shower package."

"You know, I didn't think to put that on the baby shower site." Jared tapped his safety glasses, called up his HUD, and threw a link to Charlie. "I was thinking red, yellow, and blue, to go with that table you're putting together over there."

Charlie took the table out of the box, flipped it upside down, and folded out the legs. Charlie touched his own safety glasses, pulled up his HUD, and made the selections. "When they arrive, give me a call. I'll lumber over here to help you install them."

Penny laughed. "You shapeshifters are absolutely hilarious. I love hanging around you guys."

Charlie grinned. "Libby has wanted to tell you for well over a decade now. She hated keeping any secrets from you. I remember you two, all knobby-kneed, climbing trees in the backyard."

Penny laughed so hard she almost dropped her screwdriver. "I always wondered why she was a much better climber than I was!"

Jared smiled. "Wolf children run. Everywhere, all the time. It doesn't stop when you're done being a toddler, either. It's an absolute nightmare keeping track of us, and we tend to have twins, like the bears."

Charlie unfolded the four small chairs and put them around the table. "I think it's why so many of us ended up going poly. It's much easier to handle such active kids when you've got multiple parents keeping track of them at the same time. Not that it's a reason for falling in love with more than one person at the same time. I believe that love is infinite and that it's stronger when it's shared. But, you've got to use your brain. Three of the best bear shifter women in the world chose me in particular. I have no idea why, but they did. I am the luckiest man alive."

"If they chose you, how did you use your brain?" Jared asked. He grabbed the last shelf and started screwing it on.

"I became the man they needed me to be."

Corinne and Jared worked in absolute silence after that, mulling it over. Charlie smiled, saluted, grabbed the box detritus, and left the room. His work there was done.

~

*D*inner was at the Camber household. Everyone had run themselves through the showers to the point there was no hot water left in either house. Penny and Libby wore their gym clothes, the washers and dryers going full tilt. Absolutely no one cared who was dressed in what with the sheer number of children running around. Bobby, Adam, Ricky, and Denver had a very complicated spaceship thing going on in the corner with a lot of action figures, starships, and buildings. Beau, River, and Bethany had a chase game going on that involved crawling under tables at the same time that people were loading them with food. There were no accidents, but the kids got chased out of the kitchen. Charlie got his hands on Beau, and Mitch grabbed River and Bethany, one under each arm. The captured children were all hollering so loud that no one could carry on a conversation.

Jared took Penny's hand and led her into the living room. They found a corner and constructed a sizable den with sheets and pillows.

Jared handed Libby a pillow. "Are you coming tomorrow? I apologize. It just occurred to me that I never asked you to Thanksgiving. I assumed Libby would, or that you would be spending time with your mother, but I really do want to see you tomorrow. Besides, the food is amazing around here."

Penny laughed. "This is going to sound completely insane, but my mother is on a cruise. I dropped her off at the airport yesterday. She ships out from Galveston tomorrow morning. It's a special mystery cruise with a whole bunch of dinners, mystery plays, and pretend thefts and murders to solve. My mother loves that stuff. She went on one last year, and this was the only time when they could book the ship this year. I told her to go, with my full blessings. I like mysteries myself, but I am just not interested. Besides, it's kind of hard."

"What's hard?" Jared helped tie down an errant sheet.

"It's hard having just two of us. We're so close, we talk all the time, so by the time we're doing some sort of get together like Thanksgiving or Christmas, by the second day, we are just staring at each other. We also do volunteer work throughout the year, so that's not some special thing to do during the holidays. Plus, I live in a tiny house with no room for new stuff, and she has money now, so buying each other gifts is really difficult. And giving money is just kind of crass." Penny put on the last pillow and stood back. "Shall we call in the troops?"

"No, for two reasons. First of all, I can smell something amazing. Second, they'll find it on their own." He took Penny's hand. "Decided yes about staying with us? You don't even have to go home. Your clothes are in the laundry right now. Plus, the barn is nowhere near done, and we have a free day tomorrow."

Penny punched him in the shoulder. "You just want me for my garnet tool belt."

Jared grinned and led her into the kitchen. "Guilty as charged. Did you ever consider being a low-paid construction worker and runner during the break? Isn't this normally when you start to shut down your shop? Or, I guess on your side of the shop?"

"Yes, I could do that. I've got a lot to study for keto recipes and small business marketing, so I've got a lot of podcasts and lessons to listen to while I'm working. I take it you have a barn to complete?"

"I do. I have seen you can put together shelves. How do you feel about constructing dog pens?"

They skirted the kids' table, piled with hot dogs and macaroni and cheese. Jared pulled out a chair for Penny at the main table.

"Let's find out." It was time to sing. Libby had been teaching her the words. They were very old, about nourishment, family, love, and gratitude. Penny grinned. She finally had the large family she craved.

THANKSGIVING

*J*ared smiled as he looked over the railing. Penny looked fantastic in the lower bunk, crimson hair spread out over her dark blue pillowcase. She was on her side, face turned into the pillow, snuggled into the sleeping bag, a peaceful angel. They had run out of comforters the night before; she wore his cobalt camp bag well. Jared had slept in the upper bunk, constructed the day before, which would be accessible by side stairs in the future. For the moment, there was a removable ladder that would get locked up because toddlers shouldn't be climbing ladders when they were small.

Jared put on his safety glasses and checked the checklist on his HUD. They had gone through much of the extensive punch list for the barn and quite a bit of it on the house, so he couldn't be happier. The electrical person, Amelia, was coming to the barn early, eager to get the work out of the way so she could still have plenty of time with her family. She gladly took on the job for double overtime to pay for Christmas presents. They had to get electrical and plumbing in before they could put in the insulation, and insulation was absolutely vital in a place with deep snows. Then they had the drywall, and then everything after that.

Jared scampered down the railing, careful not to wake up Penny in his stocking feet. He grabbed his clothes from the shelf and carefully shut the door behind him, Shadow at his heels. He headed to the bathroom, ready to dress and conquer the world.

He found Mitch downstairs sipping from a mug of coffee as the elixir of the gods that it was. Jared fed Shadow her breakfast. Mitch had four breakfast muffins stuffed with cheddar and bacon in the microwave. He put two on each plate and handed a plate to Jared. Jared took the plate, poured himself a mug of coffee, doctored it, and wolfed down his muffins. He washed up, put the plates in the dishwasher, then Jared ordered Shadow to stay and watch over Penny. Shadow padded back upstairs, and Mitch and Jared both silently crept out the back door.

Amelia was already getting out of the truck. Short and squat, the contractor had huge muscles bulging under her coat, a wide face, and a flat nose, her hair in braids under her hard hat. She handed large boxes out to Mitch and Jared. None of them spoke until they were inside the barn. Amelia shut the door behind him. Mitch and Jared put on their utility belts while Amelia walked the space.

"Some bright person cut both the electrical holes and the plumbing ones too. The space is huge, and we don't have all day. I'm going to install the boxes. I've got the plans, thank you, Jared, and I know where the lights, fans, and outlets go. You guys will run the cables. Watch me install a box, we'll run the wire, I'll show you how to install the outlet box. Mitch, open the box on the right and pull out the spool of white cable. Jared, open that box over there and run the blue fiber optic cable. I'll start with the first junction box."

Mitch and Jared looked at each other, then at Amelia. "We both know how to wire and install the boxes. I know where the boxes go. Mitch, I'll send you a schematic. I'll take the right, you take the left. We'll do the outlet boxes for you, Amelia. Does that sound good?" Jared knelt, opened a box of electrical boxes.

Amelia smiled like the sun coming out. "Thank the skies I don't have numbskulls working with me. Okay, let's get started."

Charlie, Gunny, Jen, Penny, and Stretcher arrived about twenty minutes later. The dogs lay outside chewing snacks. Jen and Gunny set up a sawhorse-and-board table in the back with coffee, water, and Meri's homemade energy bars, and they divided up the space. Stretcher and Jen went upstairs with Gunny, and Charlie took the back wall. It was silent within the room except for the occasional whir of an electric screwdriver or drill. Everyone had their own individual music. Penny got an education from Lynette and Jared as they taught her how to do everything they were doing, from wiring to cutting drywall.

About an hour later, James and Lynette came over to help install the plumbing along with Lucia, Ricardo, and Linc the neighbor. Then it got a lot louder with the installation of the water heater, along with hammering and banging. The drainage pipes were plastic, but they sometimes needed torque to fit together.

Since the barn wasn't far from the main house, Dan, who was no longer needed on snowplow because the snow had stopped falling hours ago, dug both water and sewer lines to the main house. Dan looked like a powerful thief in his winter clothes, which included a puffy black full-length jacket and a black ski mask for his face. The excavator was deafening, but it was relatively fast. They took turns following behind Dan, laying the fat white sewer pipe, painting the outside, then the inside of each end with purple glue, then screwing the pipes together.

When it was Jared and Penny's turn, they found a rhythm. Penny painted on the purple glue while Jared screwed the pipes together. Shadow came out from herding the dogs to oversee their work. Jared played rap into the air about finding the right moment and was surprised that Penny knew all the words. They used the beat to get the job done. Jared approved; it checked off the boxes in his military mind. Shadow stood on the piles of dirt on the side that would be used to cover the hole, the rocks used to make paths later. Penny painted another pipe end, being sure to get the brush deep in the threads of the pipe.

"I'm being stared at."

Jared grinned. "She's wondering why the humans are in a hole painting purple glue on pipes." He held his pipe still as she switched to paint the one he was holding.

Penny knelt, getting frost on her knees. "I wonder the same thing."

"Dog adoptions. Dogs that help parents have warning when their kids have seizures. Therapy dogs for terrified children and trauma survivors." He smiled wanly. "Like me."

Penny finished, put the paintbrush down, and helped connect the pipe and hold it flat while Jared screwed it on. "I won't be stupid and assume I have any idea what you went through."

Jared nodded. "At least you didn't thank me for my service. It was my job." He rubbed the back of his neck. "The problem is, guiding a dog through a war zone to find explosives does not translate so much into the real world. The adrenaline is exhausting. I like the training here. No real bombs or drugs." He grunted as he tightened the pipe as hard as he could. He backed up, and Penny followed him with the glue. Shadow shadowed them above.

"Excited to train dogs here?"

Jared nodded. "Long way away from that old reality. This is good. Visceral. Proof that my dreams have legs. Baby steps, one centimeter at a time."

Penny knelt on the cold ground again. "I understand. I took baby steps on my way to my idea of perfection. My first shop was tiny. I saved up to move my shop next to Libby's, more tables, more service. We got our stuff from a going-out-of-business sale. Sad. Anyway, expanded. Thought I would fall flat on my face. This is very much a seasonal business. I'm still pushing to find out more stuff I can do during the winter. Sadly, my new skills laying pipe will not be needed during winter." They both laughed, then got the next segment screwed in.

"You know you are really helping dogs here, right?" Jared carried the pot of glue while she carried the brush to the next pipe. They both ducked dirt from Shadow's keeping pace overhead.

Penny grinned, then spluttered as she nearly breathed in dirt. "Yuck." She stepped up to the end of the pipe. "I do. Besides, I'd be alone in my tiny apartment if I wasn't here. Not out in the freezing air

ducking dirt, painting purple glue on my knees on the hard ground."
She grinned. "It sounds bizarre, but this is fun."

Jared raised his eyebrows. "Female, you have a strange idea of what
is fun." She picked up the pot of glue and laughed.

Dan finished digging, the entire length of pipe in, the fiber optic
cable strung through a separate tube, and they covered the hole with
plywood to keep the kids out.

Penny barked out a laugh when Jared had to stop Shadow from
trying to cover up the hole. "Tomorrow, dog."

Jared shook his head. "Don't promise my partner something you
can't deliver. What inspector works the day after Thanksgiving?"

Penny raised an eyebrow when she saw Charlie whip out his
phone and send a text. The man had connections. Dan left the excavator for when the pipe and cables had been inspected to cover the
pipe back up. The water, power, sewer, and cable inspectors would be
by the following week. They called a halt while Amelia and Dan drove
away.

They cleaned up, showered, and got ready for Thanksgiving
dinner, which would start at two in the afternoon and go on until
people felt like going home. Normally, there were outside games of
football, but since so many of the adults were sore and exhausted
from all of the construction and it was freezing outside, they did interior construction of forts and Legos instead. Jared and Penny recre-
ated their earlier fort to the kids' delight, and the kids ran in and out
of it with their various toys.

Lydia showed up with her husband Lucas, a shock because this
was the busiest time of the year for Lucas, a gangly geek. Lydia
showed her native American heritage in her dark eyes and high
cheekbones. She looked just like Stretcher, without the purple mili-
tary-short hair. Lucas created the digital sets for online games, which
had to be done by December in order to get into the hands of gamers
by Christmas.

Lucas grinned. "I worked ahead this year. And, I hired one of the
daughters of my linguist. I got a lot done because the construction on
the cabin to make it two stories made me rent one of my mother's tiny

cabins to work in. The one next to what Lydia first rented, actually."
Lynette, Stretcher, and Lydia all coughed their laughter.

"He hired a genius little girl. His linguist is a local teacher who
creates valid in-game languages," Lydia explained.

Lynette stared, narrow-eyed, at Lydia. "When?"

Lydia smiled and touched her stomach. "July." Everyone congratu-
lated Lydia and Lucas. "There's one little thing," Lydia added.

Lynette clapped her hands. "She's having multiples. How many?"

Lucas went pale. "Three."

"Then it won't be July," Lynette predicted.

Gunny sighed. "More bassinets to put together."

Rachael pushed on his shoulder. "You love it."

Gunny grinned. "I do."

Jetta patted her stomach. "Then you can help us."

Everyone looked at her. Jen looked smug, Lynette satisfied, and
Charlie smiled so wide it looked like his face would split in half.
Everyone cheered.

"Wait." Len gasped for air. "How many siblings am I going to end
up with?"

"Two more," Jetta said.

"Enough," Charlie said.

"Deal, little bro," Vic said, clapping Len on the back. "We get our
kids and little siblings at the same time."

"And no one finds that weird?"

Davis shrugged. "Normal is a setting on a clothes dryer. Pass the
potatoes." Everyone laughed.

They had two turkeys, four chickens, two ducks, baked potatoes
loaded with bacon, cheddar, sour cream, and butter instead of
mashed, stone-ground wheat country rolls, green beans, and
asparagus loaded with garlic and parmesan, and miniature pies.
Gunny and Davis carved the birds, Mary and Libby baked and cut up
the pies, Len baked the veggies, Jetta the bread.

They laughed nearly continually, cleaned up with plenty of food
for later, and divided up into separate rooms. Jared and Penny
watched over the girls with Shadow. The pregnant women formed a

cabal and exchanged checklists. Davis and Len played with the boys. The three new dogs, Shadow, and five corgis went outside, came in and warmed up, and found little ones to play with. Meri and Libby passed out hot chocolate and treats. Football was on the main screen, with Jen cheering the loudest.

Davis and Len took Jared and Penny's place at the fort. Penny joined the women laughing their heads off at the table over pie, and Jared helped Mitch on pot and general cleanup duty.

"Lots of pregnant females." Jared dried the pot Mitch gave him.

Mitch scrubbed another pot. "There are. We're all so happy we could explode."

Jared shook his head. "Enough to clean up around here as it is."

"What bug crawled up your butt?" Mitch gave Jared the side-eye. "You should be happy. Despite the enormous cost of people working on Thanksgiving morning, you're ahead weeks at this point. Why so glum?"

"I'm not down. Not really. It's just that... this is what I want."

Mitch handed a pot to Jared to rinse. "Pots to wash?"

"Well, in a way. I want kids."

"I... oh. Things with Penny going too slow?"

"No, not really. She was really busy, and she's tired a lot. I'm doing the best I can. Things have to go at her pace, not mine."

"Oh, I get it." Mitch attacked another pot. "You want your life to happen faster. Let me warn you. Life happens at its own pace. You think things are smooth on the river, then you're upside-down in your canoe."

"Ah. Hang on, when the ride seems smooth, it's all going to change?" Jared grinned. "You sound more like Dad every day."

Mitch's face froze, then he broke into a grin. "That's the nicest thing you've ever said to me."

"Don't let it go to your head, bro." Jared took the pot from Mitch and rinsed it. Mitch laughed.

*P*enny snuck away from the merriment into an upstairs bedroom to read a text from her mom.

We've got a real butler as a perk of taking this particular cruise. She hasn't been killed off yet. She may be the killer. More to follow. Penny laughed. Adelle experienced life with relish now that she had the enormous weight of financial issues off her head. This was why Penny had no debt and saved nearly half of what she earned to spend on the business. A cruise was far past her means. Her mom wanted to help, but Adelle had done enough. Penny gave her a song and dance about doing things on her own, standing proudly on her own two feet. There was some truth in that. But, her mom had done more than enough, and that was it in Penny's mind.

Eating like a pig. I think I might explode. Libby and Meri are going to have to take me to work out with Ned seven days a week at this rate. Going to help Jared some more before reopening on Monday morning. We are turning the barn he had shipped here into a dog training facility for rescue dogs. Learning to use my new power tools. Penny lay back in the glider, which Corinne, and probably Kandace, would sit in when she visited and rock their babies. She thought of her eggs while waiting for her mother's text. If it didn't work out with Jared, she had a bevy of hunky men around her who might consent to donate their...

Shifter sperm. She had a lot to learn, but she thought she could do it. Maybe. Probably. With a lot of help. She realized that was why they tended to congregate in large family groups. Packs. Sleuths. Whatever.

She sat up at her mother's text message. *Gotta go. Just lost a ringer we thought was a guest. The butler is nowhere in sight. Hmm.*

Penny laughed and decided to call Maddie. Maddie answered at once. "Hey, Pen. Wish you were here. Jack's got the kids dancing to Disney songs in princess costumes, and I'm doing absolutely nothing at all. He did half the cooking and all the dishes. Got the recorder on, so I can watch later. What's up?"

"I'm sorry I bothered you about the..." Penny waved her hand.

"I did it, and I feel free. I want no contact with her, but it kind of validated me. Shut the door on it. My therapist saw it and walked me through the memories. Jack saw it, and he was quiet for a week. Then he said that I was the best mom and the best person ever." She let tears flow down her cheeks. "We're even closer than before. It's like, we get the kids in bed. We trade off reading with Cannie and Cammie."

Candace and Cameron were two years apart, but Cameron was an old soul, so they acted like they were the same age. Both little girls had Maddie's green eyes and brown curly hair. Cannie was chatty, and Cammie more thoughtful, more inclined to think rather than do first. The sisters were like peas in a pod, only going nuclear once in a while.

"I can't wait to see them." Penny would visit after the holidays for a few days early in the new year. Jack and Maddie deserved their special family time without Penny's interference.

"See you soon, Pen. How is it between you and Jared?"

"You know, the usual, putting in a sewer line and building furniture together."

"What? Tell ya sista." Penny laughed and described the last two days. "Unpaid work, huh? So you got to use your tools? Better than the guys being tools."

Penny laughed. "The guys here aren't tools. We're having fun. Laughing all the time. I'm learning a lot about construction." She tilted her head. "I think I'll look into fixer-upper houses. It seems that they've kind of drawn me into the fold, Cambers, Westons. Huge families."

"Oddly enough, I can imagine having multiple husbands at my beck and call. Right now, I've got friends trading off cleaning the house and running errands so we can play on the floor with the kids. We can do jobs and raise our daughters right. Pay attention to them."

"You are nothing like Farrah. At all. You may have a few cells in common, but that's all. I was there, Maddie. I saw what she said and did. You are one of the strongest, most amazing women I know. And your kids are... and Jack is... I admit it; I'm a little jealous."

"Thinking it's time to unfreeze the popsicles?" Maddie asked.

"It's way early with Jared, and I haven't found a house yet. I think I need to buy a fixer-upper with my newfound skills with the money I do have. I can fix it up, then when there's no construction dust and paint fumes, go for it." Penny grinned. "I know Jared is great with kids and that he wants them."

"Oo, baby." Maddie grinned. "And he's nice-looking from the pictures you sent. All intense and focused. That's good for a man. And, you know he gets things done."

Penny snorted out a laugh. "He says the way the family works is, someone gets an idea and starts moving in that direction. Others help, and then you're in the middle of the rapids wondering if you happened to pack an oar."

"Then, take advantage of it. Casually mention your very low down payment..."

"Try nearly nonexistent."

"And let them help you. Make phone calls or something."

"And be caught in the rapids." Penny shrugged. "I'm learning how to make gluten-free frozen desserts."

"Develop a tasting menu. Get some guinea pigs." Maddie grinned. "I would taste-test for you, but I'm far away."

"Great idea, Maddie! I am also taking courses in accounting and small business social media marketing. The accounting is uber-boring, but I'm getting better at keeping my own books. And a design course, too. I'm learning how to make logos. And now learning how to fix stuff."

"Maybe you should focus on one or two things?"

Penny shook her head. "I can, but I may be piecing together jobs for a while. And, I don't know what will hit and stick. I may get an accounting degree and find out I have no clients. This way, I'm sure, and every little bit helps."

"Just remember the downtime thing."

Penny sighed. "I keep hearing my mother's voice in my head. Learn to earn."

"I did what she said, and now I have an amazing life." There was a loud crash. "Penny, gotta go."

"Love always." Penny waved goodbye.

"Always." Maddie waved back.

Penny sighed. She hated leaving the whole shifter thing out, but a promise was a promise. She ached to tell her best friend everything. She stood, giggled as she almost fell getting up from the glider.

Jared stuck his head in. "Hey, Pixie Penny. There you are! Game time is starting. We have board games, VR skiing, and a word contest." She reached out, and he took her hand. Laughing, they ran down the stairs.

They chose Monopoly, and soon Penny had Park Place. Things were looking up. She bought a house and put the green plastic on her empire.

Charlie grinned. "Girl's gonna win. She knows real estate."

"Actually, I'm looking for a real-world house. My down payment would be absurdly low, so a fixer-upper. Jared and Jen are teaching me what they know, so I should be able to finish what I start."

Kandace eyed her. "How much down?"

Len rolled the dice and moved his top hat around the board. He bought Baltic.

Penny showed Kandace in Monopoly money.

Mitch snorted. "Honey, you'll be lucky to get an outhouse with that."

James elbowed him. Kandace and Corinne eyed each other, and both poked at their phones.

Jared whispered in Penny's ear. "Be careful. Once they get in moving-forward mode..."

Mitch rolled and moved his dog. He paid rent on Atlantic to his wife, and Jared took the dice.

"I'm counting on it," Penny whispered back. She laughed as Jared landed on Park Place. "Pay up."

He did and grinned.

"Got one," Corinne passed the phone to Kandace, who grimaced and passed back the phone.

Penny landed on Chance and drew, and paid luxury taxes. She snorted; she wouldn't be doing that for at least a decade in real life.

"Got another one." Kandace passed the phone back to Corinne. Corinne nodded and handed it back.

Penny whispered to Jared, "Do I get to look at the houses?"

Jared whispered back. "These are the two of the most competent women in the world, except our mothers. They'll show you what they deem to be best, and you'll jump."

Penny nodded. Formidable women seemed to be the norm in the giant merged family.

River slammed into the back of Penny's chair. Penny got up, turned around, knelt, and picked up the little girl when she began to cry. "It's okay, honey; I know where the ice is." She made a beeline for the kitchen.

Kandace and Corinne both looked at Jared. Jared nodded once, got up, and headed to get a towel from the hall closet to wrap up the ice if there were no blue freezer packs in there.

"How do you do that?" Mitch asked.

Kandace snorted. "It's a gift. Sometimes bears are dense. Not sure about wolf guys." Corinne guffawed.

Jared came back and sat down. "Jetta's got her. No blood or loose teeth."

Penny came back with a carafe and glasses in her hand. "I made my apple cider stuff. Far less strong than Ned's bottled stuff."

"Ned drinks on duty?" Mitch asked, appalled.

"No, fool, Ned drinks cider with ginger and cinnamon and some other potent herbs. Hasn't had a cold in three years." Libby snagged a glass and poured herself some. "Can I get in?"

Corinne pointed to a chair. "My next bladder break, go for it."

Kandace sighed. "The joys of gestating." She saw the look in Penny's eyes. She looked over at her best friend Corinne, who gave an infinitesimal nod. She looked at Jared, and Corinne shook her head a tiny bit, then made an achingly slow movement with her hand. Libby noticed, looked over at Jared, and gave her own little nod. Penny, oblivious, smiled at Jared.

Mitch sighed. The women had a plan. Their lives would never be the same again.

ACQUISITION

*J*ared received the call at six in the evening while he was putting away the painting supplies in his barn from Juliet Zau, head of the Canine Prison Program in the left half of Kansas. "He's scheduled to be released at six in the morning. The warden is hoping to avoid the press."

Diego Alvarez, a perfectly normal seventeen-year-old boy, had been mowing lawns and trimming bushes as Jared himself had done at that age. Every penny for college was a serious thing. The woman living in one of the houses on the street where Diego worked, Gina Shinam-Kiao, had been killed when Diego had been home alone because his mom, Benita, worked two jobs in the hopes of sending Diego to community college. Diego's blood was on the weapon—garden shears. He had cut himself earlier in the week and had the bandaged hand to prove it. The prosecutor and jury saw it the other way—that he had cut himself committing the brutal murder. Tried as an adult, Diego had served eight years of a thirty-year sentence when Vorko Shinam had been caught cleaning up the bloody aftermath of the murder of his second wife. It took ten long days for the paperwork to go through to release Diego.

Jared was elated; he needed so much help it was absurd. Penny and the entire family had worked with him to get the inspections done, then the heating and air conditioning, then another inspection before the flooring went in and drywall went up. The kitchen was done, all the bathrooms, and two out of four of the upstairs bedrooms.

Vic and Davis had gathered couches and easy chairs that were to be thrown away or from consignment stores from all over two counties to put in the pens that were taking shape under Penny and Libby's hands. Jared wanted the pens to be like little living rooms, safe and comfortable. Mitch and Charlie had come up with some hideous but warm, serviceable rugs that Corinne washed, swearing like a sailor. Two of them had to be thrown out, but they ended up with twelve. Penny's fabulous mother Adelle came up with a practical solution; soft but water-resistant covers sewn together from special sheets the woman sewed, night after night, into rug coverings. The home economics class at the high school had converted their pillow project into a doggy bed project, and the pens were slowly becoming perfect.

A local pet store had donated doggy dishes, and Gunny had driven three hours both ways to drop off a variety load of dog food, from puppy to adult to senior food. Senior dogs were great dogs for kids to read to. There were already schools lined up to have dogs come over and volunteers in two counties if he could get the place ready for dogs. The housing inspector had signed off, and the Canine Training Unit would exist in two days.

Corinne had picked Diego herself, sure of his innocence, and she was right. Diego's loving mother had died two years before, and he had been a gangly geek with few friends before the murder. Now, he had none except the dogs he trained and would have to leave behind. Jared had a long drive ahead of him across two states in the snow if he were to make it on time to pick up Diego. If he wasn't there, Diego would be left outside on an icy late December morning with no one to help him. He jogged towards the house from his barn, Shadow at his side.

Corinne sat at the kitchen table with Penny. "I don't know," Penny wailed.

Jared patted her shoulder and went to grab a cold box and bag for the trip. He packed sodas in the cold box, then filled up two carafes with coffee. He then pulled out sandwich fixings—leftover tandoori chicken, thick, brown walnut bread, lettuce, tomatoes, pickles, black olives, goat cheese, and cream cheese mixed with curry powder and a hint of stone-ground mustard. He fed Shadow, then grabbed his traveling-dog pack. Jared filled up the water bottles and sealed the kibble tray. Then he assembled several fat sandwiches for himself and packed them.

Corinne said, "You need just a little more. It's an auction. You have to have the money upfront. There's a way. I promise you. And if you don't win the auction, then you're not out anything."

Jared gave Corinne an infinitesimal nod. Penny had put in more hours on the dog training facility than nearly anyone else, even close family. She deserved the money. But, like all the other tireless volunteers, she wouldn't accept repayment. So, he'd floated the mysterious loan money.

"It's a loan?" Penny had hope and fear warring across her beautiful face.

"Repayment at five percent, which you don't have to start repaying for two years. It's a small amount, only a few thousand dollars. You should be able to save up the whole thing in two years and pay it back. Anonymous donor wanting homeownership for single women to be easier."

"But who put up the money?" Penny asked.

"I have my suspicions." Corinne grinned sunnily. "Some single women around here make serious money now, running good businesses, side businesses, like you learning the tax, um, accountant thing. Good side work. Besides, they get repaid with interest. No one loses anything."

"I hate debt. Debt is for suckers." Penny narrowed her eyes at the paperwork for the escrow account.

"It is, but you're gaining a home." Corinne pointed to the house plans she'd finagled. "Huge living room. Enormous kitchen. Great property. I have it on good authority you'll have to gut it and start over. Meth users were there. It won't be pretty. It'll be nasty, smelly, and horrible. You'll have to wear a Tyvek suit and goggles. You'll look sweaty, silly, and stupid."

Penny sat straight up. "I can do this."

"You can do this." Corinne waved her hand at the plans. "Shall I get the funds released and move the money into the auction escrow account for you?"

Penny stared at the ceiling, then back at Corinne. "Let's do this."

Jared finished the sandwiches, packed them, washed his hands, and put everything away. He double-checked the dog bag and dragged all the bags to the front door. He got his go-bag from out of the closet, which contained his toiletries and two changes of clothes from head to toe, including long underwear and extra boots in case his first pair got wet, and put it by the front door. Jared came back into the kitchen, Shadow at his heels.

"Are you going to Kansas?" Corinne asked.

"My guy will be thrown out into the world with nothing in less than twelve hours, and it's at least an eight-hour drive, and there's going to be snow, making things a lot slower." He kissed Corinne's cheek, and held her close, then touched her protruding stomach. "Little girls, stay put until Uncle gets home."

Penny bounced up, drew Jared into a hug, and kissed him soundly. "Go get him, come back. Then the two of you can help me with my house!"

Corinne said, gently, "He may want to. But, dogs."

Penny nodded sharply. "Dogs."

Jared put on his heavy black winter coat, grabbed a second one in case something happened to the first one, and decided on the van. It would make him less maneuverable, but he would be able to pick up donated things on the way back. That could save a lot of time, and he didn't want to put Gunny out any more than he already had. His dad had always been there for each of his kids, but now he had four kids under seven and two more on the way. He packed the van while Shadow did her business. Shadow hopped into her traveling box, and Jared put up the mesh so the dog wouldn't go flying in an accident. Jared got in front in case he needed to go manual, and they were off.

Jared put in a podcast about how to run a nonprofit while on the road. He had done all the paperwork, and things were on track. They had approval, especially since Yanna was behind him. She was smart, wily, and knew everything about running a dog training nonprofit. He listened to every word Yanna said, made checklists, had her check them over, and worked them relentlessly. The Marines had taught him that.

He ate a sandwich, drank some coffee. He was tired, so he took a nap. He woke up, stretched, told the car to exit the highway at a rest stop, and took Shadow for a walk in the icy cold. The wind was like a knife, wailing against the vehicle. Shadow was intelligent enough to do her business quickly. Some water and a dog treat, and she was back in her warm back seat in the box lined with a dog bed.

The nap was enough for him to focus. He checked what he had done that day off the checklist, such as setting up the pantry and the hall closet upstairs and painting the last of the trim. He loved his work. The dogs needed new homes, new purpose, new people to be their humans. He had the training to get them ready. It broke his heart to work with a dog for six months to a year, to raise a dog from a puppy, then send that dog away, every time. But, the dogs would die otherwise. He was the right person at the right time. Jared knew the value of a purpose.

Having Diego would be fantastic. He could move out of the main house, work with Diego once the dogs came. He could help this young man live out his purpose. Diego had been in prison for nearly a decade and would need a lot of help restructuring his life, being reabsorbed into a society that didn't think much about the problems of soldierly re-entry, let alone prisoners. Diego would need structure, movement, and education. Diego had been able to take some business courses in prison and art. The kid was apparently talented with a pencil or brush.

The trip was endless, and Jared slept, ate, and did his coursework. The accounting made him cringe. Not because of the math; he enjoyed that. But, what if he missed something important, something that threw the whole thing off? He listed every single expense he could have; he might as well base his coursework on a real-world example. He texted Yanna for a snapshot of her books and was stunned to receive a full accounting at a little after midnight. His coursework suddenly got a lot more detailed. He decided not to get bogged down and kept the books to himself and Diego, with a plan to add two to three more trainers that would live onsite.

He parked at a rest stop, did his own business, let Shadow out, and got them both back in. The snow was coming down in fat white flakes. By morning they would have to travel behind a snowplow. He slept a bit, then got where he needed to go forty-five minutes early. There was no paperwork to sign; Diego would be a free man.

He was stunned to see a young man in summer-weight khakis, tennis shoes, a polo shirt, and a flannel shirt thrown over the top shivering in the cold, leaning against the gate. Jared moved quickly, got out his second heavy coat, and bolted out of the van. He ran forward, got Diego in the coat, and said, "I'm Jared. Get in the van, now."

"Whoa!" Diego said, shivering, paperwork in his shaking hands. He got the door closed. "Hey, pretty baby," he said to Shadow.

Jared got in, set the GPS for the nearest box store, and said, "Dog's name is Shadow. I carry a second outfit in the duffel. Put it on, all of it. It should fit, all but the boots. Sorry, I have no brains. I should have guessed that since the crime happened in the early summer that you would have gone in with what you had on. Trial was in the fall, right?"

"It was hot as blazes." Diego took off his coat and two shirts, pulled the long black underwear over his head, followed by a black sweatshirt with a silver Marines logo on the front. He grabbed the socks and pulled them on, then stripped to put on the long underwear and jeans while the van's computer got more and more strident about Diego putting on his belt mesh. He got everything but the overcoat on and put the mesh band across his torso. The van stopped dinging and yelling.

"The trip back is long. As I said, I'm Jared, and that's Shadow there." Shadow thumped her tail. Diego held out his shaking hand, and Shadow sniffed then licked it. "We're going to get you a brand-new series of outfits. We don't have an official uniform yet. What you were wearing would be great for summer, and what we're both wearing now good for winter. We'll get a logo. In fact, you and my girlfriend Penny can work on it together. She's taking courses on logos. The 3D ones are amazing. Penny's already sold two of them, and she's in a beginning class."

"I can take classes?" Diego's teeth still chattered.

Jared turned up the heat. "Sure. It's just you and me for now. We'll finish painting the last two bedrooms. The roofs are sloped, so they feel smaller than they are, but the views are excellent. We... Hold on; I have a call. Mary? Mary, slow down. What? Okay, I'll be there in the afternoon. No, I can't come faster. Call... Call Yanna, Mary. She'll get someone trained down there to hold down the fort until we can... No, I've got a trainee now. Yes. No. Mary, we don't have time to chat. Call Yanna, or I will, if you're caught up in... Okay. I can't go any faster, Yanna, and we need food. We'll fill up the hot and cold boxes and be on our way." Jared got off the call and pounded the seat twice. Shadow sat at alert. "Shadow, calm. We're good." He said a command in German, and she relaxed.

"That didn't sound good," Diego said, as the lights to the twenty-four-hour big-box store came up through the snow on their right.

"No, it wasn't. I'll explain when we're back in the van. Here's the thing, Diego. Try on one of each thing, hoodie, heavy coat, boots, long underwear, all of it. You can't go on the size you were going in. You'd have filled out over the years in prison, bulked up."

Jared could barely see the boy he had been out of the filled-out face. Diego was still lean, but it was muscle now. He had definitely been lifting weights in prison.

"Then, get three of everything except the heavy coat. Get two winter coats, one to the ankles and a heavy stadium jacket that covers your butt. I've made an executive decision and decided the summer colors are khaki below and dark blue up, and the winter colors blue or black with dark blue up. We'll get more clothes later; these are to hold you for now. I'm getting food for us. We'll hit a drive-by, but we need snacks. Anything you hate?" Jared parked, then grabbed the two largest reusable shopping bags he had, both inscribed with the Marines logo.

Diego and Jared got out of the truck, leaving the heater on and the dog in the van. Jared told the dog to stay.

Diego shrugged. "I hate beans and jalapenos. Got razzed for it in prison. And I prefer potatoes to rice."

"Got it," Jared said. They went as fast as they could without slipping into the front of the store. "Only one checkout. Go there when you're done. Move quickly and efficiently, but be sure your clothes fit. No use buying clothes that don't."

"Yes, sir. I'm on it." Diego half-jogged towards the clothes to the left.

Jared headed right and got some potato, fruit, and green salads, pulled pork sandwiches, and coffee, waters, sodas, and juice and put them into a shopping cart. He moved as quickly as he could, adding twice what he normally ate, then twenty percent over. Nervous people tended to eat, and now they were both nervous. He got cool ranch tortilla chips, regular chips, salsa, almonds, and dried fruit. He dashed with his cart to electronics to get a good pair of HUD glasses, a navy blue wrist comp, their charging cables, and a car charger. He walked to the men's clothing area and stood at the entrance to the dressing room.

"Diego, can you hear me?"

"Yes, sir."

Jared told Diego about everything food-related in the cart, and Jared asked for pork rinds and chocolate milk.

"I know that's weird, sir."

"Not at all. Getting that, too. Anything else?"

"No." Diego strode out, three of everything in his arm and two coats. He handed the second set to the previously-bored clerk and handed his number of items back. "I did get bigger. You were right, sir. Meet you at the front?"

"Be there soon."

Jared got the extra food, paid, and went to the front. Diego was having his three-of-almost-everything scanned. He handed Jared back his extra coat and put on a long, black, triple-lined puffer coat as it came through. Diego had the clothes folded and in the basket by the time Jared paid. They hauled the stuff to the truck, dusted off the heavy snow, and then Jared put the cart back then got in. Diego tried to climb in the backseat with the grocery bags.

"Keep the other clothes. I have plenty. Front seat. I've got a lot to tell you," Jared said.

"Okay." Diego got in front.

Jared got the address to Harris Kolja's place and put on his mesh. He drove to the closest fast food place and got breakfast sandwiches, hash browns, and sodas. They were soon back on the highway.

"Diego, stick with me for a few more minutes. I've got some calls to make. That there's the hot box, the other one's the cold box. Fill them up with the groceries, but eat first. I bet you got out too early for breakfast."

"Yes, sir." Diego began sorting through the grocery bags.

Jared started with Yanna while working his way through his own breakfast.

"I'm on my way myself." Yanna blew out a sigh. "What a mess."

"It is. We're on our way."

"Diego got out? Excellent. Well, I'll get them fed, watered, walked, cleaned, checked out, groomed as much as I have time for, and crated. If we don't have enough crates, I'll buy them myself. You have the van?"

"Yes, praise the skies above." Jared checked the dash to be sure he had the right coordinates. "The seats will fold flat. I've got Shadow. I can put her upfront if need be; I have hooks so she can get meshed in front here."

"No worries. We can call your dad or Jen in if the puzzle pieces don't fit."

Jared sighed. "I hate to do that, but we don't have much of a choice."

Yanna shook her head. "What a mess. Harris Kolja is a good man."

"He's holding on?"

"Last I heard. The heart attack was massive. Quadruple bypass. He won't be getting out of bed for months."

"Well, I'm officially certified in about two hours, so we're good. Do we have a count?"

"Twelve. You up for this? I can stay..."

Jared shook his head. "We can do this. I've got two more people in the pipeline. I've got one finishing rehab. She's getting really good with the leg. Be out in ten days. I'll fly her up."

"That would be Specialist Calanthe Nadebo? She's one hell of a squared-away soldier."

"She is."

"No second thoughts?"

"None that I'm aware of. She literally sends me daily progress reports. We're working to have her overseas dog sent here. Set up a crowdfunding page."

Yanna nodded hard. "I'll pay into it, then I'll get the word out. We don't leave soldiers behind." Military dogs were considered to be soldiers with rank.

"Good. See you this afternoon." Jared hung up, looked over.

Diego's breakfast was finished, his detritus in the trash, and both food boxes were filled with the correct items except for, of course, the chocolate milk and pork rinds.

Diego pieced it together. "I think I get it. Guy, who has an animal place with twelve dogs, had a massive heart attack last night. You called in someone, probably someone you knew from the military, to hold the fort until you can get us there. Then we've got twelve more dogs to get to your farm, and feed, water, and train them all."

"Exactly, and we don't know anything about the dogs yet. Some may need a vet. We've got to get there before the state does. We can get them adopted and moved in because Mary, his wife, gave consent. Yanna will have the paperwork done by the time we get there. She trained me with dogs overseas. My dad helped me get Shadow home. We needed time, and I was going to go back in or work with the police, but Yanna called and needed help training. So, Shadow and I do that. I moved in with my two brothers. My sister's gonna have twins in less than a month. The rest of our family is three hours away across the state."

"Wow. You tell me what to do, Mr. Jared. I'll do it."

"Diego, it's just Jared. You don't have to call me 'sir.'"

"Yes, I do, sir." Diego's face was resolute. He had black hair shorn close, huge limpid brown eyes, and lines around his mouth and eyes that had not been there on the face of the young man whose life had been stolen from him.

Jared knew Diego wasn't going to budge. "Fine. There's glasses and a wrist comp in the bag at your feet. Get them out and charge them, and you can start learning about the farm and maybe enroll in the logo class. You'll get room and board free, as well as seven day's worth of clothes. Your extra salary won't be big, but as we get profitable, it should hit reasonableness in a year or two."

"That sounds very good, sir."

Diego reached forward and snagged the glasses and charger. He folded up and stowed the bag in the side panel pocket and figured out the packaging. Soon, the glasses were charging, and the packaging was in the recycling bag hanging on the back of the center console. He put the wrist comp on while it charged.

Jared called Charlie's farm. "Sir."

Charlie waved his hand. "I work for a living, Jared. Don't 'sir' me. What's up?"

"Well, if I tell the women, Corinne won't get a nap, and you know how cranky she gets."

Charlie went still. "Tell me everything."

Jared did.

"You're right; the women would do it all. Send me a checklist, and I'll get to it. And I was planning on buying you some electronic nonsense for Christmas. Rather buy you more dog food, don't you think?"

Jared felt his eyes tear up. "Thank you. The dogs... well, sir, they have nowhere else to go. I know what that's like, and so does Diego here."

Charlie waved a hand in front of his eyes. "Don't make me blubber, boy, or I won't get jack done around here. Get me the checklist. And quit calling me 'sir' You're family. Gunny and I shook on it."

Jared sat up straight. That was big news. The bears and wolves had made a tenuous pact. Now two shifter families from different animals were joining a family over two females, Corinne and Kandace, who thought of each other as sisters but weren't related. Sometimes friendship ran thicker than blood.

"What do Jetta, Jen, and Lynette say?"

Charlie snorted. "They said, 'About time.' And I'm quoting all my wives. They've been bonding up a storm with Rachael for a long time now. Now, you all be careful and get our new boy Diego down here. Christmas is coming soon, and we've got to buy another Christmas stocking. Jetta will be all over it."

"Sounds good. See you later, Dad Two."

Charlie waved his hands in front of his eyes again and let the link go.

"Did I... did I just get adopted?" Diego's eyes were huge.

"It happens all the time in these families. Cambers and Westons. We're kinda joined by marriage and... sameness, I'd say. Part Native American, too, and half of us speak Cherokee, Crow, Navajo, or Spanish. So, family by love."

Diego, stunned, could only nod.

STEPPING UP

*P*enny stood, stretched. She'd made key lime, mocha, and chocolate peanut butter no-sugar frozen desserts, made with heavy cream and monk fruit extract. She also made rum raisin, peppermint stick, and eggnog ice creams (alcohol-free) that sold like crazy in December. She had tasting menus, as her best friend and 'sisterlike entity,' as Maddie called herself, had suggested. The new graham cracker key lime, a sugared version, did exceptionally well also. Penny had finished developing a keto chocolate mint delight, using baking chocolate, real mint, and monk fruit. She added it to the tasting menu and ended up with a line for her trouble.

She and her purple-haired sidekick, Dana, got through the line. Penny was glad she'd bought the special serving cups and cup holder tree for the tasting menu. It increased the washing but vastly decreased the waste, and now people were buying more sugar-free items. The guests rated the items, and Penny felt five new sugar-free ice creams would be good. There was a cherry fudge and a turtle sundae made with sugar-free caramel syrup she wanted to make next. After the line, she cleaned up, left Dana at the register, and went back with a load of dishes.

Penny ran the dishwasher, washed up, and began on the cherry fudge. She put rock salt into the ice cream maker, then the new sugar free caramel syrup called her name. She made the second recipe, put it in the other ice cream maker, cleaned up, and went out front to help. Forty minutes later she wrote out a completely sugar-free tasting menu on the whiteboard, and she sold out of all her sugar-free ice cream by the time the sun was going down.

Penny wiped down the tables. "I trust you to close while I make all five flavors."

Dana jogged over, put the sign to *Closed*, locked the door, and jogged back. "Fine, I'll run the report and count the money, but I want to watch you make them. I'll finish cleaning and running the dishwasher when you get them in the machines."

"Great, but they're full batches this time. Hurry up." Penny grinned as Dana rushed around. Her teenaged assistant grabbed all the dishes, put them in the dishwasher, washed up, put the extra money away in the safe, and washed up again. Penny had Dana learn step-by-step how to make full batches. They put in rock salt and filled up the much larger machines, and Penny cleaned up the back of the house while Dana finished the front.

They put away the dishes, tasted all the ice creams, put them in their huge containers, and put them away in the freezer. They ran the dishwasher again with the machine paddles, wiped them down, washed up, and separated outside the back of the store. Dana's girlfriend and study partner Rici was there to pick her up. Rici's hair was blue and shaved on the other side. She had two more earrings in each ear than Dana, her skin was a deep golden tone, and Rici's nose was more flattened. Other than that, they looked like sisters. Or clones.

Penny was paying attention this time when she went around the corner, so she didn't run into Jared.

"Hi. I'm here to steal you away for dinner and unpaid labor. You can spend the night in the third bedroom. Both the third and fourth ones are complete."

Penny sighed. "I wish I could. I bought the house!"

Jared grabbed her and whirled her around. Penny shrieked with surprised laughter. He put her down carefully. "You won the auction?"

"Obviously." She grabbed his arm and started dragging him to the diner, already stuffed with people trying to finish shopping as evidenced by the bags hanging off their chairs. "Tell all. Did the dogs like the enclosures we built?"

"Loved. We had thirteen dogs, including Shadow, but one was elderly and needed constant love and a warm fire. Sanne Garthside, who lives about eight blocks from here, is a retired mail carrier. She took Amie, a golden retriever, home for love and attention. Urdo, that's a pit bull mix, went to live with Rylan Zanzi. Rylan says Urdo helps his wife with her knitting by laying on her sweaters."

Penny laughed. "Good, so we built enough enclosures." Jared opened the door to the diner for her. "Two more to grow on later."

"One's a pregnant mama. Dalmatian. I swear, the fire departments in four counties called us and said they'd take them, training or not, and the mama too."

Penny dragged Jared over to a booth in the back being vacated by an elderly couple.

Aubree Topie came by to clean off the table, a tiny girl with a wide nose, a quick smile, and chocolate-colored hair braided to her waist. "You guys are lucky. It's a zoo here. Want coffee?"

Penny nodded. "Love it. Decaf for me."

Jared took the proffered menus, handed one to Penny. "Full octane. I've got a long night with a pregnant dog ahead of me. Riva is a great dog, follows me everywhere just like Shadow. Shadow keeps an eye on her for me when I'm not there."

Aubree rushed off, then came back with cups, two carafes of coffee with the decaf in yellow. They both ordered breakfast for dinner, farmer's breakfasts with hash browns, four pieces of extra-crispy bacon, sausage, scrambled eggs, and English muffins.

Penny poured her coffee. "Sounds like you're busy with the new dogs."

"Up at dawn, sleep when we can. We've got to stock up on every-thing from dog food to toys. They all need playing, training, and loving."

"Have you tried talking to the 4-H club or the cozy mystery club?"

Jared stared at her as if she were speaking Martian. "Many cozy mysteries are about dogs. Bet you'd have at least three or four people over at various times of day to help with the dogs, even read to them. And the 4H people will do anything for credit in the field of animal husbandry."

Jared poured and doctored his coffee. "That's wonderful. Thanks."

Penny pulled out her glasses, tapped them, and sent him two links. She put the glasses away. Their breakfasts arrived, and they dug in. "So, how's it going with Diego?"

"That young man is the hardest worker I've ever seen. The dog enclosures are spotless three times a day. Restless, though. I sent him to lift weights and do some kickboxing with Mitch. Came back with a bloody nose and a sparkle in his eyes. Now, I watch the dogs while Diego and Mitch train, and someone from the family comes to help me. If I can get anyone, 4H or mystery or whatnot, it will save me from having to call family away from whatever they're doing."

Penny put her hand over Jared's. "They're family, plus dogs. Let them help. I'll be at the new house as much as I can in a hazmat suit. My mama's gonna help."

"I wish I could help you. You've done so much for me, for the dogs. And now we get a bit of food, and one of us has to dash. That's not fair."

Penny laughed out loud. "Games are fair because they have rules. Life doesn't come with rules, so, not fair. Besides, I've got the house. A focus, like you said you wanted for yourself. I wanted it for me, too. Now, we've got what we want. We'll work hard, get our stuff done. We'll carve out time when we can."

Penny had pictures of the interior of the house, and Jared tried not to cringe. The house was a thirty-year-old three-bedroom plus loft, two-and-a-half-bath two-story with a large kitchen and a pretty good-sized yard that was dirt under the snow. There were gouges in the floor, copper piping and ceiling lights had been pulled out and sold off, doors were hanging askew, and broken windows were covered with plywood. One bathroom was a hideous turquoise, and another had smashed subway tile. There were no appliances at all.

Jared spied both mouse and rat droppings. "First, get a pest control person in. The smell must be horrible. Use menthol under your nose. Cuts the smell."

"Pest control guy's been here and gone. We're going in with space heaters, brooms, and sledgehammers tomorrow, already rented the trash bin. Your dad is coming up for that. Says he loves smashing some walls. Charlie and Jen, and I think Len and Vic are coming too."

Jared laughed. "So do I. I really wish I could be there."

Penny held up her hand. "Dogs. I get it. Anyway, we'll smash down to the studs. The wiring is mostly okay, but the missing pipes need to be replaced. Then, we're starting at the bottom and working our way up. It's my project, but I've got Jen with a plan. She's got people for everything—electrical, plumbing, inspection. We're going to wire every room with cable. I will be doing as much of the work as I can." She finished her bacon.

Jared saw an incoming text. "Dalmatian puppies on the way!" Jared began shoveling in the last of his food.

"So, you're a midwife tonight?"

Jared nodded. "Diego says Riva's in her bed, and he thinks labor's started. Shadow is licking Riva's face. I deeply apologize, but I've got to head out." He tapped his glasses and paid their bill. "You get to bed, Pixie Penny. Lifting sledgehammers will be fun tomorrow." He stood, kissed her nose. "See you when I see you."

"Goodnight. Text me the puppy details later."

"I will."

Penny ordered pie. No one could resist cinnamon apple cobbler with cinnamon ice cream. She went over her checklist, sighed, then grinned. She knew kids were looking for spending money, and the local schools were still in session. She paid a nominal amount for an ad on the consolidated middle/high school's website. She had her first reply while crossing the street back to her apartment.

Penny thought she'd be too excited to sleep. She showered and got ready for bed, stretched out in her recliner, and put on a house-flipping video. Just before she fell asleep, she got a text from Jared.

Three girls, two boys, mama, and pups are fine. She smiled and slid into sleep.

~

The next day, there were sledgehammers, and Davis showed up too, despite his surgeon's hands. They put menthol under their noses, opened the windows to the frigid air, then took turns slinging sledgehammers and carrying debris to the Dumpster. Harry and Chris, bulky high school weightlifters, showed up before lunch, ready to go. Harry had a round face, bulging neck, and deep blue eyes. Chris brought her own gloves and hard hat to cover her black curls, and her muscles rippled when she lifted the sledgehammer with ease. Gunny brought them into the living room while Davis opened up packs of Meri lunches, tandoori chicken sandwiches with veggies, hummus, and olives, and passed around the waters, cherry and lime.

Davis cleaned himself and his area up and headed off. The teens were unstoppable, so they got the entire downstairs demolished. They took a break and ate Libby snacks, and went after the ripped-apart banister, strung up mesh to prevent a fall, and tackled the upstairs. Penny checked her list and was delighted to smash the horrible turquoise bathroom tile while the teens demolished the cracked yellow subway tile. The bedrooms were next; there were holes in nearly every wall, shelves destroyed in the closets, wood and nails poking out. Penny exchanged her sledgehammer for a crowbar and attacked the master bedroom closet, a very small walk-in.

Jen stuck her head in and grinned. "We are really bashing things out today! The kids are great!"

"Cleanup crew is coming in..." Penny tapped her safety glasses, then squeaked. "Now!"

Jen laughed. "Benny is the skinniest kid I've ever seen, but he's got a mask, gloves, and a suit, and he's using a shop-vac hooked up to a generator on the nasty stuff. His friend Becky is doing the same thing, getting the crap out of the kitchen. Literally."

Penny relaxed. "Good. This smells terrible, but I'm having fun."

Jen smiled indulgently at Penny. "Stay on your pink cloud as long as you can, girl." She waved, and Penny waved back.

Penny attacked the closet, then what Jen said began to sink in. What was a pink cloud? And what happened when it floated away?

～

*P*enny bought a staggering amount of pizza for dinner. The interior smelled much better. Teen girl Bobbi, of the flat nose, wiry black hair, and prepared thinking, brought an air filter and plugged it into the generator. Penny paid her for the rental. She paid all the students, fed them, and they went through liters of cherry water, soda, and hot cinnamon apple cider. They did cleanup, and Penny went home happy. The trash bin was full, the house was down to its studs, and the animal droppings and sadly some deceased rodents had been cleaned up. The traps were humane, but some had nested in the insulation. They had to suit up to get the insulation out.

Penny went home and rushed to take a shower. She nearly fell asleep standing up. She made it to bed and remembered Davis' tip to rub her body with the massage stick so she wouldn't be sore in the morning.

Despite the tip, Penny was still barely able to stand up in the morning. She stood up anyway. She was on shortened hours at the store, and she had to get one bedroom, one bathroom, and the kitchen ready so she could move in.

She sold tasting menus and cheated by having hot water in the scoop rinses so she could get the frozen desserts out. Dana put her boss on the cash register and cleanup, stole Libby's coffee, and poured it down Penny's throat.

They got rid of the line, then Dana said, "I'm getting lunch. BLT and fries? Sit on the stool. Think of new frozen desserts."

"Duh." Penny was unable to form actual words. She stared into space, then remembered to lock up her midday money.

Libby came over when her rush died down with a small pot with a screwtop lid of something that smelled heavenly. "Davis swears by this. It's a peppermint balm you put on sore muscles. It has something or the other in there that takes away the pain."

"Bless you."

Libby laughed as Penny realized she wouldn't be able to rub it into her shoulders without taking off her long-sleeved shirt. "Go in back, rub it in, wash your hands, come back out."

Penny groaned, fell off her stool, and went to the back. She was back on her stool by the time Dana came back.

Dana put the sandwiches down on a table and stole more of Libby's coffee. "I am so sorry I wasn't there for your house smashing thing. I had a church thing, then band practice. Both of them got pushed back because of snow."

Penny nodded. "We had a lot of people, got pushed forward a total of three days. Gotta get... bedroom done. Gotta sleep."

Dana waved a finger in front of Penny's face. "No talk of sleeping. Work first. You've only got two hours left."

"I'll walk the deposits down. Nat will walk with me," Libby said, bringing over her own coffee. She and her assistant had already eaten. "Let Dana close."

Penny nodded. "I want to…"

"I get the obsession. Really, I do. But you need the wiring and plumbing inspected before you can put in insulation and hang drywall, huh?"

"Drywall." Dana moaned. "I worked with Habitat for Humanity for three projects now. Drywall is not my thing." She pushed her purple hair out of her eyes.

"I think I fell off my pink cloud." Penny fell on her sandwich like a starving person.

"That usually doesn't happen until three weeks in." Libby stole a fry.

Dana tilted her head quizzically. "What's a pink cloud?"

"That gorgeous feeling of something new until reality sets in." Libby grinned. "Penny thought she could swing a sledgehammer yesterday and be able to wash her hair today."

Penny laughed. "Did so." She ate more fries.

"You'll be eating more, drinking lots of fluids, and sleeping a lot harder. I'm going to advise buying me out of my snacks. Put them in your pocket and consume when needed. Have high protein bars in your new place, sealed tight." Libby shuddered. "I saw Jen's pics. My stars, woman, you chose the nastiest house in town, didn't you?"

Dana shrugged. "Seen worse. Some of those houses Habitat receives have to be torn down and made new."

Libby nodded. "Houses left in wills, that sort of thing. I worked on some houses in high school."

Penny groaned. "I need the kitchen, one bathroom, and one bedroom. Then I can move in and do the rest."

"Not without water, power, and drywall, you won't." Libby stole a chip. "Dad said he'd be at your place going down Jen's checklist. Don't be surprised if something is done."

"I can't let them work without me!" Penny wailed.

Dana shook her head. "This is your job, right here, right now. Those ice creams won't make themselves. Well, I could, but I still need you to supervise. Plus, you can barely stand up."

Libby nodded. "Preach it, sister." They bumped fists.

Penny groaned. "You two are no fun." Her employee and her other best friend laughed at her.

~

*T*he drywall wasn't done, but the electrical, plumbing, and sewer had all been tested out and inspected. Luckily, no animals had chewed through wiring. Jen, Charlie, and the high school girl Bobbi with the snub nose and huge brown eyes were in white suits, heavy gloves, masks, and safety glasses putting in rolls of insulation. Penny suited up and rushed to help Charlie while Jen worked with Bobbi. They blasted Southern rock while Charlie and Penny worked clockwise and Bobbi and Jen counterclockwise.

Penny grabbed her end of the pink insulation. "I can't believe the electrical stuff tested as good."

Charlie nodded. "Homeowners upgraded electrical, plumbing, and sewer before they sold this home ten years ago. They sold it to an out-of-state woman using it as an investment property. She didn't check out who was staying very well. She repaired the property a few times, but then became behind on her property taxes, and tweakers did the rest."

"Sad." Penny rolled out more insulation.

Charlie grinned. "Not anymore. You still want to build that room over the garage?"

Libby nodded. "I do. I want kids."

Charlie measured twice, then cut the insulation. "Good house for 'em. Good bones on the house. Just needs a lot of work."

"This is great, all the help."

Penny unrolled more insulation. Charlie made another cut, and they made sure it was in tight before unrolling and cutting more.

"I can't thank you enough."

"You're family now." Charlie cut as Libby rolled out more insulation. "You'll be helping with all the babies we got coming, won't you?"

Penny grinned. "Absolutely."

"Christmas Eve, you spend with your mama. Spend Christmas with us."

"I'll be there." Penny hoped a very busy Jared would come, too. If not, she'd just have to go to him.

HOLIDAZE

*J*ared met Mitch in the wide shopping street two towns over.

"Glad you could make it, bro." Mitch hugged Jared. Mitch was not normally a hugger; Jared put it down to the impending babies.

"We've got 4H helping twice a day to feed and walk the dogs, the Deep Mystery Society people sit with the dogs, read books aloud, and pet them, and the firefighters won't stop checking out the Dalmatians." Jared blew out a breath. "I just have to have coffee and human snacks and sign the people in and out."

"So little bro Diego is with the pups now?" Mitch saw a necklace in a window, imagined it on Corinne's neck, and led the way into the store.

"He is." Jared saw a scarf in a deep blue that would bring out the red in Penny's hair. He bought it, and Mitch fumbled through buying some silver hoop earrings to go with the necklace.

Jared brought Mitch a silver scarf for Kandace, Corinne's sister-friend. "Nice save, bro. Thanks."

"No problem. I'm heading to the home store. Going to buy a line of credit for my woman."

Mitch stared at Jared in awe. "You are really good at this, bro."

Jared grinned. "I try." He put in the line of credit at the store, then met Mitch again. "Who do you have?"

Mitch shrugged. "Bobby. Which means both boys, really. No use courting jealousy."

Jared nodded. "Easier than mine. I've got Stretcher."

Mitch groaned. "Toy store for me." He headed down the street at a fast clip.

Jared was freezing, so he went back into the hardware store. He was tired. He'd been neglecting his woman, and he had dogs to love. So many. He was finally getting help, but... He shook off the cobwebs. Jared remembered Stretcher complaining about glare when going skiing. He took off for the good outdoor store, packed with both tourists and local shoppers. Jared found a pair of excellent snow glasses with an interior HUD to help navigate difficult terrain.

Jared stood in line and heard a guy named Carl tell his buddy about a cross-country ski route he liked. One step closer, and he heard Henrietta Dawson of the Deep Mystery Society invite Rooke Coate, the cashier, to read at the farmhouse with the dogs.

Rooke laughed. "I don't know whether I'm coming or going this season, but once it slows down, I'll be there." Rooke cashed her out, deftly wrapped her presents, and sent Henrietta on her way.

Jared got to the front of the line. "Rooke, you're busy most of the year these days, except in mud season."

Rooke bellowed out a laugh. "Then I'm selling tow winches. This for your girl?" He wrapped the present with deft hands in glittery red paper.

"Nope, my sister, Stretcher."

"She a corpsman?"

"She was."

"Tell her thank her for her service. And you, too. Ten percent discount. Now, get outta here; I have a line."

"Thank you." Jared never knew what to say when people said that. He had survived, that's all. Like Gunny said, you did what you had to do and got out with your ass intact if possible.

Jared spied his brother putting packages into his vehicle; he did the same. "We done?"

"Yeah. Coffee?"

"I was thinking something Irish." Jared nodded.

They headed to Paddy's. They ordered Irish coffee, stout stew, and soda bread.

Mitch sighed, sipped his coffee. "That went well. Found the boys a train set. Magnetic, not electric. Couldn't stand to not get the girls something, so I got them their own track. Then I got little people to go with the trains."

Jared held up a hand. "Bro, slow down. At this rate, the parents won't have anything to buy for the kids."

Mitch guffawed. "Even in bad years, never had a naked tree."

"True."

Their stew came, and they dug in.

They were on their last slice of buttered bread when Mitch said, "So. You've wanted to date Libby's ice cream shop partner since you got here."

"Have." Jared nodded.

"But you couldn't because she's not one of us."

"True."

"And now that she knows our secret, you're both too busy to see each other."

"Also true."

"That's messed up."

Jared could only nod.

"Then quit sitting here." Mitch bit off his words. "Jen has the punch list. Go work on your woman's house. She needs the one bedroom and bathroom and the kitchen done. And you're doing the painting. My woman is determined to go down there and breathe paint fumes."

Jared swallowed the last of his bread. He touched his sunglasses, gone light in the restaurant, but Mitch shook his head.

"I've got this. Go."

Jared went.

Jared found Jen's list and saw that they were putting in cabinets and fixtures in the bathrooms and kitchen. He called ahead.

Jen said, "Speak."

"You need any hardware?"

"Jared! No, but bring sandwiches and sodas. How'd you get out of dog duty?"

"Volunteers and 4-H animal husbandry hours."

"Good. I know you know how to lay tile."

Jared tried not to groan. "I do."

"Good, you can do that later. Get over here, nephew." She let the link go.

Jared smiled. Apparently, they were joining, bears and wolves. One pack or sloth or whatever the hell they were. He had aunts. It was kind of nice. He panicked a bit, thought about Christmas, and sent a text that suggested Mitch swing by for more winter scarves and gloves for Christmas for Jen, Jetta, and Lynette. Charlie was easy. He loved grilling, so he sent a text to Mitch about that. He got an angry emoticon back. Jared laughed.

Jared swung by the deli for sandwiches and got to Penny's new house. It was an eyesore. It was painted an unfortunate pink and yellow. The porch was sagging. Outside lights were broken. Jared made a note to get that front porch mess fixed. He couldn't have his girl break an ankle in the dark of winter.

"Hey!" A woman wrapped head to toe in black wool leaned against the fence dividing Penny's yard from the house on the right. Her face was round, her cheeks rosy with cold. "You own that place?"

"No, but I know the owner. Why?"

"Your construction is gonna take forever? 'Cause Ritchie's barking up a storm." She pointed to the window of the next house, a tidy blue house with white trim. Ritchie was a dachshund, who was indeed barking up a storm.

"Ma'am, I'm Jared. My aunt Jen is in there, installing cabinetry. My girlfriend owns this property. I assure you, we're working as fast as possible."

"Brought property values down. Tweakers breaking into houses, stealing stuff. Police coming out at all hours of the night. You gonna rent this place out?"

Jared shook his head. "No, ma'am. This house has good bones. Be stupid to treat her like that."

"Good." The woman nodded her head once, twice. "I'm Mabel. Mabel Forthright."

"You certainly are." Mabel grinned at him. "Ma'am, if you'll excuse me, my aunt needs food, and I've got it." He held up the sack of sandwiches. "You have a nice day now."

"You too." Mabel nodded.

Jared tapped in the garage code and entered. There was nothing in there but dust and broken shelving. He shook his head; another project. He closed the exterior door, coded his way into the interior one, and went in.

Jen took the bags from him the second he walked in the door. "Mabel's nosy, but a good sort. That little dog had a big job protecting her from the drug addicts that used to live here." Jen stalked into the kitchen.

Jared shed his coat, looked at the mesh being used for a banister. He cautiously went up the stairs and was horrified by the conditions of the rooms. The bathrooms had new cabinetry and hardware but he shuddered at the job they'd need to do on the tile. He went to the master and saw it was a good space. He shook his head at the small size of the walk-in closet. He wondered if he could steal bedroom space to enlarge it.

He looked out the grimy windows and saw a completely dead backyard. The neighbors had put up tall fencing, probably in self-defense from thieving guests. The backyard had potential.

He made his way downstairs and looked at the kitchen cabinetry. It was all in, brushed nickel hardware, spray nozzle. Classy, like his lady. The cabinets were cherry. Penny was obviously going for black, red, or grey countertops. Or maybe something glittery. There was a brand new kitchen island made up of several cabinets put together.

"Floors next?" Jared said, pointing at the boxes of interlocking bamboo flooring.

Jen nodded. "Drywall's in. So, we're painting today. You up for spraying?"

Jared shrugged. "One of my best things." He stole Jen's screwdriver and opened a can of paint. "Lovely." The paint was a soft gray, pale, like a dove's wing. He closed it up, then opened the primer, grabbed tarps and tape, and began covering up the lovely new cabinets. He did the same with the floor all the way to the windows. French doors had been installed instead of the sliders, the broken glass replaced with double-paned windows that showed the glare of the sun on snow. Jared gloved up, put together the sprayer, filled it up, plugged it in, put on the white suit, goggles, and mask Jen had ready to go, and began to paint.

By the time Penny arrived with dinner and Libby, Jared was done and had made it all the way to the living room.

Libby's jaw dropped. "My word! Your honey does good work."

Jared finished wrestling his way out of his moon suit. He kissed Penny. "Sorry, I'm sweaty and smell like paint."

She grinned. "You painted for me! I don't care if you smell like…"

"Don't finish that sentence." Libby held up the boxes in her hands. "Pizza. Personal ones. Got ones with both meat and veg."

Jared grinned. "Great!" They ate, standing up on the plywood laid over the kitchen island, which was draped with a tarp. "Penny, what are you putting in for the countertops?"

"I've got this silvery granite for behind you, butcher block for this kitchen island. I've got two freezers and a huge refrigerator on order. Would have been way over budget, but they were bought then discarded when the build on another house fell through." She grinned. "Tiling tonight, bathroom in the master. The tub is so nice! Couldn't have afforded one that big but…"

"Let me guess. Already bought, but the homeowner changed course." Libby grinned at her friend.

"Better, a floor model. Not like people are taking baths in the store." Both women laughed.

"How was your day?" Jared put the empty containers in the trash bag.

Penny smiled. "I cannot believe I'm selling so much eggnog, peppermint stick, and rum raisin ice cream. Sales are beginning to drop off; mostly everyone has done their shopping. One more day, and I get to spend two days getting this place done!"

"Yay you. I've got kids that know school is going on break soon, and Christmas is coming. Their mom didn't do..." Libby choked up. "This is their first tree with presents underneath. I think it's freaking them out. Caring isn't normal to them. Who doesn't give their kids presents? None of them knew when their birthdays were!"

Penny rubbed her friend's back. "Now, you have a tree. And they're getting family time all over the place."

Libby nodded and wiped her eyes. "I know. Nat makes snow forts with them. They're complicated, with snow slides. Meri can't get them to come inside for dinner."

Jared grinned. "We used to go up this hill with a ditch on either side. Drove mama nuts. Gunny, that's our dad, had to clean out that ditch every fall so we wouldn't impale ourselves on sticks. We would spend all day there tobogganing."

Libby grinned. "Good times! Did that with my brothers too."

"Maddie and Morgan and I would go to the park. Mama was working two jobs; she couldn't come. Farrah blamed Mom when Morgan turned wrong and broke her wrist hitting the swingset. After that, I didn't want to go alone, so I just..."

Libby hugged Penny, then Jared did.

Jared smiled at Penny. "I wish I could stay and tile with you, but I've got..."

"Fur babies." Penny kissed him.

Jen grinned. "I've got human ones."

"And more on the way! You and Jetta and the rest of the family must be delighted!" Penny handed Jared the trash bag. He took it.

Jen shuddered. "Jetta's nesting. Charlie and I come here to escape the cleaning. Our house hasn't been this clean since we moved in."

Everyone laughed.

∽

*J*ared woke early. He showered, dressed, and dashed downstairs, Shadow at his side. The dogs were polite, taught not to bark, but tails were wagging, and they were politely sitting at their food bowls. Ravi from 4H was already there on that dark, cold morning, measuring out the food in scoops. Ravi was tall and gangly, with too-big feet and a shock of black hair. He was the most conscientious, and he had a snowmobile, so he got first crack at the dogs. Many of the other teens were already on vacation. Ravi and his family were staying put, their huge family traveling to them for the break.

Minnie the brown Chihuahua, gorgeous in her little blue winter coat, was the only one on the small-dog diet. They had two beagles named Charlie and Lucy, two chocolate labs named Milo and Hetta, one golden lab named Bella, the dalmatian Riva and her five pups Ringo, John, Paula, George, and Peeta. George and Paul were the boys. Lola was a German shepherd mix, a black and white dog with a little tan. Archie was a black chow, and Bailey was... something. She was black, gray, and rust-colored, with big brown eyes. Toby was a hound mix and already excelled at the training.

"Good morning, Ravi. I'll take left, and you take right." Jared eyed the coffee but wisely chose to feed the dogs first.

"I've got the cart, Mr. Camber." Ravi's voice was light, melodious. The boy was in choir, and angels wept when he sang. "You get Miss Shadow there."

Jared sighed. "Mr. Camber is my dad. I'm Jared."

"Mr. Jared, got to go!" Ravi wheeled the cart out, wisely going for the Chihuahua first, vibrating at the gate to her enclosure.

Jared fed Shadow, poured the coffee, and signed off on Ravi's hours. Ravi wanted to be a vet, and he certainly could be with his brains and talent. He knew he would be giving the kid a job, offering him a formal internship with pay. Yanna had sent Jared the forms, and Jared already had the paperwork ready to go. The school was delighted at the number of businesses hiring local kids with internships. Ravi was only fifteen, but Jared already had the principal willing to sign off on an exception. Jared reheated himself two egg, bacon, and cheese muffins, had them with his coffee, and went to clean out cages.

Nuna and Jun were there early. Nuna, which meant 'older sister' in Korean, went by Violet, the color of her hair. Jun's real name was Byong-Jun, but he'd gone by Jun since he entered school. Jun was autistic and had a lot of trouble reading aloud. He had no trouble understanding what he was reading; he was two years above grade level. He had a lisp and a monotone. 'Making the story exciting for the dog' was helping him speak less like a robot. He held Minnie in his arms and reclined on the bean bag chair while Violet did the last of her homework before school break in an armchair. Jun was reading from a science textbook to Minnie. Minnie sat in Jun's arms, huge brown eyes focused on her human, ears up. His monotone didn't bother the dog. She just knew her human was reading to her. Jun's HUD gave an audible chime, and Jun modulated his voice. The chimes were reminders.

Violet stood up, walked over to speak to Jared, and pointed towards Minnie's enclosure. "You did a great job with this."

Jared shrugged. "I had so much help. If I listed all the names, you would fall asleep by the time I finished." He went in, started piling up Minnie's toys and her little coats.

Violet laughed. She had intelligent brown eyes and sharp cheekbones, which hinted at the woman she was becoming. She wore a chocolate-brown sweater and blue jeans; her snowsuit was dripping at the door. "I know it's too soon. You just got the dogs. You haven't had time to train them yet."

Jared shook his head. "Minnie is training your brother. Not me training her to help your brother. She knows her job already."

Violet shook her head, confused. "She's already trained?"

"You want to know if you can take her home." Jared reached for her harness and leash, hanging on the back of the little gate. "The answer is yes. But I've got to talk to your brother first."

"Okay." Violet stared at her brother, then smiled.

Jared put the harness and leash on the pile of toys and coats. He strode over to Jun and sat across from him in the red beanbag chair. He waited until Jun was done with the article he was reading. "Jun, can I speak to you for five minutes?"

"Yes. It is impolite to interrupt, but I was at a good stopping place."

Jared stared just over Jun's shoulder. "Jun, do I look you in the eyes? Do I touch your shoulder?"

"No, you do not."

"Why do I keep from doing that when I do those things with your sister Violet?"

"I don't like those things."

"I treat you differently because I respect you. You are a being with feelings. If I touched your shoulder, you would feel bad. I don't want you to feel bad."

"Okay."

Jared noticed the careful way Jun held the dog. "Jun, did you read a book on Chihuahuas and how to care for them?"

"No. I read two books on the breed and how to care for them."

"Where did this dog breed originate?"

"Mexico."

"Does Mexico and where we live in Missouri have the same weather and temperatures?"

"No. That's why Minnie has to have a coat."

"Do you know how much to feed her?"

"The amount is in grams in the book. I did the conversions. So yes, I do."

"Do you know how often she needs to see the vet?"

"Yes, I do. She needs a vet every six months. If she were my dog, I know that I must put the times in my cell phone so I remember."

"Do you know that she needs to play and to be walked outside when it is warm and the weather is not bad?"

"Yes. Now you will ask me about picking up after her pee and poop. I know how to do that. I have gloves and plastic dog bags. They are blue." Jun was getting impatient. He had a little knot between his eyes.

"Good. Now, Jun, this is the most important question. Do you want to take Minnie home with you today?"

Jun smiled. Violet sucked in a breath, and Jared worked to not have his jaw drop. Autistic kids didn't smile often.

"Yes, I think I would like that very much." Jun dropped the smile and looked down at Minne. "Minnie, I will follow the dog book very well and take care of you. I will put alarms to feed you two times every day and give you clean water. I will read to you two times a day and play with you two times a day. Would you like to be my dog?"

Minnie barked once, then a second time. She licked Jun's hand.

Violet grinned. "I think that's a yes."

"Her outside coat and carrier are right there." Jared pointed. "I'll get a bag for her things." Jared watched while Jun carefully got Minnie into her dog coat, then went to find a bag.

~

*D*iego was an excellent dog trainer. He was smart, patient, and knew not to give confusing signals. The dogs were already being played with and read to; that was part of their training. The dogs first had to learn *sit, stay, lie down, come, heel, back,* and other commands, using both voice and hand signals. They all learned quickly. They trained in twos normally, but they could train in threes since they were all good at the sit and say commands. All three labs were focused, although Bella, the golden, liked to be silly. They taught the dogs the 'back' command, then played with them as a reward. Milo, Hetta, and Bella were focused and on target.

The very happy new mother, Riva, was exempt for the time being, but she knew most of them already. Harve Juneau, a firefighter with steely blue eyes and equally steely muscles, was in with her. The firefighter and the new mother were really bonding well.

Mika Sorensen came from the book club, a woman with the blue eyes, dark blonde hair, and no-nonsense attitude of her heritage, and the labs and the retriever trotted into what was now the reading room. They brought out the low-to-the-ground dogs, and the sessions went well.

Karen and Donald from the reading group came and got some basset hound love in the form of Charlie and Lucy, and Toby was a hound two. He had the distinctive 'roo' call. They finished out with Lola, the German shepherd mix, Archie the black chow, and Bailey the mutt. Bailey was even more focused than Archie, and Archie could have a treat on his nose and wait to be permitted to eat it. They hadn't done that to the dogs more than once. It was doggie torture.

Everyone got treats and were cycled through a jog when Asha from 4-H came with her best friend Ravi. Asha kept half her head shaved and dyed the tips hot pink. It was unusual to see brother and sister as best friends. They were only a year apart, but Asha was much shorter than Ravi and the more straightforward of the two. The run was around the barn's interior. Then, the dogs could go in the snow, then they would be towel-dried and given dinner early.

"We've got to go," Jared told everyone. "You've all got the door codes. Happy holidays!"

Harve came up, tears in his eyes, while Jared and Diego were putting on their coats. "It's Christmas Eve."

Jared knew what was coming and realized putting it off wasn't helping anyone. "You know you can keep only one puppy, don't you? Your brothers and sisters at the other fire departments need them."

Harve nodded. "I do. We'll see them at every picnic, volleyball, and baseball game. So it's not so bad."

"You've got the printout on food, vet care, all of it?"

"I do. I've got new toys and a big bed for her and the babies, and…."

Jared held up a hand. "I get it. I think you're qualified. But if I hear one word in six weeks about not getting those puppies where they belong, that they didn't receive their training or the vet visits didn't happen…"

Harve's great wide face with the squat nose split open in a huge smile, his eyes shining. "She can come home for Christmas?"

"Yes, but set up a visitation schedule for the others to visit. You'll have a busy house." And their own home/facility would have far fewer firefighter visitors, at least until they adopted more Dalmatians.

Harve picked up Jared and hugged him. Jared felt his back pop. "Thank you! I'll get her to all her vet visits, you'll see."

Jared had Diego help get the dogs and puppies to Harve's van while Jared filled out the paperwork. Harve signed with a flourish, including the addendums on which fire departments got adorable black-and-white spotted puppies.

Jared sighed. "We're going to be late."

Diego grinned. "Many adoptions today, huh?"

"Yep."

"When are we getting more?"

Jared sighed, glad he'd gotten the presents out to the van before that bear hug. He still felt breathless. "You really want more work, don't you?"

Diego hitched a thumb out the kitchen window at Harve driving away. "That stuff, that's heart-hurting and heart-helping at the same time."

Jared nodded. "That's the best way of putting it I've ever heard. Let's get out of here before moms, sisters, or dads kill us."

They turned and went out the door, the sounds of people reading to dogs carrying out into the night.

CATCH

Christmas Eve was sheer chaos. The noise hit Jared and Diego like a wall. Meri had Bobby and Adam faced off against Denver and Beau on the kitchen island. All four had cookie scoops in their hands.

"Go!" Meri shouted.

They began to scoop and put the cookies down on cookie trays. Ricky and Meri leaned over the boys and squished the cookies with crossed forks. Charlie was manning the stove; something in a huge pot smelled heavenly.

"Unca Jared!" River smashed into Jared as he was wrestling himself out of his coat.

Diego grabbed Jared's shoulder with one hand to keep him from toppling and got the coat untangled with the other. Diego threw the jacket atop the bulging jacket tree and struggled out of his own coat.

Five corgis, a greyhound, and a russet dog came barreling at Jared as he picked up River.

"I'm Wiber," she said to Diego. "The boy dogs live wif Papa Gunny an' Gamma Rachael and Stretcher. The girl dogs live wif Aunt Corinne and Unca Mitch an' Unca James. The other dogs live with the boys." She crinkled her nose.

Jared grinned at the rush of words. "This is your uncle Diego. He and I raise dogs that go to their forever homes later." Jared sighed. "River here thinks she is her own personal Demolition Derby."

River leaped out of Jared's arms and into Diego's. "I'm Wiber!" she announced again and gave Diego a huge hug.

Diego looked poleaxed. Jared grinned and pulled off his boots. Diego did the same, despite having a little girl attached to him like a limpet. Jared petted each dog, receiving dog kisses.

Kandace came up, red hair streaming behind her, her pregnant belly cleaving the air like a prow. "River, I thought you wanted to read books."

"Unca Diedo can help me."

"Diego. With a 'g.' Where will we read them?"

"My sista Bethany and I are reading in the ship."

Jared grinned. "I was going for a tree, but I got outvoted."

At Diego's perplexed look, Kandace pointed. "Down the hall, past the living room. Big playroom, doors are open. The big ship is a reading and sleep nook."

Diego nodded. "Yes, ma'am."

Kandace patted Diego's back. "Breathe, little bro. It gets easier dealing with this wildness over time." Diego gasped in a breath, and River pointed the way he should go.

Kandace sat down at the kitchen table, puffing. Her long black hair was coming out of its braid. "Don't just stand there, Jared. Get me some juice and some potatoes."

Jared found himself in front of the refrigerator, not entirely sure how he got there. The refrigerator was stuffed with meats, vegetables, fruits, and sodas.

Meri pointed. "Pomegranate juice, on the door, second shelf, left."

Jared got the bottle of juice out, and by the time he had the door closed, Meri handed him a steel bowl with potatoes inside, a peeler helpfully pushed into the side. Jared handed over the juice, put the bowl down, washed his hands, carried the potatoes to the table, then went back for a bowl for the peels.

The door crashed open in a gust of wind. "We're here!" Penny crowed. The woman she dragged in behind her had silver hair, a mass of wrinkles around her eyes and mouth, and a twinkle in her periwinkle eyes.

Jared strode over to Penny. "Let me help you with your coat. Gotta be fast getting it off."

Adelle shut the door while Jared helped get Penny's coat off and took her bag. River came flying out and threw herself against Penny's legs. Jared held Penny up while she *oofed*. Penny knelt, and River held Penny close.

"Auntie Penny!"

Jared moved to help Adelle with her coat. "That would be River. Part welcoming committee, part battering ram."

Adelle laughed from the belly. "Wonderful!"

"Who are you? I'm Wiber!"

Penny introduced her mother. "This is Grandma Adelle."

Adelle laughed as Penny launched herself at Adelle.

"I'm Wiber! Hi, Gramma!"

Jared pointed. "Reading is that way. Past the living room, on the right, in the playroom."

Adelle gasped. "Oh, I have such wonderful stories! Let's go!"

Penny laughed and took her bag back as River and Adelle headed down the hall. "Let's get these snacks set up. I've got candied pecans and cranberries, bacon-wrapped little cheesy hot dogs, and chocolate caramel pecan popcorn balls."

"Give." Kandace stood, arms outstretched.

Meri handed a bowl out into the air, and Jared moved to take it while Penny went to the breakfast counter with her goodies. Meri handed over three more bowls and a bright orange silicone baking sheet. Jared put a popcorn ball and some of the pecans and cranberries in a bowl and put it on the kitchen table. Kandace nibbled on both while Jared filled more bowls and Penny washed her hands, arranged the hot dogs on a silicone baking sheet, and popped the sheet into the oven.

Kandace whistled, and all the dogs showed up. Jared laughed and gave them all dog treats. The dogs ran back to the kids. Kandace followed so the slow-moving Nyx could have a treat too.

Corinne lumbered in. Kandace came back, pointed at the bowl of treats, and Corinne sat.

"Bless you."

"Anything for you, sister of my heart." Kandace touched her chest dramatically. Corinne rolled her eyes.

Jetta came in and sat down at the table. She took a potato out of the bowl, and Meri threw her a peeler with deadly accuracy. Jared wisely brought over more snack bowls and another bowl for the potato peels. He found the bag of red apples, washed them, and brought them to the counter, along with two paring knives, a bowl, and a cutting board. Penny took out the pigs in a bacon blanket, put some on a little plate for themselves, and put the rest on a larger plate. The boys had them gone before the tray of cookies went in.

Penny and Jared sat on high stools and stared at the apples. Jared waved at the counter. "This is Christmas Eve here. We have to cook and trade off on child care because we have so many people. I know you must be tired and your arms sore from scooping ice cream. Just relax, I can do this."

Penny smiled tiredly at him. "Get me a peeler, and I'll peel while you cut."

Meri checked a drawer and handed one over. "Heard from my sister Libby that you only worked four hours, but you had a line and had to make more ice cream."

Penny smiled. "Sold out of rum raisin, peppermint, and eggnog ice cream. Sold them by the bucket. We closed when the line stopped, cleaned up, and took off."

"That's great!" Jared peeled an apple.

Meri sighed. "Libby's on her way. She had to make more treats in the middle, and had a bear of a time cleaning up." Jen snorted.

Penny narrowed her eyes. "She said she would be right behind me."

Meri shrugged. "You were out of ice cream, so there was no sense in your staying. She sold out of nearly everything, even the gluten-free stuff. I have been up since four in the morning, making sure all my shut-ins had plenty of holiday food."

"Penny, I'm so glad you came, and that you brought your mom." Jared made quick, precise work of cutting up the apples. "I wasn't expecting to see you until tomorrow."

Penny laughed. "I wasn't either, but I told Mama that Libby invited us, and that was it. We took our snacks and ran."

"How is the house going?" Jared brushed her fingers as he took another apple out of her hand

Penny huffed out a breath. "My mom got involved. It's why she hasn't been by to read with your dogs. I told her she has to stick to my plan or she's out. She agreed, and I let her go nuts in the downstairs bedroom. She got everything done, even added some items I wasn't going to go with, like trim. Stuff beyond the budget, but she said it was a Christmas present. Since she has everything she wants and my apartment is so small, we don't buy gifts anymore."

Jared nodded. "Good mama."

Penny handed Jared a peeled apple, then put her head in her hands. "Then, since she's been off work since yesterday, completely behind my back, she hired a moving service while we were so busy today and moved me lock, stock, and barrel to the new house. I don't know whether to cry at having that load literally off my shoulders, or to yell at her for being presumptuous. Nothing is where I want it, either. I'll have to spend the holidays finishing rooms and putting things to rights. Only the kitchen, dining area, downstairs bedroom, and downstairs bathroom are done. I've got boxes... just sitting there." Penny's voice was a mix of amusement and exasperation.

"She what?" Meri bellowed.

"Penny, who did you ask to move into your old apartment?" Jared made a little motion with his hand and Meri subsided.

Charlie kissed his daughter Meri's cheek. "Downtown is popular. Mark my words, someone will want to move in despite the snow." Meri was eager to protect her sister, Libby, who owned the building.

Jared smiled. "Be happy, sis. Lots of people work downtown. Someone will want it."

"Ghost town after the holidays, remember?" Meri groused.

Charlie touched Meri's shoulder. "Christmas Eve, attitude of gratitude."

The cookie timer dinged, and the boys jumped up and down at the thought of peanut butter and chocolatey goodness.

"I'm sorry," Penny said, stricken. "I haven't put in my 30-day notice yet."

Libby came in the door, and for once River didn't attack someone. "What?" she said, at the stricken look on Penny's face.

"My mom moved me out without telling me."

Libby shrugged, then took off her coat. "She told me. She also told me to hang onto the deposit until I got a new tenant. Brooke's been after me for that apartment for two years now. I texted him, and we took a look-see. Your mama cleaned up so well that Brooke closed up and went to his brother's place to move out. He and Garret have been fighting up a storm because Garret's started... doing stupid stuff." She pantomimed putting something small in her mouth with two fingers, and everyone nodded.

"See," Charlie said to Meri. "Don't you owe someone an apology for making her feel bad on Christmas Eve?"

"You made Penny feel bad?" Libby glared at her sister, hands on her hips. "I love you, but Libby is my heart-sister too. I own that property, and I can make my own decisions."

"I'm sorry." Meri hugged Penny, and Penny hugged back.

Libby turned her glare on the boys, who were staring open-eyed at the hugging women. "Sisters fight, like brothers do. You apologize, hug, and move on. Got it?"

All five boys nodded their heads.

"Okay, Meri, back on cookie duty. The buckeyes won't make themselves."

Meri stepped back into the kitchen. "Who wants to learn how to dip chocolate?"

Five hands went up.

"Denver, you get the really big jar of peanut butter out of the pantry." Denver turned and lurched towards the pantry.

Libby hugged Penny. "Why are you working? You've been going nonstop for weeks!" She glared at Jared.

Jared held up his hands. "I tried to talk her out of it."

"He did." Penny pointed her peeler at him.

"Come. You need little girls reading to you." Libby pulled the peeler out of Penny's hand and pulled her upright. "Boys, I want a plate of buckeyes in the reading room when you're finished, you hear?"

All five boys nodded, even Denver, struggling under the weight of the huge peanut butter container. Meri grabbed the plastic jar before he dropped it.

Jared wisely took the apples and bowls for himself.

Kandace pointed at Jared with a peeler. "What did you get for that woman for Christmas? We have to approve."

Jared sighed. It was going to be a long night.

The meal was more tapas-style with bowls of nuts and fruit, olive, cheese, and cracker plates with toasted pepperoni and prosciutto for the meat lovers, sausage and cheese stuffed in biscuit dough, pastries loaded with crab, mushroom caps stuffed with shrimp, cheesecake bites, and the promised buckeyes. The appetizers and bite-sized desserts were made and eaten in between the massive session designed to prep everything for tomorrow's monster meals.

Then it was time for a fireside gathering, and the kids all got to choose one present. They chose the biggest boxes, and soon a train set was set up in the playroom, running over books as hills and bridges. The dogs watched carefully to be sure the children were safe. The dogs got their own snacks.

Beau walked up to Penny and kind of fell on her lap. He put his hands on her face. "Auntie Penny, you gotta go now."

Penny held the sleepy boy. "I know. We need to get enough sleep for tomorrow." She looked over at her mother who was cradling River in her arms. "Don't know how to drag my mom away, but I'll try."

"Hurry up, 'cause Bobby's about to go bear."

Penny stood and went to her mom. "Mom, we've got to go. Big preparations for tomorrow."

"We do?" River was asleep.

"I'll carry Bethany, but yeah, bedtime for young ones, and we've got to go. Private family ceremonies, you know." Penny hefted Bethany, dead asleep on a giant stuffed bear. She smiled and hauled the girl upstairs to her bedroom. Her mother followed. They got the girls into their beds—Bethany loved blue, River shiny silver. They put on the night lights, then Penny said goodbye to the distracted adults and half-dragged her protesting mother to the cars.

"We need to get the bowls!" Adelle waved her hands as if they were leaving prized china behind.

"We'll get them tomorrow." Penny grabbed her mother's wrist.

Jared came out, bowls in hand. "Have a lovely evening, ladies!" He kissed Penny. "So happy to see you, Adelle." He gave her a hug and handed her the bowls. "Good evening. Come by tomorrow, and we'll put you to work again!"

"Sounds good." Penny got in her van.

"Omigod omigod!" Adelle screamed. A black bear cub came toddling around the corner. "Aren't they supposed to be hibernating?"

"Mom, where there's a cub, there's an angry mom. Get in the car. Now. Go home." Penny closed her own door.

Another baby bear came crashing into the first. Then, a huge, lumbering mother bear came around the corner of the house. Adelle squeaked, got into her car, and shut the door. Jared ran back out onto the porch. Adelle finally got her car programmed for home, and both vehicles peeled out.

Jared waited until both sets of tail lights were out of sight, then he brushed off the glider swing, took off his clothes, put them on the glider, and went wolf. He ran down to circle the bears. The baby bears, Bobby and Adam, pretended to swat at him. He chased them, and they bumbled off to chase him instead. Jetta sighed and followed her offspring into the forest.

*A*delle was halfway home before she called Penny. "They were shifters! You told me there were shifters, that there were wolves. And bears. You made me panic for nothing."

Penny sighed. "Beau is really protective of the family and its secret. Knowing a secret and hanging out when they change, those are two different things. If you were a shifter, would you want people standing around in the snow staring at you? And what if neighbors showed up because they had a flat or something, and you were standing around acting like bears in the yard when they are supposed to be hibernating isn't a big deal?"

"You're mad at me. I wanted to surprise you. You are so excited about the house. You've been chatting about moving in so you could hammer in baseboards or screw in outlet plates in the mornings before work, spray rooms and lay down flooring at night. I got excited by the season."

Penny sighed. "I'm not mad. But you are paying to have the refrigerator put back when my new one comes in. You kinda stole it. The laundry room isn't done, so you're doing my laundry, too. Right now, the washer and dryer are just sitting there in the garage, and they have to be moved in and hooked up."

Adelle blew out a long breath. "I didn't think things through very well. I'm sorry. No wonder you keep telling me to hold off, hold back on me spending money on you. It's just that, we had so little for so long. And now that I have money, I want to give it to you to make your life better. You deserved so much more."

Penny refrained from either crying or smashing her face into the dashboard. "I get that, Mom, I really do. But I was loved unconditionally, and I have a clear notion of what living without that would be like. I promise if there is some sort of emergency, I will ask. Mom, quit crying. Really, I'm not mad. My stuff is off limits, you hear?"

"I hear. I really stole the refrigerator?" She laughed a little.

Penny chose to laugh. "Yeah, mom, you really did."

~

*P*enny parked in the mostly empty garage, glad that Jen had made sure the outdoor lights worked. She put in the code and entered through the side door. She stripped off her outerwear and, having no other place to put them as there was no hanging bar in the unfinished downstairs closet, left her shoes at the door and her coat on the stairs. She went into the kitchen and saw a figure hunched over at the plywood-covered breakfast bar. Penny got into a fighting crouch and turned on the light. Bobbi sat there, ice pack against her eye, an empty bowl with a spoon in it, and a box of cereal next to it.

Penny pitched herself forward, righted herself. "Bobbi?"

Bobbi turned to Penny. "I'm so sorry. I didn't know you were moving in so soon."

"Neither did I. My mom jumped the gun." She moved closer. Bobbi's beautiful brown eyes were filled with tears, and her right eye was beginning to swell shut. "Who did that to you?" Bobbi had the sleeves of her sweatshirt rolled up, and Penny saw bruises there, too. She ran to the stolen refrigerator and pulled out an ice pack. "I have a first aid kit... somewhere." Penny grabbed a kitchen towel and tied the ice pack onto Bobbi's arm. She scooted back to get another ice pack from the freezer. "What happened?"

"If you want me to go…"

"No, don't be foolish. You're kind, smart, and my best worker. Plus, it's Christmas Eve, and it started snowing again. I bet your friends are on holiday trips." Penny wrapped both of her other ice packs in kitchen towels that peeked out from a box, then handed them to Bobbi.

Bobbi nodded. "I don't have many. We're geeks. Band geeks, science fiction, fantasy, and gaming geeks, science fair geeks. The school here is really small. Mostly everyone was gone on the last day of school. Anyway, Chrissy, she's in the band too. She kissed me in the band room when we were putting away all the music."

"Your first kiss?" Penny got juice out of the refrigerator, took out a glass, and poured it. Her mom had filled the cabinets with the glasses, at least.

"Yeah." Bobbi smiled and got a wistful look in her one good eye. The other one was swollen shut.

Penny put the bowl and spoon in the sink and put the cereal box away. "Do you like Chrissy?"

Bobbi smiled. "She's amazing. Tall, great smile. She runs track, skiis. She plays the flute. I've got the violin. I guess I'll have to stop. I can't afford lessons."

Penny felt her stomach free-fall as she connected the dots. "Did you tell your mom?"

"My mom joined the Sacred and Precious Blood of Christ Church when they had a revival meeting come through here. Revivalists often don't take people of our skin color in, but these did. Mama trusted them because of that, I think. Anyway, they preach all sorts of bad things. Hate. Lots of talk about if your eye offends you, pluck it out. Mama made me go to the meetings. I hated them. They kept screaming about sinning and going to hell. I know they meant... me. Who I am. So I kept my head down, began working any job I could, and hid the money from Mama behind a loose brick in the wall of my room. Mama started searching my room for drugs and magazines and contraband. I don't know what contraband she expected to find. So, I started carrying the money around in my shoes, under the soles, and in my socks. I gave money to Paul, who I used to game with, and he hid it for me. No more gaming, no music except my violin, which I had to keep at school. I couldn't practice."

Penny sat at the counter on her pilfered bar stools. She put it on the list for things to return. "How did your mom find out about the kiss?"

"One of the parents came to pick up her band kid. She told her best friend, and it got around to my mom. We did the church thing. She stayed to pray, so I read stuff from our school's required reading list. Then we got home, and she started screaming about sending me to a camp to pray the devil out of me. I told her it was just a kiss and that I'm not going. Her brother Donnie came over. He drinks a lot. He said he was taking me tonight. I said I wasn't going anywhere with him, and if he touched me, it would be an assault on a minor. He punched me, and Mama hit me and scratched me, and Donnie took out his belt, and I got out the door. They both screamed for me to never come back, that the devil was in me."

"Let me see the scratches." Penny tried to keep her voice even, but she was ready to go over to Bobbi's former house herself. She wondered where she'd packed her baseball bat.

Bobbi showed her the scratches, some on her arm, two grooves on her neck.

Penny sighed. "It's Christmas Eve. I can choose not to report until morning, but then..." Penny pulled out her phone and called Meri. "Do you still have a foster license?"

"Yeah."

"Have an empty bed?"

"Absolutely. What just happened?"

"Can't say yet. Hypothetically, assault on a teen. Black eye and scratches, and homeless."

"Can Nat hypothetically come over tomorrow?"

"Yes. Please send me the stuff about the parenting classes."

"On it. Do you need anything? Toothbrush, medical kit?"

"I have to find it, but I have a kit. Extra mattress, not so much. Bedding, I've got somewhere. Food's good."

"Someone will come with an air mattress. Was this a parental thing?"

"Yes."

"Religious nonsense?"

"Yes."

Meri sighed. "Nat got called to the site of a disturbance. A mother and her brother admitted to assaulting a teen and throwing her out of the house. Nat arrested them. They'll be locked up until after the holidays. Nat explained this very circumspectly, and I don't know any names. Nat was calling around to try to find the teen. I'll put a hold on that with Nat. You need anything tonight, anything at all, call me."

"I will."

"Then, we're going to all be together for the holidays. What does your teen want?"

"A violin locked up in school for the next three weeks."

Meri sighed. "We'll figure it out." She dropped the link.

Bobbi raised her eyebrows. "Parenting classes?"

"I want kids. I thought it would be bio-kids, and that might happen. But..."

"I just need a room, food. I can work, fix your house for that."

Penny felt the shock of a much better idea hitting her in the head. "You can and will do that. But I've got a friend. A really good one since high school. Something happened to her. It was this time of year. A guy was felling trees and cutting them into logs illegally on government property while Karissa was hiking by on the main path. A log rolled down and crushed her. She can walk with crutches, but no kids."

"That's horrible! Makes this seem less... I don't know. Like I'm whining or something. I think my mom was turned into some sort of zombie. Her brother became an elder in this church. She just kind of took her free will and turned it over to other people. Became a pod person."

"Let's not compare horrible things. Bad is bad. There is no scale. Now, you sit here while I find the first aid kit. Are you still hungry?"

"No. Just sore and tired."

"Okay. Let's hope my mom put the first aid kit in the bathroom box."

By the time Penny found the first aid kit and cleaned and bandaged the scratches, Diego came in with an air mattress and the pump. He tried to take it into the downstairs bedroom.

Diego came back out and said, "There's not enough room in there. Mind if she sleeps near fresh drywall? Smells a little, but it's not wet. The laundry room is big enough."

"Sounds good. Tomorrow, I'm going to have to get in there and paint. My mother brought over my washer and dryer, but that room isn't finished yet."

Bobbi stood up. "I can help."

"Fine, let's find the sheets."

They found the sheets, put them on the air mattress when Diego was done blowing it up, and Penny moved in a nightstand and the first aid kit along with a carafe of cold water. Diego left.

"Let's go to bed early. We've got a lot of Christmas celebrations to go to tomorrow. You're going to be sucked into cooking," Penny warned. "And probably child care. Three boys from one family and two from another, and two girls. And be careful of River. She has perfected the attack hug."

Bobbi grinned. "As long as it isn't a church. I've had enough of that for a long time."

"Nope. Merry Christmas."

Bobbi burst into tears, and Penny held her close.

$\sim$

*P*enny got up, got coffee first, and let Bobbi sleep. Then, she put on a moon suit and sprayed the inside of the downstairs coat and linen closet. Bobbi woke up, rolled up the sheets and comforter, deflated her bed, got a sweatsuit from Penny, and took a shower while Penny sprayed the laundry room. Out of paint and gumption, Penny took a shower.

Penny dressed and came out to find Karissa and Bobbi chatting over a cherry coffee cake. Penny had sent a short text the night before asking if Karissa would consider adopting a teenager. There had been no reply, which was strange, so Penny thought that Karissa must be out of town. Instead, Karissa was bright-eyed and smiling, wearing intricate braids, her crutches resting against the kitchen island. Karissa was a beautiful woman with a square face, penetrating black eyes, and a huge smile. She wore jeans and a lovely red sweater, and little red Christmas ornaments dangled from her ears.

"When are the police coming?" Karissa asked.

Penny looked out the front window. "Nat is here now."

Penny ran to the garage to open the garage door, then held the interior door open for the deputy. The officer took off his boots, hat, and coat, and, wary of paint, left them on the stairs.

Nat strode in. Penny made sure the door was shut, then went to go pour Nat some coffee.

"Karissa! I haven't seen you since the ice cream social!"

Karissa hugged Nat. "Had another surgery. I have more range of motion in the right knee now. I'm hoping to ditch the crutches."

"That's terrific! Bobbi, I'm Deputy Nat Sandawan." They shook hands.

Bobbi gave Nat a small smile. "I know who you are. You've been coming to the school since I was a little kid talking about fire safety and later on about avoiding drugs."

"Well, what you need to know is that your mother and your uncle clearly made statements incriminating themselves after I warned them that anything they say could be used against them. I arrested them both. I caught everything on camera. There's not a judge in any of the three counties that will let them go after they assaulted a 15-year-old girl and kicked her out into the snow on Christmas Eve. I can see that you've got a black eye. I already have a body cam on, and I just want a closeup of your face and any other injuries you might have."

Bobbi obediently rolled up her sleeves and pulled down the neck of the sweatshirt to show Nat the scratches and bruises.

"Before I call Child Protective Services, Karissa, did you have any urge to adopt an older child?"

"It broke my soul when my overseas adoption fell through. The program closed down very suddenly, leaving a lot of adoptions in limbo, mine included. I spent last night on my knees, praying, asking why this happened to me, praying for the country to open up again, which was a mistake. Never pray for what you want. Found that out when I got Penny's text at three this morning when I came to from all the crying."

Penny nodded. "I want to adopt you, don't be confused about that. And you can work here until this house gets done. But Karissa here wants you more, and it has wanted you for longer than I have. It would take me six weeks to get everything I need to adopt you, but you need someone a whole lot faster. Plus, she's awesome."

"And I'm an interior decorator. You wouldn't think there would be jobs in a holler like ours, and most of the time, there's not." Karissa laughed. "I primarily work online, helping clients with no time or fashion sense order what it is they want, and I work with services to get everything in the way they like it."

Bobbi grinned. "I know who you are. You go to the church we used to go to. I've always loved the way you dressed and how you hugged everybody. Can you show me how to do the house fashion stuff? Penny needs a lot of help."

Karissa grinned. "I sure can! Penny can pay you. It will be your first design job."

Bobbi squealed, then hugged both women.

Karissa laughed, a sound that filled the room. "I'll take that as a yes."

Nat made the call, sent the footage from last night and this morning, and sat down to wait for the social worker. Penny served coffee and coffee cake.

The man they sent was thin, reedy, with a prominent Adam's apple, wearing a gray suit and a red sweater. Penny rushed to usher him in through the garage.

"I am John Scott. That porch is unacceptable."

"Of course it is," Penny said, tartly. "I'm not adopting Bobbi. Karissa is."

"Karissa is here! Girlfriend! You finally decided to join us!" They hugged and air-kissed each other's cheeks.

Karissa passed the social worker a piece of coffee cake and a cup of coffee. "Just the one, for now. Bobby is going to help me help Penny."

John looked around. "Penny definitely needs help."

Nat motioned for Penny to calm down. Steam was beginning to come out of her ears. "John, hello. I sent you the video, the mother and the uncle are in custody, and everything has been logged. Now, if you'll excuse me, I have other matters to attend to. Bobbi, I cannot begin to tell you how sorry I am that this happened to you and how relieved I was to find out you were safe. Karissa has a beautiful home. Karissa, congratulations." Nat hugged Penny and Karissa and left.

Karissa waved a hand. "John, chop chop, let's get the paperwork done and get this girl on the road. We've got to swing by the Urgent Care while it's still open, make sure everything is good. Then, we have to go shopping at the box store before it closes. This girl needs plenty of clothes."

Penny nodded. "You both are still invited to Christmas at the Cambers. But, I understand if you would like something quieter. You've been through a lot. The last thing the Camber house can be called is quiet."

Bobbi smiled shyly. "Quiet would be great today."

"Okay, I'll work on my punch list while you guys do your thing. Bobbi, if you ever need anything, give me a call. Plus, the whole work thing. You can log in as many hours as your new mom lets you."

Penny left them to the social worker interview and unpacked the bathroom things into the downstairs bathroom. She came out for hugs and found a clean kitchen as well. She sent everyone on their way and headed out for Christmas madness. And food. Lots and lots of food. She tried not to cry. It was the best solution. But why did it feel like there was a hole in her heart?

CHRISTMAS

*J*ared was drunk with exhaustion, not alcohol. Dogs, food, training, then family, gift-giving and receiving. Penny, with her flame-red hair, had loved the scarf. Jared had wisely circled back to buy another scarf for her mother, Adelle. Adelle had a big laugh and a bigger heart. Jared could see why Penny was pissed at her mom. People in wolf packs were very sharing of their things, but moving someone without their permission was beyond the pale. Adelle was contrite and hesitant around her daughter. Penny didn't act pissed, but Penny had a bit of tension in her shoulders and between her eyes from time to time.

Then, Jared heard the story about Penny's almost-adoption, the real reason for her tension, and he felt the wolf and bear packs' ripple of anger. Bobbi would be protected. Meri had gotten a teacher to let her into the closed school, found Bobbi's violin, and dropped it off with Bobbi and her new mom. According to Meri, Karissa glowed, delighted at being a mom at long last.

"No one deserves being a mom more," Penny said, a bit choked up. "I would have adopted her, but Karissa is just perfect."

Adelle patted her daughter's hand. "I know you would have. On the grandma front, River seems to have adopted me."

River wanted Adelle's stories, ones of wolves and bears who saved nerds in forests. Adelle had an excellent imagination. Adelle was also adept at braiding hair after raising a daughter and half-raising two more. Unlike other grandmothers who had perms and hair with so much hairspray it never moved, Adelle's hair was shoulder-length, a silvery gray. During the appetizer of cheese, wheat crackers, and pesto, Adelle lost her braid because of River and Bethany's busy fingers. Before Christmas dinner, River gave Adelle's hair twists with sparkly pink barrettes at the bottoms. Adelle also sported a poofy bracelet made of silvery fabric, a present from an enthusiastic River.

"Nice hairstyle, Mom." Penny smiled at her mother.

Jetta defended her girls. "Actually, they're good with twists."

Penny passed the biscuits and accepted the honey butter. "I was serious. In fact, after dinner, I'd like my own twists."

Mitch, James, and Jared eyed each other, then burst out laughing.

Charlie put his head in his hands. "I thought you wolv... people were intelligent." Charlie lowered his eyes in apology. He'd forgotten that Diego was at the table, happy with his new red sweater and scarf, a harmonica in one pocket, and a bag of candy in the other from his Christmas stocking, oblivious to the shifter secret.

Jetta, Meri, Jen, Lynette, and Penny glared at the three men.

"Just for that, you're on kiddie duty rest of the night," Jen said, her voice wintry.

Len, Davis, and Vic, surprisingly off for the afternoon, all turned flat stares at their new brothers.

"You guys have a lot to learn," Vic said.

James held his hands up. "Raised by wolves."

Everyone laughed, even Penny and Adelle.

After dinner, it was coffee, tea, or lemonade with little plates of tiny squares of lemon pie, blackberry cheesecake, peanut butter chocolate chunk cookies, and the buckeyes, which had to be made again after the females had consumed most of them. Penny got twists in her hair once the girls had consumed the cookies.

There were Christmas movies on the television. They were on "It's a Wonderful Life." Jared made it up to Penny, River, and Bethany by rubbing Penny's feet, making sure the girls had lemonade in sippy cups and taking off his shoes and socks to have his toenails done in blue sparkly nail polish. Mitch and James had their hands full with five rambunctious boys on a sugar high and created a new fort with levels. They bundled the girls up in snowsuits and took them out to make snow people. The kids made snow dogs, wolves, bears, and families.

Penny came out, created a new snow fort, and hid snowballs behind it. She used a trowel from the garage to carve out arrow slits— or in this case, snowball slits. Jared noticed, created his own castle with another trowel lifted from the same garage, and filled it with snowball ammunition. Charlie came out to referee. Davis and Vic went to their shifts—Davis had to work on an accident victim who had luckily survived an impact with a tree, and Vic had an ambulance shift for the same reason. But, Len was ready and able to fight, then Jen and Libby came out to help Penny fight. Lynette got the girls in before they were caught in the crossfire; they made the first batch of hot chocolate. The girls got naps while the boys and adults threw snowballs at each other. Adelle watched the girls sleep, and Lynette joined the fray. They all got soaking wet, and Charlie went in first to put the towels just inside the back door.

Finally, it was time to go in. Penny, Jen, and Libby got the boys dried off, then themselves, then they all consumed hot chocolate and the last of the buckeyes. They got the boys changed into dry clothes and put in a superhero movie. The boys were asleep within minutes. The adults toweled off, collapsed in front of the television, drank hot chocolate laced with cinnamon, and watched more holiday movies.

Penny was falling over when she announced she was leaving. Adelle stayed to help make sandwiches, wanting to play with the girls when they woke up.

Jared walked Penny to her car. "Want help with a project?"

Penny laughed. "No. I'm going to fall over."

Jared sent her a link. "This is a gift card for the home store."

Penny's eyes filled, and she sent a link to him. "It isn't much, but you can get some dog food for free." She smiled at him. "When I'm farther in, I'll read to the dogs. Heck, I'll sing to them." She sang a soft but gorgeous rendition of 'Silent Night' as snow fell on her shoulders.

Jared managed to clear his throat. "That was beautiful. You can sing anytime to them."

Penny smiled shyly. "Have a great night. This was fun."

"I'm sorry you didn't get to adopt Bobbi."

Penny shrugged. "It's about her, not me." She kissed him. "Merry Christmas."

"Merry Christmas."

~

The next three days were a blur of dogs, feeding, training, playing with, and loving on them. One of the labradors got a stomach ache; a spilled bottle of fabric softener the culprit. Shadow alerted them to the sick dog and the fabric softener.

Diego was in tears. "I didn't spill anything.".

"We're going to have to lock the laundry room door. I suspect someone is leaping over the enclosure at night."

A call to the company who made the product and the vet made it clear the dog would be okay. The silly golden lab vomited and pooped blue but was fine. Diego was a mess, blaming himself. Jared got a lock for the door and a dozen child safety locks. They put them everywhere and hung the keys high up so the dogs couldn't reach them.

Jared shook his head. "It's my fault. I did not think of this. We lock up the dog food, but I should have thought of household chemicals."

Diego's eyes got wet again. He had patiently cleaned up after Bella and was very careful to be sure she was all right. "Bella is a great dog. I should have thought things through."

Jared sighed. "Why you? I'm the one with more experience. Let's let it go and move on. We'll keep a sharp eye out for anything that can hurt the dogs. Bella is fine, and we have a job to do." Diego agreed.

Diego needed structure, and so did the dogs, so a regimented life worked well for him after nearly a decade in prison. After the Marines, Jared had formed his own structure. But Diego's constant neediness was wearing on Jared. Diego was alone. He'd lost his mom and all his friends, lost years of his life due to a miscarriage of justice. He had absolutely nothing in the world except what Jared paid him—clothes, food, that sort of thing. Diego needed more to do.

So, when they made some BLTs and sat down to eat their sandwiches, Jared asked, "Why don't you write a blog about dog training, care, that sort of thing? Or videos. You can compile all the information into a book or documentary. If you can make a little money, that would be good. If you can help people treat dogs better, why not?"

Diego said, "My English…"

Jared snorted. "You speak English better than I do. Why don't you do it in Spanish? There are over eighty countries that speak it."

"What about the vet, grooming, business, and animal husbandry courses I'm taking?"

Jared's eyes widened. "Whoa. How many classes are you taking?"

"Canine anatomy and physiology, grooming large dogs, accounting, and life cycles of dog breeds. The VR glasses you bought me are very helpful."

"Okay." Jared was stunned at Diego's initiative and drive. "It can't hurt us to record our training sessions. If you feel like making a vlog, you can do that later."

"If people can see what the dogs can do, they'll be lining up like the firefighters." Diego grinned. "I've been looking for more dalmatians at the shelters, but no joy there. I do have a line on two German shepherds. They're really the smaller American ones."

Jared sighed internally. He didn't want more work, headaches, vet bills. It would be a long time before they would see any more money coming in, but the dogs needed a home, and Diego was taking the initiative.

"Okay, go get them if the shelter is open."

Diego smiled like the sun, taking Jared at his word. After washing the plates, Diego took a carafe of chocolate milk, two Cokes, and some pork rinds with him to the van to go adopt the dogs.

It made dating or even taking time away to help his girl paint, hang tile, or switch out all the air filters difficult. Duke and Queenie were highly intelligent German shepherds, but both had mild respiratory infections. They had to be quarantined upstairs in one of the unfinished bedrooms until the antibiotics could work. Jared had painted in there, but nothing else.

Jared's list of things to do got longer and longer. So, he delegated and asked Diego if he knew how to make a captain's bed. Diego didn't, but Mitch and James did. So, Jared got time to change air filters and lay out golden-and-blue tile in the two upstairs bedrooms for Penny while his brothers helped Diego make beds for himself and the future dog trainers. Diego preferred a mattress on the floor when he first arrived. No one could hide under it.

Oddly enough, his brothers didn't bitch about it, not even Mitch. "Dude is wound pretty tight," Mitch observed. "He has a major hero worship thing going on for you, bro."

Jared had taken them out for a drink; Penny was shooting pool with Meri and Libby because Ned had the boys.

Jared snorted. "I'm no hero."

"You served." James used his serious voice.

Jared cringed internally. He knew Mitch still felt guilty that, after their parents died, James had not joined the military because he didn't want to leave Mitch without a brother. He decided to confront the situation. "You could do it now."

James lifted his beer. "I could. But I love my life in these valleys. Taking Boy Scouts on trips as a guide, skiers in the winter, fly fishers in summer. Being one with the land, you know? A land worth defending. But, I help in other ways. I know of a wounded warrior you might like to know."

Once again, Jared cringed inside. He had a vet named Calanthe Nadebo getting out of rehab soon. She had to prove she could climb stairs and stand for hours with the dogs. Her bionic arm was working great. In fact, Callie could probably lift heavier bags of dog food than Diego or Jared. They needed the help, but one more would... He stomped on his fears. If he had to, he could borrow from the Pack, and if there was a fellow soldier he could help, then that's how it would be.

"Oh?"

"Her name is Beatricia Munoz. She goes by Trish. Tech specialist, a Marine. Has an artificial leg. Says she gets migraines when she does anything with computers. They can't find anything wrong with her head or eyes. She has worked with dog handlers. She's from Texas. She had no family, no job. Tried to take or train for about any job but everything uses computers these days."

Jared raised his eyebrows. "When can she get here?"

James pointed with his beer. "She's over there. I took the liberty of putting her on a plane. I'll hire her to freeze her ass off with me if you don't take her."

Exhausted and poleaxed, Jared got off his stool and went over to the woman with close-cropped black hair shaved on the sides. She was short and muscular, with a wide face and dark eyes. She was wearing jeans and a Marines sweatshirt and was nursing an apple cider drink, the same one Ned drank. There was a go-bag at her feet.

"I'm Jared." He sighed. "I apologize for doing a job interview with a beer in my hand. I had a bomb dog. Still do, Shadow. I'm training dogs to detect seizures, drugs, bomb residue, even dogs kids read to. Whatever the dogs can do that will save them from..." His voice trailed off. Jared sucked in a breath. "I pay medical, room, board, clothes. Can you do the work?"

"Absolutely." Trish spoke clearly without a moment of hesitation.

"Then you're hired. Your bed is newly painted. Don't know if the mattresses got there today or not."

"Don't care. I'll sleep on the floor if I have to." Trish's voice was low, a little smoky.

"I've got a guy named Diego working for me who didn't murder anybody who was in jail for nearly a decade. Lost everybody."

"Rough." Trish finished her apple juice and stood up. "I'll keep an eye on him, sir." She hefted her go-bag on her back.

"Good." Jared left the beer bottle there. "One second, got to say goodbye." He strode over to Mitch and shoved his shoulder. Then, he pushed James in the shoulder. "No wonder you two numbskulls wanted to build the beds. Did the mattresses arrive?"

"Yes." James rubbed his shoulder. "What was that for?"

"Making me do a job interview with a beer in my hand. I looked like an unprofessional ass." Jared sighed and went to say goodbye to his woman.

Jared waited until Penny lined up her shot, took it. She muffed it. He went over to her, hugged her, smelled her pomegranate shampoo. "I've got to go home with another woman."

Libby glared at him. "You what?"

Penny laughed and kissed Jared. "Is it a dog?"

"No. James lined up a job interview without telling me. A soldier needing a berth. I'm going to train her to train dogs."

Penny nodded. "Go take care of your soldier."

Jared felt his gut jump and wished he could take Penny home. "We still on for New Year's Eve?"

"We are." She smiled up at him.

He kissed her again and jogged out the door before his heart, or another body part, exploded.

Outside, Jared led the way to the vehicle. He shoved down hard on his anger. He didn't want to take out James' dick move on his new recruit.

"Do you need anything from the box store?" Jared snorted. "Scratch that, you do. Dark blue shirt or sweatshirt, jeans or khakis. Three of everything, including underwear and long underwear, and get boots, trainers, one heavy and one stadium length coat. Try it on first. Sizes can be crazy in these stores. We don't have a logo yet. We have basic items, bread, milk, yogurt, meat marinating that we cook up, bacon, baking things. Get whatever food or drinks strike your fancy. Don't eat Diego's pork rinds or my Cool Ranch Doritos, or drink Diego's chocolate milk. You will get more clothes later. Eat any diet you like."

Trish nodded. "Yes, sir."

They got in, shut the doors. Jared programmed in the route and started the van.

Trish hooked up her mesh. "I like meat, veggies, and fruit. No bread except the kinds I make with almond and coconut flour."

Jared nodded. "Good. I like healthy people."

"You have a gym setup?"

"No, but there has to be something for sale. People get stuff for Christmas, get rid of their old stuff. We can put it in the van, carve out a corner of the barn. Should have done that a ways back. Got busy."

"I understand, sir."

"If you can find kickboxing equipment, Diego loves it."

"I'll get on it, sir."

Trish was effective and efficient. Her entire trip, including trying on clothes and a grocery run, took forty minutes. The food was so healthy that Jared felt a little ashamed of his diet. She even found a kickboxing stand, gloves, and knee pads.

At the barn, Trish introduced herself to Diego, put the food away, then introduced herself to all the dogs. Diego acted as if new people showed up every day. Then, Trish gave belly rubs and loved on dog heads. They were all in love with her, no exception. Then they all stumbled upstairs to bed.

The next day, Trish cooked mug bread and a mug omelet and made a breakfast sandwich. Diego and James both wanted to learn how to make a mug breakfast, so she showed them. The bread was delicious; more almond flour went on the house grocery list. They cleaned up, fed and watered the dogs, and cleaned the cages. They took turns—James, Diego, then Trish. Training three dogs at once made things go much faster. Trish learned the dog commands and signals quickly.

Trish was delighted to meet Adelle, who came with Ruby from her book club to read to and love on the dogs. Ravi had the day off to go snowboarding with his family. They had another BLT lunch with a delicious almond flour bread Trish made in the microwave. Adelle gave Jared the side-eye but said nothing.

Jared, delighted that things seemed to be under control, did the intelligent thing and went to see if he could make it up to his girl for leaving her the night before. He had left a bar with another woman. Tongues would be speaking his name all over town. He hoped to avoid being eviscerated by angry townsfolk. They might respect him, but they loved Penny.

He got Penny two mirrors on the way in and a lot of almond flour for home. He caught a few glares but got out unscathed. He bought over-door hooks so his woman could hang her things.

Penny had unwisely decided to demo the porch without a mask. Jared hopped out and ran over to her. "Penny, do you need more masks? I can buy some. I got mirrors for the bathrooms."

Tears of anger stood out in Penny's eyes. "I am mad at you because my mother heard a rumor that you left with another woman. You put me in the position of having to defend you."

"I'm sorry, Penny. James apparently thought it was funny to spring a veteran who needed help on me in a bar when you were right there. Sometimes brothers are assholes. If I had a baseball bat, I'd hit him with it."

Penny handed James a sledgehammer. "Don't use this on James. Instead, get your gloves and a mask. You can beat up your brother by proxy. But first, let's hang the mirrors. Then I have silver caulk to lay out."

"Yes, ma'am."

Trish was extremely competent, healthy, and made amazing food. She was a find. Jared no longer cared about borrowing from the wolf pack funds if it meant keeping Diego and Trish happy. But, he really was going to kill his brother. He carefully put down the sledgehammer, grabbed the mirrors, and followed Penny. He let his anger rise. That porch didn't stand a chance.

NEW YEAR'S BLESSINGS

New Year's Eve was lovely. Penny had her mom over to admire the new countertops, a red marble with flecks of silver, gold, and black. It was stunning. They had a tiny bit of bubbly and strawberries dipped in chocolate. Jen had helped Penny install the lights in the kitchen, dining area, and den, all brushed silver like the faucets throughout the house.

"When does the rest of the furniture arrive?" Adelle asked her daughter.

"For downstairs, two days. The upstairs other than my bedroom and one bathroom will not miraculously be finished today, tomorrow, or next week. Painting, floors, lights. I can do that on weekends when we open after the new year. No use opening my shop until after school starts again. That porch was a beast and an eyesore, pissing off the neighbors. The demo is done. Jared attacked it because he was pissed at James for springing a job interview on him at a bar."

"Pish." Adelle waved off the neighbors and the gossip caused by Jared leaving a bar with another woman. "You're doing the best that you can."

"I can't believe I swung the loan. Plus, this instant-family thing has gotten me deep discounts and so much free labor. I can't thank them enough."

Adelle shook her head. "Why won't you let me swing a hammer?"

"I wanted you to relax. You did so much for us growing up, me and Morgan and Maddie. But, if you insist, tomorrow you can put on a moon suit, grab a sprayer, and help me paint the upstairs. We need a good layer of primer everywhere, floors and ceiling."

Adelle grinned. "Works for me!" They clinked glasses.

Then, they went to Corinne, Mitch, and Kandace's house. The kids had their own party at the farmhouse, the adults circulating there on kid duty. They had a lovely dinner, tortellini stuffed with cheese and sun-dried tomatoes and covered with pesto, with a soft Italian bread baked with Parmesan and herbs. Mitch was with Len on Corinne and Kandace duty, their wishes obeyed. Both women seemed ready to go into labor, but thankfully the babies held off their arrivals.

Trish and Diego came for dinner, then went home to be with the dogs, citing exhaustion. Adelle went to the farmhouse to read to the kids, then came back once they were asleep.

The preggers people danced with their husbands. Jared danced with Adelle first, then Charlie danced with Adelle while Jared danced with Penny.

"I cannot tell you how sorry I am for ditching you."

"You destroyed the porch, so you're forgiven." Penny smiled and held Jared close.

Jared kissed her forehead. "I am also sorry about all the gossip."

Penny shrugged. "I think the neighbors were more mad at me about the state of the porch. The thing was so rotted! Plus, burned in places. Weird."

Jared nodded. "You never know what drug addicts will do."

Penny swayed. "This is nice."

"It is." Jared stroked her hair, then, when the song ended, he gave her a gentle kiss. Time stopped as Penny melted into him.

The next few songs were '40s music, and Charlie led his sons and wives into some swing dancing. Adelle joined in, and Penny was stunned to watch her mother fly in the air, red dress swirling around her. Penny regretted the silver sheath dress she wore until she remembered the look on Jared's face when he saw it.

They ate chocolate almond popcorn dusted with cinnamon, drank champagne and non-alcoholic sparkling cider, and toasted the new year. Then, Adelle took her heavy coat and went home. Jared trailed Penny to her house.

The kisses started once they shucked their outerwear and put it in the hall closet. They sat on the stairs, kissing like teenagers.

"I want to make love. Right here." Penny struggled to get Jared's button-fly jeans unbuttoned.

"Penny, if you want to make love on the moon, I'll get us a ticket and a rover." He kissed her smooth expanse of neck. He fumbled blindly for his jeans, grasped a condom.

His jaw hit the floor as Penny kicked off her low silver heels and shimmied out of her tights.

Penny took the condom from his nerveless fingers. "Now." She rolled the condom on as Jared struggled out of his button-down gray shirt.

He threw the shirt on the mesh and wondered why the railing wasn't in yet. Then he was drowning in sensation. She knew what she wanted and took it. She slid two of his fingers in between her legs, grabbed him with the other hand, and guided him in. He held her, looked into her eyes, her hair falling out of its clip.

He kissed her, stroked the top of her breasts peeking out of the sheath. He was careful not to pull on the dress with its beading and delicate zipper. He guessed she had to save up for it. He used those extraneous thoughts to keep from coming too soon. She tasted like chocolate and cinnamon, spicy and sweet. Then, he was lost and let himself feel. They moved in rhythm, Jared's hands in her hair, her fingers splayed on his chest. She took the lead, took him completely inside her. Jared lost breath, lost the air in the room. He lay his head back and moaned as she screamed.

Penny stood, carefully rolled off the condom, and said, "Wait, I'll be right back."

Jared leaned against the wall. He couldn't have moved if he tried.

Penny came back with a warm washcloth and wiped him down. She went away and came back. "Can you stand, love?"

Jared took his clothes completely off, stood, and said, "Lead on." He took it slow; his head was spinning with champagne and sex.

She led him to her bedroom, done in blue with magenta trim. She pulled back the sheets, and Jared struggled to lay down rather than fall into the bed. She took off her silvery dress and hung it up, along with her slip and bra. She grinned, took out the clip in her hair, let it fall in waves all around.

"Beautiful." Jared's tone was reverent.

"Flattery will get you everywhere." Penny took out her silver earrings but left on a silver chain.

"Come back to me."

She crawled in bed, and Jared kissed her, held her close. She put her head on his shoulder, and Jared's heart stuttered.

"I love you." He stroked a finger down her arm. "Make a list, tell me what you want, what you want me to do. I'll do anything for you.

Penny looked up into his eyes. "I love you back. Lists are nice, though." He kissed her forehead, stroked her hair and back. He wondered if he were dreaming, then slipped into sleep.

❧

*P*enny awoke to the smell of bread, bacon, almonds, and coffee. She stumbled to the bathroom, slid on a silk robe, then went out to the kitchen. Jared was slicing and buttering a spongy round bread.

"What is this?" Penny stumbled in the direction of the coffee. They had made love near dawn, and she was pleasantly sore.

"Mug bread. I brought in the almond flour from the truck in the garage. Got a lot. Anyway, pleasantly nutty flavor. We have butter and blackberry jam. Plus bacon cups. Bacon in a silicone muffin pan, bake it or zap it in the microwave, then add an omelet in the middle. Egg, mushrooms, red bell peppers, cheddar and mozzarella, and Italian spices."

Penny sat at the breakfast bar. "Incredible." She bit into the bacon cup and groaned.

"That's a ten-minute breakfast using the microwave, including prep. I've already had mine and cleaned up most of it."

Penny kissed him. "Mmm." He tasted like coffee.

"I hate to do this to you. But…"

"You have to leave," she guessed.

"No, the exact opposite. The storm that was supposed to miss us ended up here, and now we're in deep snow. Blizzard, no visibility. You're stuck with me for a few days."

Penny grinned. "Whatever will I do with you?"

"Hmm. I have some ideas." Jared's kiss was slow. Penny felt it all the way to her toes.

They made love, constructed sandwiches, binge-watched television, and made love again. Then, the dreamy hold wore off, and Penny was restless. So, despite the fact they could only crack the windows, they went upstairs, took sprayers to opposite sides of the hallway, and sprayed the rest of the upstairs with primer. They took a hot shower together, and Jared found the strength to make love to her in the shower. Then, they went back to bed with condoms, juice, and more shows to watch. They sprayed again, and the bedrooms looked beautiful.

Jared left the minute the snowplow went by, following in its wake. Penny felt bereft and satisfied at the same time. She showered, then tackled tiling the upstairs ensuite bathroom. She showered again and went to stock her empty cupboards. She hit up the barbecue place, ate pulled pork and chips, washed it down with lemonade, and headed to the grocery store.

Corinne had the same idea, but she was walking very slowly and was sweating a little.

"Let me do that for you." Penny held out her hand. "Give me the list. I bet I need most everything you do. I'll just put two of everything in the cart, and we'll divide it up." Penny squeaked and jumped back when fluid hit the floor.

Corinne went red and clutched her back. "Oooh."

"Okay, one second." Penny ran, grabbed a giant towel from the home part of the store, and ran back. She wrapped the towel around Corinne's waist.

Corinne was huffing like a freight train. "Okay, slow steps."

Penny took Corinne's arm. "Do you want to lean on the cart?"

Corinne nodded, and Penny pushed over her empty cart. Corinne leaned on the cart's bar, and Penny pulled it. Step by step, they walked to the nearest door. Penny sent the money for the towel to the bug-eyed cashier via her link, then called Mitch.

"Yo," Mitch said. "Busy, can't help you with the house today."

"Your wife is in labor. Her water just broke."

"Shit! Bro! Get the hospital bag! On our way." Mitch dropped the link.

The contraction let up. "Stupid. Husbands." Corinne huffed. "Wife. Says. Get. Groceries. In. Snow. About. To. Drop. Babies." They got up to the door. Corinne winced at the cold. "Mitch. Should. Have. Gone." She huffed some more, and the contraction let up. "He said he had to finish some bike. James was helping."

Penny pinged the four-wheel-drive open and got Corinne into the seat. Penny got the mesh over her, shut the door, and carefully got into the other side. She put in hospital emergency, and the vehicle flashed blue lights and headed to the birthing center.

Penny linked with Jared while Corinne huffed and tried to break Penny's hand. "Corinne's having the baby."

Jared sighed. "And I'm picking up a dalmatian because of my overeager worker. I may be back in time."

"See you at the hospital." Penny let the link go, then answered another call.

Vic's calm voice settled Penny's jumping stomach. "I've got the car's passenger information, and the contractions seem to be three minutes apart. Put me on speaker."

Penny fed his call into the car's dash.

"Hey, Corinne, Vic here. You've got some time. Doctor Chastain is here. Just delivered another baby, in fact. Your vitals are awesome."

"Good. To. Know. Contractions. Very. Strong."

"The hospital is close. The vehicle is going as fast as it can. The other drivers are out of your way, all lights green. Breathe. In. Out. In. Out. Okay, again. In, out, in, out."

Penny found herself breathing along with the huffing Corinne as Vic instructed. She sent a link to Libby, one to Kandace, another to Charlie, then Gunny. Replies flooded in, all of them meet-you-at-the-hospital variations.

Vic was there in his ambulance when Penny's vehicle pulled into the entrance to the birthing center. He came out, helped Corinne into a wheelchair, and wheeled her in. Penny went back out. Hospital coffee was hot, but it had no other redeeming qualities. She drove to a convenience store, loaded up on drinks and snacks, swung by a coffee shop, and was back in time to find Libby demanding to see Corinne. Penny went to the waiting room while Libby went to help Corinne. Penny stole a table and set up the coffee, cream, sugar, and other drinks and snacks.

Penny poked her head out at the noise in the hallway and saw Mitch panicking and James trying to get information from a nurse. Penny whistled, pointed, and got out of the way as both men took off at the speed of sound. Penny got her own coffee, doctored it, and set herself up as the greeter and pointer.

Libby came out, and Penny directed her to the coffee.

"How's she doing?"

"Total pain block." Libby poured and doctored her coffee.

"Good idea." Penny smiled, stuck her head out, and pointed Lynette in the right direction.

"Wait, this is Kenyan roast. You did this! How great!" Penny braced herself in the doorway as Libby gave Penny a River-style attack hug.

Charlie came in, loaded down with baby gear—a diaper bag, car seat, balloon, and a tiny stuffed bear and wolf pair. Penny smiled and waved him in. "How's the labor going?"

Penny helped him put down the baby stuff while Libby got him a coffee. "A few hours, looks like. Total pain block."

"Good idea." Charlie took his coffee black and sipped while Penny resumed her station in the doorway. "Wait, this is Kenyan!"

Libby pointed at Penny. "She's brought real coffee, good snacks, and apparently appointed herself cruise director."

"Thank you, love." Charlie's hug was far less attack-like.

"Since I can't help anyone give birth, I'm the support staff." Penny was surprised to see Jetta, and she waved her over.

Charlie laughed. "Since none of us are Corinne, we're all support staff."

Jetta came into the room, kissed her husband on the cheek, hugged Libby, and poured and doctored her coffee. "Jen and Adelle took the kids to read to the dogs. It's a special treat while they wait for the babies."

"Doesn't my mom have a job?" Penny was surprised to find out that she was hungry and got herself a bag of chips.

Jetta laughed. "She worked ahead during the snowstorm to spend more time with the dogs. She says she's really happy that she did because now she can be helpful while the babies are born."

James came flying into the room, poured himself a cup of coffee, and held up his hands at the barrage of questions. He doctored his coffee and swallowed. "We are going to need a new crib and more onesies. There's the baby hiding under the first two."

Charlie gasped and hugged James. Jetta gasped and cried. Penny found herself crying and laughing at the same time. They did a round-robin of exclamations and hugs. Penny wiped her eyes, finished her coffee and snacks, and went to wash up as Charlie ordered another crib and Jetta counted diapers and onesies in the diaper bag.

Despite her joy, Penny felt a deep pain that Jared wasn't there. She knew rescuing another dog was also a time for joy, but it would absolutely kill Jared to not be there for his brothers. She debated whether or not to send him a text, worried that he would abort picking up the dog and break his heart that way. She decided to wait. Instead, she sent him a text that said it would probably be a few more hours and to text her when he was on his way back.

Over the long hours, Kandace went in to be with Corinne, and Len came to support Kandace. Penny went back to the convenience store and coffee shop for coffee and snacks because food and drink went like snow under the summer sun. Charlie talked to James, Mitch, and Kandace when they cycled in for a break, shaking out their hands from holding Corinne's hand. Meri delivered lunch.

Penny ate her chicken salad sandwich, then went in to see how everything was going. She found Corinne reclined a little, eating ice chips and cracking jokes.

"They've asked me if they want to cut me open or have them come out. I asked if all of them had their heads down, and they said the babies are good to go. Should be pushing in about a half-hour or forty-five minutes." Corinne's hair was matted with sweat, her skin had a sheen to it, but otherwise, she looked very good.

"How do you feel about having triplets?"

Corinne waved her hand, pushing the question away. "Fine. Whatever. Can't stop now, can I? I'm high on drugs and probably talking to you at the wrong time about this. Jared approached us with a question. We would really like for you to be a very close part of these babies' lives. You do so well with the other kids in the family. And your mother absolutely dotes on the kids. We would like for you to move your house onto our property. It isn't any farther to your work, and when you decide to have kids of your own, you'll have plenty of people that are willing to help. Plus, none of us like the neighborhood you're in. Libby is worried, and so is Jared. And, when Libby worries, so do Meri and Nat."

Penny tried to parse the onslaught of words and wondered when Corinne would take a breath. Corinne just plunged on.

"The thing is, Jared says moving it before he finishes the porch is probably better. He swears he's not jumping the gun, just getting you closer. You can be on the other side of our house. In fact, you can probably be in the position where you can't see the main house at all. But the house is pretty big." She sighed. "We need hands. Kandace is having her own babies. And your mama loves kids, so more help there."

"Shut up. Yes. It is jumping the gun, but I don't care. I love him. I will live in my own damn house and date him. But the house does have to be close enough to where he can see the barn in a blizzard. Or have a line to it." They hugged, both crying.

"I'm so glad you came into the family. Corinne wiped her eyes. "Where is Jared? With Mitch and James?"

"He sent a text about half an hour ago, something about a fire-fighter. He's on his way back. He went to go pick up a Dalmatian."

"A boy and his dogs. If you do keep dating, or whatever, you know you're going to have house dogs. I suggest corgis. They're not too big, and they're smart, very sweet, and wonderful."

"I'm absolutely certain that if things progress, Jared will bring dogs home."

Corinne pushed on Penny's arm. "I want my men. Go get them."

Penny laughed. Queen Corinne had spoken. She went into the waiting room to get the husbands and saw Jared hugging James in the hallway. She saw the moment when James told him that they were having triplets; Jared's whole face lit up. There was a lot of back-pounding, and James and Mitch headed in to be with Corinne.

Jared went up and held Penny close. "You've been keeping secrets from me."

"How is the dog?"

"Dogs. A mom and eight puppies, if you can believe it. The fire departments around here are absolutely in love with Dalmatians. I had a firefighter meet me to pick up the dogs and take them the rest of the way to the barn."

Penny punched his arm. "And you have been keeping secrets from me. You want me to move onto your property. I suspect you want me to move on that concrete slab you had poured. But I want a basement. I can get a playroom or an extra bedroom that way."

"Wait. What? You are willing to move the house?" He grabbed her in a crushing hug, and she gasped. He let her go, stood back. "I will pay for it, I swear. I don't know how I'm going to dig a basement in the middle of winter, but I will move you."

"You better." They kissed, and he held her tight.

Jared let Penny go when Gunny and Rachael ran towards them.

Penny pointed to the waiting room, and they both smiled. Stretcher, Lydia, Lucas, and Nat followed at a more reasonable pace.

Jared sighed. "We need another hallway. And a bigger waiting room."

Penny laughed.

$\sim$

*A*thena, Bree, and Damia were born within minutes of one another. The family took turns passing them around like very delicate footballs, then Jared stayed with his brothers while Penny escaped the din of excited adults to get a huge order of sandwiches, a veggie plate, chips, and dip. The sandwiches were a hit.

Penny took a second run for more food and sodas with her mom. "Big day," Penny said to Adelle. She grabbed six bags of chips and a bag of almonds and put them on top of the sodas and juices.

"You asked me to help you, and you're too independent for that. You'd rather take seven trips. Out with it. Are you running away and joining the circus?"

Penny laughed. "Sort of. Mom, I'm having the house moved to be next to Corinne, Mitch, James, and the babies. I'm gonna be an auntie."

Adelle clutched at her chest. "Moving? The house? Oh, good. The neighbors told me that your 'tall, dark, and handsome' left you for another woman, then shacked up with him. I don't like them."

Penny blew out a breath and nodded. "Okay. You know the other woman is really a new hire. There's another one coming next week."

Adelle shrugged. "More help to move your house."

They checked out, staggered out with the load of food and drinks, and headed to the vehicle.

Back at the hospital, Penny and Adelle set up the new trays of sandwiches, potato chips, and assorted salads and added to the soda and juice assortment. Penny went to have one last look at the triplets.

Kandace passed Bree in her yellow blanket to Len, took two waddling steps back, and pointed at Penny as fluid fell down between her legs onto the floor. "It's her fault! She stands next to pregnant people, and their water breaks, and they go into labor!"

Len handed the baby to Penny. "Sorry, Penny, we're just a little shocked."

"I better not be having three! Two is plenty!" Kandace raved.

"Methinks someone needs pain meds," Len calmly observed. "Come on, I think the room next door is open."

Penny looked at Jared, stricken. "I have a teen break into my house, and she ends up with one of my best friends. Then I am with two women in one day whose water breaks."

Len spoke in his calm voice. "Would someone call Davis? I think he's in surgery." He walked out towards the waiting room, and gasps and shouts came from inside.

"How is it going with Bobbi and Karissa?" Jared asked Penny, his voice soothing, while Mitch went to the nurses' station to have Davis paged.

Penny sat down and slowly rocked the baby. "The adoption's on track. Bobbi's mom and brother are going to prison for two to six years. When Bobbi's mom found out she'd have to pay child support, she signed the adoption papers."

"Good. Let's put the baby in her bassinet. She's had a hard day, being introduced to the world and all."

Penny was reluctant to put the baby down. She rocked Bree, then sang a startlingly beautiful "Rockabye." Corinne slept, and James held Athena in his arms. Damia slept in her mother's arms.

Charlie stuck his head in. "Kandace is on her way to the OR. She barely got into her gown and was scanned when the fetal heartbeats fluttered. Davis is going to be in the room with Len. Vic is coming back with a patient who fell while taking down his Christmas tree. Broken arm."

Penny nodded. "Okay. We'll take care of Corinne and the babies."

"Good. I'll send someone to update you." Then, he was gone.

The kids arrived to see the triplets, and they spent a few minutes each seeing the babies and Corinne. Gunny and Charlie texted each other the entire time, Gunny in the waiting room and occasionally cycling into Corinne's maternity room, Charlie just outside the operating room.

Gunny sighed, and everyone looked at him with laser focus. "Holden and Hunter are fine. Kandace had some bleeding, but they put a stop to that right quick. Kandace is sleeping due to anesthesia and blood loss. She'll be fine, but she will be in the hospital longer than Corinne."

Jetta, Lynette, and Jen all stood, then Jetta burst into tears. Lynette and Jen held her, then Jen led Jetta to wash up while Lynette explained to the children that Mommy was crying because she was happy.

Bobby shook his head. "That doesn't sound right. You cry when you're sad or mad, not glad."

"Aunt Kandace got sick, and the doctors made her better, and the babies came out," Adam explained to his brother. "Mama cried because she got really scared for a minute. But now she's okay."

Jen and Charlie shared a glance as they hugged the kids. Their kids were perceptive as hell.

Libby nodded. "Okay, we will see the new babies when they let us, and kids go home. We need a roster. We rotate adults to take care of the new parents and the new babies. Meals, snacks, breaks, whatever they need. Hospital food sucks, so they get whatever they want."

Penny held up a hand. "I can do meals."

"Tomorrow, you bring breakfast. You and Jared see Holden and Hunter and go home. You're wiped. Stay and eat, then home for you two. Meri and I will rotate; Nat is on duty through the week."

Adelle held up her hand. "I can do child care. Give you guys more rotations."

"Thank you. We have a lot of kids. We need one adult here at all times. I do suggest we hole up at the farm. Easier with eyes on all of them."

Penny held up her hand again. "Bobbi can help. And Karissa is a licensed foster mom. She would jump at the opportunity."

"Text them, please," Jen said. "Plus, there are both high school and college kids in town on vacation who would love the chance to earn some extra money playing in snow with kids." They sent some texts and soon had six people to help with the kids.

Penny and Jared saw the boys, both with shocks of black hair. Charlie held Hunter, Len held Holden, Vic stroked Kandace's hair, and Davis took her vital signs.

"How is she?" Penny asked.

"Fine. Just needs sleep and a really big steak when she wakes up." Vic smiled. "Our woman is strong."

"I'm taking breakfast orders for tomorrow. You're probably too exhausted to think of that now, so text me."

Davis smiled. "Divvying up the workload already, I see. Thank you. I suggest you make it easy on yourself and get us steak, eggs, hash browns, and English muffins with butter, and four sides of bacon, crispy, and sausage for Kandace. We'll take the same."

Jared grinned. "Forgot how much bears eat. We'll be here at eight. Congratulations."

They hugged everyone except the sleeping Kandace, kissed the babies, and headed to the parking lot.

Penny stared at her vehicle. Jared rubbed her back. "If you can't sleep, we have puppies."

Penny grinned. "Enough excitement for one day, I think. It's time for a book and bed. See you at the diner at seven tomorrow. You can go home in the middle, then help me with lunch."

Jared kissed her. "You were wonderful."

Penny sighed. "Just don't let me around any pregnant people. I tend to make them all give birth at once."

Jared laughed. "Taking on godlike powers, huh?" He kissed her again. "See you tomorrow." He walked her to her vehicle, kissed her again, and shut the door behind her.

APOLOGIES

The team came to move the house during a false spring in mid-March. Penny took a video with her HUD all over the house. She got a taciturn reply from the movers. "Doable."

Penny was glad there was so much she hadn't put away because most of her things went back in boxes. The conjoined shifter clan came with boxes and trucks and moved her things the day the house movers were supposed to arrive. The water, power, and cable people shut everything off and disconnected the house. The movers came and pumped up the house on giant jacks, like a car jack, only large enough to raise an entire house. They put it on the truck and moved it once the town started to close down around 7:30 at night. They drove slowly and used wide roads. Nat drove ahead and had the other deputy drive behind to eliminate accidents. By nine, the house was on its new foundation—with her promised basement. They put in steps; the new porch would come later. The water and power hookups went in, but they had to wait for the cable guy.

Bobbi came over with her mom Karissa to put everything to rights at eight in the morning the next day. "Your countertops are fine!" Karissa crowed. "I told you all that worry was for nothing."

"You can break or steal my stuff, but my countertops are sacred."

Penny grinned as she cleaned and plugged in her kitchen appliances one at a time.

Karissa laughed. "I'll get these dishes washed before they go into their new rack. I do have taste, if I say so myself."

"My taste, Mama." Bobbi hauled a box of sheets upstairs to put in the hall closet.

"Things seem to be going well there." Penny moved the red ice cream maker into alignment with the blue one. She'd come up with a half dozen new frozen dessert flavors, from sugar-free chocolate chip cookie chunk to a line of berry ices. She tested at home, and fed Mitch, James, a very hungry Corinne with two hungry babies, Jared, a ravenous Diego, Trish, and the hypercompetent Calantha 'Cal' Nadebo, Jared's new hire. Cal was still recovering but walked solidly and was ready for anything. Penny also made peanut butter ice cream for Kandace, who had monster cravings.

While Penny prepared for a spring opening, Jared trained the trainers to care for and train the dogs. They'd already had the second set of Dalmatians adopted and two of their reading dogs who had been trained and certified to work with both children and adults, their silly, happy golden lab and their mutt.

"Bobbi is amazing. The only problem is, she'll go to college within a year. She's been taking advanced placement classes all along, and she worked even harder when her other mom went wonky. No apology from that side of the family, unfortunately. Bobbi's resilient. But, I'm going to have empty nest syndrome really fast. There are no colleges or community colleges in the immediate area except for agriculture, programming, and medical and vet tech, and Bobbi wants to study 3D technologies and minor in interior design. She says she wants to design spaces." Karissa put the dishes in the dishwasher.

"She gets it from her mom." Penny smiled and was alarmed to find Karissa's eyes filled with tears.

"I get her for such a short time!" Karissa said.

Penny stopped fiddling with power cords and held her friend close. "I have a solution, but it's radical, expensive, and you're going to need help."

"I'm listening." Karissa sat at the breakfast bar.

Penny got out two cherry waters and said, "I have some frozen eggs. I'm keeping some, but I'd like to donate some to you. You would need to find a sperm donor and a surrogate..."

"I can carry a baby." Karissa's words spilled out like coffee spilling out of a carafe into a cup. "I have no viable eggs. The uterus is still intact. The Fallopian tubes were damaged too, but the uterus itself... but it is safer to choose a surrogate. I can find one. I can. Thank you!" Penny found herself enveloped in a hug. "Thank you!"

Bobbi came down the stairs. "I heard that. Wait. A little brother or sister?"

Karissa stood. "This is your decision, too. It would take a lot of time..."

Bobbi jogged over and threw herself in her mother's arms. "I was so worried about you when I went away to college! Do it!"

Penny caught her breath after her friend's enthusiastic hug. She grinned, then finished the box with the plates while mother and daughter took turns opening boxes while the other one looked up sperm services.

The doorbell rang. Penny opened the door to find a well-dressed lady in a red suit, and gold at her earrings, neck, and wrists, including a huge diamond engagement ring. She had a wide face, huge green eyes, and a cherry-lipsticked smile.

"Hello. May I speak to Penelope Frachelle?"

"I'm Penny. How may I help you?"

"My name is Desiree Trainor. I'm a real estate agent from St. Louis. I'm here about the property you had this house on."

"Come in," said Penny, bewildered. She shut the door behind the woman. "I don't have coffee right now, but I can make it. I do have cherry water and some sodas for the movers."

Desiree Trainor smiled sweetly. "Nothing for me, please."

"Is there some sort of problem?" Penny stood in the entryway staring at the woman, stunned.

"No, the exact opposite. You see, the story about your house moving made the local online news outlets. I did my research, and I know what you paid for the house and property at auction. A family in the city wants to do what you did, move a property. They want to live in a small town. Their son got into some trouble with some bad friends, and they need a new start. They want to move their house, which they own and love very much, here. They are willing to pay five percent over what you bought for the property. Considering housing prices where they are from and the fact they own their house outright, it's cheaper for them to do it this way."

Karissa came in behind Bobbi. "I'm Karissa DeShawn, and I am an interior designer. I work with real estate agents all the time." She took a card out of her back pocket and gave it to the woman. "The property is a very nice place to live. Please, drive around a little and record what you see for the family, and send me the offer to my link. We'll discuss it and get back to you within the hour."

The real estate agent smiled. "I already did the driving-around part and spoke to some neighbors. I'll head to the coffee shop. If you want to proceed, we can make a cash transaction. No escrow. We can sign the papers today and get you the money back from your auction."

"I'll see you in an hour, Ms. Trainor. Now, if you will excuse me, I have a few more boxes to open before I meet with you."

"Of course." The woman gave Penny a cherry-lipped smile. "The family will be so happy if you agree. See you soon!" She waved good-bye, and Penny shut the door behind the woman.

"Are you going to do it?" Karissa asked.

In reply, Penny put her hands over her head and did a victory jog around the entryway. "Now I can purchase the land under this property outright! And pay off the other stuff!" Karissa laughed.

"Mom! I found a surrogate! She lives near here, she's had four kids of her own, and she says her pregnancies are super-easy." Bobbi jumped up and down with glee.

Karissa laughed. "I never thought my daughter and I would be working on my reproduction together."

"Is adoption off the table?"

Karissa shook her head. "Never close a door. Learned that one the hard way."

Penny grinned. "You can say that again."

Karissa looked over the paperwork when the real estate agent sent it in and pronounced it good. Penny finished off the kitchen and left the mother and daughter to alternately put the house to rights and order sperm online. Laughing, Penny went to see a woman about the property.

~

*T*he surprises kept rolling in. After the signing, Penny bought sandwiches and little mini pizzas, then went grocery shopping for her denuded refrigerator. The vehicle drove her back. One the way home, Penny was surprised to get a rambling video from the address of a women's prison upstate. Penny thought it might be Bobbi's mother, but it was a very changed Farrah. Farrah had lost a lot of weight. Her helmet hair was gone, replaced by a soft cut that framed her face. She wore jeans and a sweatshirt with the insignia of the prison on them.

"Penny, I can't really make amends. I know I can't. I said horrible things to people. Plus, you grew up next to me and saw me be a horrible mama. I can't hurt you, and after this, you won't hear from me again. I know that's best."

Penny let the video roll. The woman was right; Farrah couldn't hurt her anymore. She might as well let the woman have her say.

"Let me explain a bit if you'll let me. I am in a psychiatric wing, in a special program for people like me. They have videos of everything I was arrested for over the years. They have people's victims send videos explaining what they did and what the effects were. They call 'em victim impact statements. Whenever we say something stupid about it not being that bad or fail to take responsibility for our actions, they play them. They make us talk about how our victims must have felt when we deliberately hurt them."

Farrah sighed. "They also put me on meds. At first, my mind was muddy, but now I realize I'm really sick. They won't let me be disrespectful to anyone for any reason or use negative emotions or manipulation to get what I want. They played the videos, had me act out what I said and did again. I didn't remember saying exactly those things. They sound a lot more horrible now."

Penny stopped the video, letting her anger cool. Farrah would have to be an idiot or really sick to not realize how awful her words and actions were. Then, she started it again.

"I don't have that much from when my kids were little, a few photos. Most parents take pictures and videos all the time. I didn't. I got pregnant young, and I had no idea how to be a mama. My mama was weak and let my daddy pound on us all."

Farrah held up a hand. "That's no excuse, just goes to the point that I had no idea what I was doing. I was angry at the world, and I was sick in my head. They got a bunch of names for it. They mean that I hate myself and want to make other people hate me. A lot of well-meaning people tried to help me and my kids, including your mama and you. I blew them off. I didn't want to look at me, because I would have to change. And I didn't want to change. And I hit my kids, and you, and I was a terrible mom. Your mama was right to keep me out of your house. My mouth was a sewer, and so were my thoughts."

Penny blew her breath out through her nose. She'd wanted an apology for years, but this one fell flat. She should have felt vindicated. Instead, she felt sad.

Farrah nodded. "You were right, what you said. My psychiatrist told me to put a little girl in front of me in my imagination and asked me if I would do those things to that girl. And I realized no. Most of the stuff I've done in my life I would not do again. I made Morgan hate me so much. She joined the military to pay for college, but the main reason was to get away from me. I know that now." Tears streamed down Farrah's face. "I didn't want the responsibility, and I knew my kids hated me. I wanted them to go. So, they did, and I will never, ever get either one of them back."

The recording cut out, cut back in. Farrah had stopped crying and washed her face. "Maddie will never forgive me. She shouldn't, except to give herself some peace. I doubt she'll see my video. Just, could you tell her that every single thing was my fault? Tell that girl... that woman. Tell her every word out of my mouth was a lie. She was and is beautiful and smart. A fine person. The exact opposite of me. I hated how good she was and saw how much better she was than me. I tried to crush the goodness out of that girl. I was a monster."

Tears streamed down Farrah's cheeks. She wiped them away with the heel of her hand. "Your mama may delete my video, too. She should. We were both poor, and she ended up raising my kids too. They turned out the right way because of her and you. I thank you for that."

The video cut out, then went back in. The light was different, obviously hours later. "I have to make restitution for my crimes. You can't make restitution for a horrible childhood. Or for how I treated people. Nothing I ever say or do will do that. What I will do is work. I have to pay back the cost of treatment and pay for my meds from here on out. I've got to get a real job. I'm taking classes here, trying to find something to do that will be good. I'll get a tiny apartment and keep it real clean, and go to church. A real one, not one of those hate-preaching ones. Unitarian, maybe."

Farrah looked directly into the camera. "I need your help. I'll move far away. I can't leave the state. Just sent me a text that says left or right side, top or bottom. I'll stay as far away from my daughter as she wants me to be. One or two words, that's all I ask. Wherever you tell me to go, I'll move there. I'm thinking Kansas City, one of the towns near there, so I can get my meds. Or St. Louis. Just tell me where you want me to go to stay away from Maddie. She deserves ten thousand times better than me."

Penny had to strain to hear the last words; they were spoken so softly.

"And, if you can think of any kind of volunteering thing that pays a little, send that link to me too. I just need to pay all this back some-how. You know? Anyway, this is a piss-poor video to say I'm sorry. I was horrible, and I'll get out of your life now. I hope you and your mama have the happiest life ever." The video ended.

Penny arrived home, took in the groceries, sat down at the table, and told Karissa what happened. Penny cried while Karissa handed

Penny a box of tissues, then saw the video. Karissa threw some punches in the air, then sat down.

Bobbi came downstairs, alarmed. "What's wrong?"

Karissa tilted her head, thought before speaking. "A nasty woman that used to be here got some psychiatric help in prison. She made a lot of people's lives a living hell, like people I grew up with, Maddie and Morgan, and me too sometimes." Karissa's eyes filled. "She called me a cripple. And a darky."

Bobbi dropped her jaw and cringed. "What? I can't believe she said that."

Penny hugged Karissa. "I'm sorry. I didn't know. I wouldn't have let her in my shop if I had known." She shook her head. "Sometimes I'm too nice. I should have stood up to that woman long ago."

Bobbi hugged Penny and her mom.

Karissa pushed them away gently. "I'm fine. She was such a bad mom that our friend Morgan joined the military to get away from her, and then she died. Maddie moved far away. Penny here is like a sister to Maddie, and this woman's apology is like salt in a wound. Brings up old pain. But, this woman might, just might, have actually changed, which is good."

Karissa hugged Bobbi, then Penny. "Go take a shower, Penny. I'll put the groceries away. I'll also send that witch a link to tell her to move to Kansas City when she gets out. Maddie's nowhere near there."

Penny wiped her eyes and stood. "Good idea. And to heck with sandwiches. Let's go out to a nice restaurant and celebrate. I'm out of debt, and I can pay off my mysterious loan."

"Mysterious loan?" Karissa asked.

"I borrowed a few thousand at a very low interest to make that payment."

"From whom?"

"I kind of hoped it was you. I was told... no, Corinne insinuated that the mysterious benefactor was another woman who wanted to pay it forward."

Karissa shook her head, confused. "Wasn't me. Although that is a good idea."

Penny smiled. "I'll pay it back and start my own loan."

Karissa grinned. "I'm in. The Female Pay It Forward Fund?"

Bobbi snorted. "Too long, Mama. Women Pay It Forward. And, pay me for my design services with some of that money. I've got to go to college."

Penny raised her eyebrows, and Karissa laughed.

~

*A*fter a very fun girl's lunch at a cafe, Penny called Maddie in the vehicle and gave her a very short synopsis of the video.

Maddie grimaced. "I deleted mine. Apologies from that woman's mouth are dirt. I wanted them years ago. Now, my husband and I and our girls just want to be left alone. Thanks for steering her to Kansas City."

"I hope she changes. But, not my jungle, not my monkeys."

Maddie nodded. "So, tell me about moving the house." Maddie squealed when Penny got to the part about having five percent over her auction price paid, including all taxes and fees, in cash. "What are you going to do with the money after paying for the land and the move?"

"I have a basement to furnish and two empty bedrooms upstairs!" Penny's vehicle pulled up at Kandace's place, and Penny hopped out. "I've got to go. Babysitting duty."

"Triplets." Maddie groaned. "Better her than me!"

Kandace was visiting, so all five babies were in need of love. Each baby was in different colored onesies and blankets, making it easy to determine which baby was which. Corinne gave a little wave and went to take a shower with slow, heavy steps, obviously crushingly exhausted. Adelle was there, happily rocking Hunter in his green onesie in the downstairs living room, which had been turned into Baby Central. Penny kicked off her boots, hung up her coat, and went for a screaming Bree in her yellow onesie. After a diaper change, Bree cooed in Penny's arms.

Adelle came up with a sling. "Let's get her in as a papoose. We have more babies to change."

"Where's Kandace?"

"Shower, then nap."

The sling held the baby snugly. Adelle put Hunter down, and they checked and changed the rest of the babies. Athena slept under a sky blue blanket, Damia wore pink and waved her hands at her crib mobile, and Holden screamed bloody murder in burgundy and tried to pee on Adelle during a diaper change. Penny patted the papoosed Bree and sang to her. Penny went into the kitchen, put the dishes away, and transferred the sleeping Bree to her crib. Damia got papoosed next while Penny wiped down the counters and swept and mopped the kitchen floor.

Penny had just washed up and brought her mother a lime water when Athena woke up and screamed. The infant got a diaper change and a bottle of mother's milk from the refrigerator, and soon everything was right with the world again.

Penny told her mother about her day while rocking Athena. Adelle was stunned to hear about the money.

"Now I can pay off my loan, and I have a nest egg for the future!"

"What loan?" Adelle grimaced, irritated. "I would have loaned you anything you wanted."

Penny sighed. "I know, Mom."

Jared stood in the doorway, then shut the door behind him. "I gave you the loan, love. I swore the family to secrecy. You spent so much time helping me with the barn, and I couldn't help you with the house. Are you mad?"

Penny shook her head. "No. I wish you'd told me upfront, but no." She smiled to see him check on the babies. "And, now I can pay you back. I already paid Corinne for the land." She sighed. "I have to tell you about Farrah."

"Did she hurt you?" Jared went over and hugged Penny and kissed her temple.

"Nope."

Jared cleaned the downstairs bathroom while Penny told him about the videos. Jared washed his hands, then kissed the woman he loved. "This has been a very interesting day. After baby duty, shall we celebrate the new house?"

"Yes." Penny kissed him back. "Yes, we shall."

EPILOGUE

Fourteen Months Later

*P*enny had a line five people deep when Gareth and Dana spilled in. They both went for their aprons.

"Sorry, we got hungry," Dana explained.

Gareth had moved into town when his parents moved onto Penny's old property. He changed from a terrified teen with long, stringy hair and a paunch to a boy with muscles, clear blue eyes, and short hair dyed to match. He had dabbled in drugs and burglary and had witnessed an attempted murder when he broke into a house. He went to rehab, testified in court, and his parents moved the entire house to a small town far from danger.

Gareth had found several new obsessions to replace his bad behavior—canoeing, skiing, swimming, and robotics. Gareth had been shocked that Penny was willing to trust him to work at the ice cream counter, but she had never regretted it.

Penny handed over two sundaes with pecans and waited on the next customer. "Did you win?" She rang up a cherry ice cream cone.

"Came in second!" Dana crowed. She washed her hands in the sink.

"Congrats! Cherry cone." Penny rang up the next customer.

"Our robot was two seconds behind the team from Bennet's Hollow." Gareth washed his hands. "What's next?"

"Two cones, one coconut, one orange." Penny rang up the next customer.

Penny did a quick cleaning when she was done with the line.

Gareth came up to her and said, "Get out of here."

Penny smiled. "Okay, I'm going. Are you coming to the reception?"

Gareth grinned. "We only have two more hours here. Go!"

"I'm going, I'm going," Penny said. She hung up her apron, washed her hands, and jogged around back to her vehicle. She stopped by the doggy spa. Minnie the pug had fallen in love with Penny when Jared brought her to the farm, and Penny fell in love back. The dog had gone from emaciated to fat and healthy. However, she tended to sleep on nearly anything, so she was simultaneously being pampered and prevented from hurling herself down in the dirt to rest.

Gina at the doggie day spa came out and rang Penny up. "Teeth are clean, nails buffed, body washed. We even washed and dried her pillow."

Renna came out with Minnie on a pillow. Minnie wiggled her tail and turned soulful brown eyes on her mom. Penny put her arms under the pillow and cradled her dog. Minnie kissed her cheek.

"Come on, love. We've got a wedding to get to."

"Congrats!" Gina and Renna both said.

Penny waved and took her dog to the vehicle.

Libby met her at Shear Beauty. "Get in here, you two." She took the dog, still on her pillow, and put her in a special Pet Pampering enclosure. "Verna, wash and style." Verna, a willowy blonde, was an excellent stylist.

"Updo, I think." Verna pointed to her chair and whipped out a cape. "I've got some gorgeous combs." She put the cape on Penny. "Let's get this done, love."

Lisa, a tiny teen with black hair and huge hazel eyes, did Penny's nails as Verna blew Penny's hair out and pinned it using beautiful silvery combs with wisps of Penny's hair hanging down.

"Out of the way." Tan rolled over his box of makeup. "I love your cheekbones, girl." Tan had a gorgeous golden skin, high cheekbones, and huge brown eyes. He had an edgy cut with his black hair cut to different lengths on each side.

"Make her wedding gorgeous," Libby ordered.

"She already is, honey." Tan picked out his favorite moisturizer. "Just bringing out what's already there."

Penny sighed. "The man is awesome." Tan grinned and gave a little bow.

Libby glared at Penny. "I can't believe you worked on your wedding day."

Penny shrugged. "The robot thing was important to them." She touched her stomach.

"Oh, do you need a drink?" Libby asked.

"Ginger ale," Penny requested.

Tan narrowed his eyes. "No wonder you're glowing!"

Penny laughed. "Surprise!"

"Indeed."

After Tan finished, they carried the sleeping dog to the dress shop. Penny put her wedding dress on, and Libby gasped. The beadwork on the top of the simple sheath was gorgeous. Myna, the seamstress, clucked, making sure the fit was perfect.

"You're lucky you're in your first trimester." Libby grinned. "You may have had trouble later."

Penny shrugged. "We were way too busy to have this wedding earlier. Most of the dogs went to their new homes this week. Poor Jared finally got some sleep." Penny accepted a silken robe to put over her dress.

Libby got a call. "Meadow. Now."

Penny grinned and paid. "You do excellent work, Myna."

Myna grinned. "Your new family will kept me in business." The woman was in her sixties, her silvery hair in a short bob. She possessed an eye for exactly would make a bride cry with joy.

"Let's go." Libby picked up the dog on her throne-pillow.

The meadow was festooned with flowers, roses, calla lilies, and baby's breath, plus the violets all around the periphery that grew in the sunlight. The immediate family was there—all of them. Libby handed the dog to Adelle, who took her with a huge smile and tears in her eyes. The dog didn't bark at the bear sitting at the edge of the meadow, the owl blinking at being up at an unaccustomed hour at the top of a pine, or the panther in a tree at the edge of the meadow.

Jen wore a golden robe. "Who brings this woman into the family?"

Jared stepped forward. "I do."

"Who speaks for her?"

Libby stepped forward. "I do. She is my best friend. She makes me laugh. I trust her with our businesses. She's known about us for years. She has kept our secret. She knows us. She has helped us raise our children together. She is a beautiful person."

"Your words are heard. Do the Clans object?"

The bear raised a paw, the owl flew away, and the panther leaped down and stalked away. Jen began singing the first song, ancient words about the joining of lives and families. They all joined in. The bear lumbered off.

Jared took Libby's hands in his. "This woman is the most kind, gentle, generous woman I've ever known. I want to share our lives together. I want her to join our ever-growing family."

"This man saves lives. He helps dogs find new homes. He has taken in the people who need him the most. We helped each other build our lives with our hands. We want to build our lives with our hearts."

Penny smiled at Jared. To her surprise, the babies didn't cry. Adelle did.

Jen wound cords around their hands and spoke about joining. They were unwound, the gold, red, green, and russet cords handed over to Meri to be braided. They sang, and then they walked to the backyard of the Camber farmhouse.

They ate a buffet lunch, cut and devoured their slices of ice cream cake (layers of cherry chocolate chunk, chocolate mint, and lemon fizz), and then the band set up.

Penny stood, walked up to the microphone, and said, "To the most incredible man in the world." She sang "Thinking Out Loud." The band kept playing while Jared carefully helped her down from the bandstand, then danced with her. There wasn't a dry eye in the house.

Some of their friends joined them, those that didn't know about the shifters. Bobbi, up from college, danced with her little sister, Alyssa, the baby in a pack on her stomach, as Karissa watched. The Camber and Weston kids danced, ran around, and exhausted themselves. Diego, Trish, and Cal were able to attend because Ravi, half the 4-H club, and two off-duty firefighters were at the dog training center. They danced and ate like everyone else. The five toddlers toddled and were passed from hand to hand, to parents and grandparents, brothers and sisters, aunts and uncles. Dogs waddled or ran around, stealing food from under tables. It was a riotous, joyous mess, and Penny and Jared loved every minute.

Finally, it was time to say goodbye, so they made the rounds. The party was still going strong, but Jared could see Penny was exhausted. Jared picked up Minnie the spoiled dog, still on her pillow, and took his wife to the truck.

"Would you like to change out of the dress before we go to the shifter bed and breakfast?"

Penny shook her head. "I love my dress, and I'd like to wear it longer. Let's just go."

So, they did.

<<<The End>>>

THANK YOU

Thank you!

Thank you for being one of my beautiful, amazing readers! I can't do what I do without you! If you liked the book, please leave a review! I read them all, looking to improve my craft so I can write more fun stories for you.

Thank you to my beta reader team. My editors Lynda and Talented_Fixer are amazing, and so is my critique partner, Alyssa. Crooked Sixpence created my incredible covers. Any errors left in the manuscript are entirely my own. Please let me know what they are so I can fix them in your online review! Or, you can contact me on social media at Facebook: Facebook.com/lj.hawke, Instagram: Instagram.com/ljhawke, and Twitter: Twitter.com/Hawkelj, and my website: ljhawkeauthor.com.

Books in the Forever Loved series:

Forever Challenged (novella, prequel, male point of view)
Forever Charmed
Forever Claimed
Forever Wild

THANK YOU

Forever Challenged
Forever Fierce
Forever Untamed

ABOUT THE AUTHOR

L. J. Hawke is an author, university professor, and an avid reader. She writes what she loves to read—paranormal romance, urban fantasy, and science fiction, as well as some nonfiction titles in her fields of expertise. She can be found petting her cats while writing, or with a backpack on her back, traveling the world—after calling the cat sitter.

One last thing...

If you enjoyed this book or found it useful, I'd be very grateful if you'd post a short review on Amazon. Your support really does make a difference, and I read all the reviews personally so I can get your feedback and make this book even better.

If you'd like to leave a review, then all you need to do is click the review link on this book's page on Amazon.

Thanks again for your support!

facebook.com/lj.hawke
twitter.com/hawkelj
instagram.com/ljhawke